The
First Plague

Written by Kevin M. Port

PROLOGUE
Constantinople, Europe 1351

Gray clouds littered the still sky, casting almost otherworldly shadows across the baron field. The air was light with a hint of premature autumn chill on what would normally be a humid, sundrenched August afternoon.

Three men in their early thirties stood in a staggered formation, wearing tattered and dirt ridden clothes. Their faces were thick with soot and grime in any place visible past their unkempt hair and unshaven beards. Although they stood with steel resolve there was no denying the level of exhaustion they wore on their faces. They had been complete strangers to one other only a few months prior but have since formed an unbreakable bond. The trust among them was forged from the blood and tears they shared in this short period of time. A time of endless and unforgettable violence.

The man in front stood with a relaxed posture. His name was Eli. His face conveyed determination and his right hand sat idly on the hilt of his sword resting in its sheathe on his side. However, his visage couldn't be further from how he truly felt. Under his controlled exterior, the man's heart beat like a locomotive, while almost every ounce of strength was being used to maintain control of his trembling limbs. Sweat lined his forehead and palms. He glanced back at the ally on his left, then turned his head to the man on the right, who nodded once at him.

They stood twenty feet from the shape of another figure who was facing them. He was tall and thin, covered in off-white bandages stained with varying shades of color from yellow to black. He wore an aged, torn waist-high, white sarong that contrasted his ashen-hued torso. Dark green and black spots littered various parts of the man's body. Red sores protruded from his skin and leaked a viscous, puss-like liquid. And although a hood which matched his attire covered his face, the three men could tell that his eyes were fixated on them.

The sickly man slowly stepped one bare foot forward, the small, white mist that surrounded him shifting with his movement. The three men across from him tensed visibly as he stepped further forward, but they did not withdraw. The sickly man stopped progressing and tilted his head to the side as if perplexed to see them holding their ground.

When the bandaged man spoke, his voice was unnatural. "You know who I am?", he inquired in a low shrill.

"Aye," Eli said with certainty. "We know who you are, First Plague."

"And are you all so eager to receive crippling affliction?", he taunted with an ominous smile creeping across his hidden, disfigured face.

The sickly man snickered and raised a sore-ridden palm up as he moved even closer. "Ah, the old names. You do know who I am." He rasped, clearly impressed. "Pray tell mortals; how do you plan to defend yourselves from the suffering I am about to inflict upon you?"

Eli unsheathed his sword slightly, "Stand down," he said defiantly, ignoring the question, "or we will strike you down."

With one hand still outstretched the sickly man removed his hood, revealing a grotesque yet featureless face. Green and red pock marks littered his bald head, puss and wax oozed from swollen ear canals. Deformed black eyes expelled mucus and rheum. In the center was a single hole where his nose should be. The most distinguishing malformation, however, was his mouth, where dry and torn lips gave way to jagged and rotten teeth. Plaque lined the gums of his permanent skeletal smile.

There was no hair, but his brows furrowed in anger as he growled "You dare threaten me?! You humans are the disease plaguing this Earth. My liberation will be your enslavement."

The mist that surrounded the frail man's legs began flowing from his outstretched palm. Like a snake, the mists moved in unison, surrounding each of the men. They all drew their swords as the mist enveloped them but refrained from striking.

Eli locked eyes with his adversary through the mist. The absence of any humanity in his adversary's expression terrified him. "Your magic won't work on us, King of Retches. We are protected."

The disfigured man snarled through gritted teeth. He was enraged that his mist was not entering every orifice of these mortals' bodies as it was supposed to. Their skin should be blistering and boiling as he was serenaded by the cacophony of their screams. The sick thought of this alone brought a twisted smile of satisfaction to his mutilated face. Yet there they stood, seemingly unaffected by his assault.

He lifted both arms together and separated them hastily causing the mist around the men to dissipate. "You have the shroud?" he barked incredulously. He moved towards them; each step heavy with rage. "It won't stop me from tearing your flesh from your bones!" he snarled, picking up pace and shaking the ground with each colossal step forward.

As he advanced, the men could see just how tall the pale creature was. He was almost a giant, easily exceeding seven feet in height when slightly crouched and running.

Eli dug his back foot into the soil and lifted his sword, "Silas," he yelled to the man on his left, "flank."

Without question Silas moved, sidestepping in a wide arc to the side of his target. With his weapon also raised, Silas never took his eyes from his adversary as he moved.

The mutilated monstrosity caught a glance at his flanker but never broke stride. He wanted Eli for mocking him with such arrogance. He relished in the thought of watching the life fade from his frail, mortal body as he sank his teeth into his flesh and fed on him.

The man in back sprinted past his leader with his sword above his head, letting out a battle cry as he closed the gap to his threat. The creature swung his bandaged fist out at the warrior, missing as he ducked under it and brought his sword up and across the thing's colorless torso. The warrior stepped back to regain footing and observe the damage he had inflicted, but the creature moved with him, grasping his forearm.

The wound would have been fatal for any mortal man but left their foe seemingly unaffected. Thick black liquid oozed like rotten syrup from the laceration. However, he paid the wound no attention and twisted the warrior's arm violently, causing an audible snapping of bone. The man dropped his sword and screamed in agony.

"Barak!" Eli shouted, shifting left and lunging forward, thrusting his sword up and into their foe's sore covered neck. Silas came up from behind the creature and sliced the outstretched arm holding his ally.

The creature dropped Barak to the ground and turned to Silas with fury in his blackened eyes. He backhanded Silas and sent him rolling like a ragdoll across the ground. He pulled the blade of the sword from his neck as more black liquid spewed out with it and threw it to the side, far out of reach of its wielder.

"Your metal sticks are useless against me," he bellowed, placing a massive hand over Eli's face and lifting him effortlessly off the ground.

Barak sat on his knees, cradling his now useless arm and grunting in pain. He glanced over at the creature holding Eli and realized his moment to act was now while it was distracted. He let his shattered arm hang to the side while he hurriedly fidgeted through the satchel on his side. When he found the item he needed, he pulled it from the bag to the front of his face to verify it was what he had hoped. In his hand sat a six-inch sliver of rusted metal with jagged, bent edges.

The giant hand covering Eli's face muffled his screams. His legs thrashed about wildly several feet above the ground as his hands punched and dug into the creature's fingers and wrist, hoping to loosen the grip. The creature's skeletal grin widened as he opened his mouth. Saliva and bile stringed across the gap between his upper and lower teeth. He moved Eli's head in closer to take a massive bite of the man's neck and shoulder, which would ensure decapitation.

Suddenly the creature recoiled, letting out a supernatural howl in pain, and discarded his potential meal. He shot an angered glance down at his left leg which burned with the fires of the sun.

There was Barak, staring up at his foe with almost as much surprise that pain had just been inflicted on the creature. With his still functioning hand, he had driven the small metal into the side of the creature's leg.

As the creature recoiled and raised his fist to strike down at him, Barak quickly removed the small blade and struck again. This time he dug deep into the beast's calf and dragged the blade across it, tearing flesh like nothing more than paper. The creature howled in pain again and dropped to one knee, already noticeably weakened.

"You swine," the creature bellowed at Barak as he still managed to grab him by his neck and lift him away from his wounded leg.

At that moment, Silas had run up from behind the creature and leapt into the air. The height he gained still only put him just below the head of the monster. Silas struck down into its back and dragged a small piece of metal similar to Barak's down the spine of the creature.

Sores split open and flesh tore away with the blade, but instead of blood or bile, bright light shown from the wounds made with this strange metal. The creature howled again and pulled his teeth back to further protest the pain. With a low growl, he fell over on his side, slightly bladed. The audible thump of his large frame kicked up dust with the impact.

The beasts' breathing was laboured. The wounds on his back and leg radiated with white light as he lay there, barely holding onto life.

Eli stared down at his adversary and met his black eyes. Barak stumbled over to Eli's side, still holding his mangled arm. Silas then stepped to the opposite side and held the strange metal firmly in his hand, ready to strike out again if needed.

The creature glanced at Silas' weapon and let out a gurgled cough that sounded eerily similar to a chuckle. "I underestimated you, mortals." the creature said between labored breaths.

"How is it that you are here, Monster?" Eli asked, ignoring its statement.

"My seal… was compromised…" he said almost lamentingly. Blood and bile ran down the side of his mouth as he spoke. "Just enough for me… to escape."

"End times are centuries away," Barak said to Eli with a worried expression. "How can that be?"

"He had help," Silas interjected as the creature let out another cough filled laugh.

Eli's brow furrowed. *Who would be so cold as to wish this torment on people?* he thought to himself. "Who?" he said forcefully, leaning closer toward his fallen foe. "Who would summon such a vile creature?!" The anger in his voice was unmistakable, yet his sick and wounded adversary gave him nothing more.

"Your world," the creature mocked in a low growl, "belongs to my brethren and I." His skeleton like grin widened slightly and his head lowered to the ground.

The three men stood quietly, regaining their composure as they let the creature's warning sink in. Eli turned his blade over and examined the rustic metal. There was no blood on it, no bile, nor any discoloured bodily fluids. No evidence that the blade had ever been used on anyone, human or otherwise.

"We need to fasten these into weapons," Eli said, addressing both of his allies.

"And what of the shroud?" Barak asked, untying a ribbon of cloth from his abdomen.

"We'll think of something," Eli replied with a sigh. "First we need to rest and regroup. We'll give ourselves two days... then we can address this... mess." He said waving a hand over the field towards the hill-line.

"What of him?" Silas asked pointing to the creature.

"We know these weapons will not kill him," Eli replied, "So I will send him back and repair the seal."

"We'll need more help," Barak said plainly.

"We will," Eli agreed. "At weeks end, we all ride to our designated destinations. Search out allies and leads. We need to find those responsible for this."

"And to what purpose," Barak added, grimacing in pain. His adrenaline was beginning to fade, bringing attention to the excruciating pain shooting throughout his broken arm.

"Aye," Eli confirmed. "See to your arm my friend. When this is done, go west and seek out information on the relics." Barak nodded with affirmation. "Silas, you have allies to the East, yes?"

Silas nodded, "I do, and friends in the Order I will speak with." He turned and began a slow exhausted walk towards the town over the hill.

"We have many challenges ahead of us," Eli told his comrades. "And I fear this is only the beginning."

Chapter 1
Willow Valley PA
Present Day

"Shit, I died," Logan said into his headset as he slammed his controller down on the coffee table. "I told you to cover me, Luke." He chastised his slightly older brother for letting him suffer digital death at the hands of their rival online team, *Bushwhackers.*

"I thought you were talking to Matt," Luke replied with a defensive tone.

"No, I'm covering the side like I've been doing for the past five rounds," Matt deflected, slightly irritated.

Luke and Matt began a minor verbal spat when Logan spoke over them, "It's cool, I'm getting a beer real quick." The two never acknowledged him and continued bickering as Logan removed the headset and stood up to stretch.

They had been having a marathon of their most coveted first-person shooter, *Horde Z.* It had been a while since the three friends had the same weekends off from their respective jobs and could slay zombies and mercenaries together. In recent months they have developed a friendly rivalry with this particular team.

Logan walked into the kitchen and opened the fridge. He reached in and grabbed the last *Gingerfish* beer. He wasn't a beer snob by any stretch of the word, but sometimes, he just couldn't deny the superior taste of an expensive local brew. He popped the cap and took a mouthful of the delightful nectar of the gods. The hops invigorated his taste buds as the beer soaked his palate. *Damn that's good,* he thought as he took another swig.

"You die again?" his wife asked, stepping into the kitchen and taking the beer from his hand. It was such a simple action but when she met his eyes, he almost found himself lost in her gaze. Jen was beautiful. She stood five foot six with a thin frame but an athletic build. Her dark red hair flowed like crimson silk and was contrasted by her hypnotic emerald green eyes. She took a mouthful of his beer and handed it back to him.

Logan caught himself staring blankly at her and chuckled as he took the beer back. "Sure did.", he finally managed to respond.

"Luke's fault I'm guessing," she said with a humoring nod and suspicious smile.

"Of course," he replied. "It sure as hell wasn't my fault. What do you wanna do for dinner?"

"I ordered a pizza," she said turning and walking to the sink. She stopped when she felt Logan's eyes on her and turned to see his head cocked to one side, clearly staring at her backside. "Can I help you?" she asked coyly, raising an eyebrow.

"Well now that you mention it," Logan started as he attempted his sexiest catwalk towards his potential conquest. He put his beer on the counter and pursed his lips together, making his own soundtrack with his mouth as he stepped.

Jen laughed and turned to face him with her arms outstretched. "I'm sorry, is this your attempt to seduce me?"

Logan nodded and continued to strut towards her. He licked the tip of his finger and put it on his chest only to quickly remove it and shake it, as if he had just burned it on himself. Jen laughed harder and closed her arms around him.

"So, whatcha think?" he asked quickly raising his eyebrows at her. "There's like fifteen minutes until my next match."

Jen placed a hand on his chest and made puppy eyes. "Aww honey, what would we do with the next thirteen minutes?" she jested.

"Ouch," Logan replied, feigning rejection as he pulled away and picked his beer back up off the counter. He headed towards the doorway knowing that there would be no intimacy to be had for the time being.

"Don't forget we have brunch with the Sams tomorrow," she said stopping him in his tracks. Logan looked over at her with protest in his eyes but said nothing. "We planned it like a month ago," she added in response to his stare.

"God damnit," he lamented in a friendly whine. "They're just so…" he trailed off for a second, trying to find the right word.

"Awkward?" Jen finished his thought. "Yea, that's why we have to go to brunch with them."

"That doesn't make any sense," Logan said squinting suspiciously. "First of all, why do *we* have to have brunch with them because *they* are awkward? And secondly, who marries someone with the same name? It only adds to the awkwardness."

The Sams were their neighbors, Samuel and Samantha Gilbert, who lived a few doors down. They were in their early thirties, about the same age as Logan and Jen and were the only other couple on the block without any children. Although they made nice with the small daily interactions, saying "hello" and "have a good day," they seem to lack any credence once placed in a full-blown social situation. To their credit, they seemed to embrace the moniker of *The Sams* that the neighborhood allotted them by going so far as getting *The Sams* emblazoned on their mailbox instead of just The Gilberts.

"Because they don't have any other friends and we don't have any excuses not to be their friends," Jen scolded him, "so, behave yourself." She pointed a finger at him, as if giving him a friendly warning.

Logan sighed, knowing he wasn't winning this argument. "Yes mam." He walked back into the living room and put his headset back on. He noticed his whole team was still alive in the match, himself notwithstanding. "How's it looking?" he asked into the headset at no one in particular.

"Not good," Luke said, "we have too many... SHIT!" he said a little louder than he meant to as his character was gunned down by an enemy he couldn't see.

"Luke's down. But there's only one threat left." Logan said to Matt, encouraging him to change the tides of the match.

Hales of gunfire erupted onscreen and digital chaos gave way to realistic tension as all three teammates were holding their collective breaths, anxiously waiting to see who would emerge the victor.

Without warning there was an earsplitting waling that erupted throughout Logan's head. He snatched the headset off, believing it to be some type of feedback or interference. When he found the thunderous noise was even louder without the headset on, he knew it had to be coming from outside. The intrusive waling caused a massive throbbing in his head and he threw his hands up to his ears in an attempt to alleviate the pain.

"Jen," he screamed, unable to hear his own words over the deafening blare. He ran out to the dining room and saw his wife standing with her hands over her ears as well. She was wearing a confused look on her face as Logan ran up to her. She raised her shoulders as if to convey the universal sign for *I don't know.*

The two of them opened the front door and stepped outside. They looked frantically up and down the block for the source of the resounding, trumpet-like roar. The normally quiet and quaint suburban block now had most, if not all, of its residents standing on their respective lawns wearing the same, tense expressions on their faces.

Logan and Jen slowly loosened their hands from their heads when the waling softened slightly. The sound began to fade further as everyone slowly straightened themselves and exchanged confused glances.

"What the hell was that?" their neighbor Brian yelled from his lawn across the street. His words were muffled but could still be made out. Logan wouldn't have known Brian was asking him directly if he hadn't been staring at him, a grave expression pasted on his face.

How the hell would I know? I have just as much information as you, Logan thought to himself. But instead of saying anything, he simply shrugged.

The sound was as perplexing as it was unnerving, but it paled in comparison to the unsettling quiet that followed. Lips began moving as families started speculating to each other until inaudible murmurs could be heard throughout the block. Some families returned to their domiciles while others just stood around.

"That was weird," Logan said to Jen, "Maybe the fire house up the road or something." He didn't believe it but there didn't seem to be another logical explanation at the moment. Jen nodded unsurely.

Their attention was then directed to the end of their block as a white smoke-like fog crept around the corner of the houses at the end of the street. Glancing over, Jen noticed it also snaking down from the opposite end of the block. Even though it was clearly visible, the fog itself seemed to move stealthily and with purpose. It slinked along lawns and in-between the houses, slowly bridging the gap to meet in the middle of the suburban thoroughfare.

The silence was finally broken by what sounded like a distant scream farther in the confines of this mysterious fog. Looks of confusion turned to looks of unease as more screams of torment erupted from the neighborhood. People could be heard shouting in defense and protest at some unknown encroaching threat. Only select words like "no" and "stop" could be heard over the booming cries of agony that ushered through. Car horns could be heard blaring from several streets over as either a warning to those in the street or a cry for help. The cacophony of screams that filled the air shifted closer and closer, seemingly spreading with the fog.

Some residents were standing in the street and became enveloped by the ominous mist. Within seconds they were each bending over, coughing furiously and grabbing at parts of their bodies. Some fell over completely, others only partially. Air eluded their lungs as they began gasping between heavy, labored breaths. Their bodies began twitching violently as their skin pigmentation began to change from darker, healthy tones to ashen and pale. Sores and pustules immediately began to materialize on their arms and face, among the rest of their clothed bodies, as if they were being boiled from the inside out. Just as quickly as they started thrashing wildly in pain, the bodies became still.

Logan, Jen, and several of their neighbors looked around at the chaos, trying to grasp just what was happening. Several of them squinted as they could begin to see silhouettes of people through the fog. As the shapes drew closer into view, they all appeared to be running. There were at least a dozen of them, adult men and women sprinting full speed. They looked gravely ill but moved like track stars. Logan and Jen watched as one of them ran right towards Brian, never slowing. The man slammed into him with all of his forward momentum and landed on top of Brian as they fell onto the lawn. Brian screamed and tried to push the man off to no avail. The man scratched and punched Brian savagely, then stuck his neck out and opened his mouth. He leaned over and bit down on Brian's face with such force they could hear the wet crunching of skin and bone across the street.

"Oh God," Jen said as she watched the man pull his teeth away from Brian's face, sending flesh and sinew flying in the air. The man looked to the sky and chewed with a look of euphoria as Brian's eyeball hung from his mouth, still attached to the optic nerve. Brian's screaming had stopped alongside his struggling. The man saw this as an invitation to go down for a second serving as he leaned in to put more teeth to flesh.

Logan stared transfixed on the horror across the street but found himself subconsciously reaching for one of the gardening tools leaning on a wall of the house. His hand was struggling to grip anything without the help of his eyes. Jen took the handle of a shovel and moved it closer to his flailing hand. Logan gripped it and swung the shovel around in front of him, choking the handle and swallowing heavy.

The number of attackers grew as a steady stream of people continued to emerge from the fog like professional runners. More of them slammed into the confused and defenseless residents standing outside. Once the neighbors began to realize they were all fair game, many of them began running back into their homes, slamming the doors shut. Some jumped in their cars and drove off, leaving their remaining family members to fend for themselves.

One woman was torn from her car in her own driveway by three of the crazed attackers. They were on top of her the moment she made contact with the pavement, viciously slashing and biting her. She screamed in vein until one of them bit down into her jugular. A wet ripping noise and a shrill gurgling were all that could be heard as flesh bits caked the attackers' mouths.

"This is nuts," Logan said in disbelief, "We need to get inside," he added turning to Jen with haste in his voice.

As they turned to enter their house, they heard a low growl come from one of their neighbors who lay on his lawn a few houses down. They stopped and watched as he stood up without the use of his arms. He craned his neck unnaturally to the side and looked in their direction as the fog that once surrounded him seemingly disappeared.

His name was John and even though they had always exchanged pleasantries in passing, Logan thought he was kind of a dick. John was a crotchety, middle-aged man with glasses and a pedophile mustache. He would often complain to any of his neighbors about anything and everything. He once beat Jen's ear for forty-five minutes about the number of kids who rang his doorbell and asked him for candy one particular night. The fact that it happened on Halloween was either lost on him or he just didn't care. As long as they had known John, he had lived by himself and had been miserable. Logan just couldn't figure out if John was a jerk because his wife left him, or the other way around.

John's green t-shirt was tucked into his khaki cargo pants, which were now dirt laden from his brief nap on the ground. His eyes shot open and were covered with a thick white film. He opened his now plaque-lined mouth and let out a deafening shrill. Without warning, he bolted towards their next-door neighbor Mary with what could only be described as a murderous rage. Her spastic, panic-stricken hands prevented the middle-aged woman from successfully opening her own front door. She was staring at the knob pleading for it to open with her back turned to John.

Logan glanced back and forth from Mary to John, hoping he would just veer off but seeing his bloodthirst would not waver. When Logan saw that Mary had no idea that she was being honed in on and John had no intention of stopping, he moved.

"Shit," was all he could get out as his legs went into action before his brain could regret the decision. John was only feet away from Mary and Logan could tell that something was clearly wrong with the man. But God be damned if he was about to try and reason with any man who was charging at a woman with murderous intent. John's teeth clacked as he repeatedly opened his mouth and bit down, as if waiting for a meal to voluntarily jump in and be consumed. His arms thrashed out violently as he closed in on her with unwavering tenacity.

"John don't…," Logan shouted as he pivoted with the shovel and brought it up and across his body, slamming it into John's face and making a cartoony *BONK* sound. John's momentum was halted, and the impact whipped his head backwards as blood and teeth took flight. His feet left the air as if he had slipped on a banana peel and his back slammed to the ground.

Mary jumped as she shrieked in both terror and surprise. She stared down at John for a moment then focused on the shovel in Logan's hand, putting the scene together. "Thank you, Logan." she said, swallowing nervously and collecting herself. She steadied her hand and finally managed to turn the handle. Once shut, Logan could hear her securing the locks and bolts from inside.

"No problem." he said to the door, trying to catch his breath. He was bent over with his hands on his knees and threw Jen a thumbs up.

"Hey hon…" Jen said calmly raising a finger and pointing past Logan. He turned and saw John clambering to his feet, fresh blood flowing from his now broken nose and mouth. He let out a predatory growl that sounded more like a low, wet gurgle. His white emotionless eyes were now speckled with blood droplets as they peered through shattered bifocals with bits of glass embedded in them.

"Door." Logan murmured to Jen without turning around. He gripped the shovel in both hands again and carefully stepped backwards. Jen pushed the door open and hurried inside. She peered out at her husband anxiously waiting for him to get in. "John," Logan said apprehensively, "Don't come closer or I'll have to hit you again."

John let out a wet snarl and extended his neck as he bit at the air like a wolf intimidating his prey. Logan was a few steps from his door when John leapt at him with gnashing teeth and spittle flying. Logan put his right foot back and got into a defensive position, readying his shovel and bracing for impact.

Logan and Jen had been so enthralled with the confrontation that they hadn't noticed a black older model sedan that had been speeding up the street, swerving and weaving uncontrollably. John was just about in arms reach when the vehicle turned right into John, sending him flying high in the air and over the car with a loud thud. Logan jumped from the sight and heard Jen let out an involuntary gasp behind him.

The vehicle came to an abrupt stop when it crashed headlong into a small tree on Mary's lawn, only feet from them. The driver side door swung open from the impact and revealed the lifeless driver slumped over at the wheel. John lay on the ground, no longer moving.

Jen was now yelling for Logan to hurry up when he spotted something from the corner of his eye. "One sec," he said to Jen, stealing a quick glance in both directions to see if he was clear.

"What?" Jen responded hastily in protest. "Where are you going?"

Logan didn't even answer as he ran as fast as he could over to the black sedan now resting against the tree. He glanced in the driver side window and noted the drivers' apparel then pulled on the handle to the backseat passenger door. It was unlocked and pulled open freely. The item he had hoped for sit unperturbed on the seat. He dropped the shovel and claimed his new prize in both hands, then turned back to the house.

"You gotta be fucking kidding me." Jen said as she watched Logan sprint full speed back towards her, not slowing for anything. She opened the door slightly and he barreled in as she slammed it shut, muffling screams from the outside. In his hands Logan held a still hot and fresh pizza box.

Jen looked at him angrily as she fidgeted with the locks. He put the box down and helped her barricade the door with some furniture close by; an entryway table, some chairs and a loveseat. They stepped back to catch their breaths and Logan opened the pizza.

"Shit." he exclaimed involuntarily.

"What's wrong?" Jen replied in an almost panic, studying the barricade.

"It's pepperoni." Logan said, holding up a slice of the meat covered pizza.

Jen breathed heavily. "What the hell is wrong with you?" she yelled quietly, clearly pissed. "Did you see what just happened out there?"

Logan bit the slice and dropped it back in the box, wiping the grease on his pants. "Yea I did," he said with irritation, "and I got a real good look at John. Whatever that was just scared the shit out of me. And you know I'm a stress eater." She knew all too well about his coping mechanism and could not fathom how he stayed so fit considering he was always eating. She would be kind enough to let it go for now though.

They pulled back the ivory curtain of the window and peered at the chaos outside. What was just a peaceful, suburban community moments ago now had the familiar faces of its' residents running frantically throughout as they were being slaughtered by neighbors and friends. The roles of predator and prey clearly distinguishable.

"Are all the doors and windows locked?" Jen asked, not looking away from outside. She already knew the answer. Logan was borderline paranoid. As long as he was inside the house, everything stayed shut and locked. A window would only be open if they were currently occupying that room.

"Yea they're locked," he responded. "But we should still barricade everything until we know what's going on. Would you want to ready the guns and I'll reinforce down here really quick?"

"Yea." she said firmly and headed upstairs. Jen was great with firearms. When they had first started dating, she wanted Logan to teach her everything he knew about them. He wasn't an expert on the subject by any means, but he had training with some sidearms and rifles from his previous job.

Logan went from window to window tugging on the latches and closing blinds when the sound of digital gunshots and computerized screaming came from his den. He had completely forgotten that he was in the middle of a match when all the commotion started. The loud sounds were coming from his TV and Xbox console.

"Crap." he muttered as he darted into the room, almost falling over. He put the headset on and listened for a second, hoping his friend and brother might be unaffected from the madness outside. There was only silence. "Matt, Luke?" he said pressing the headphones tighter against his ears. "Matt, Luke? You guys ok?" His eyes darted back and forth on the floor as he began to feel panic well up from his throat.

There was a hiss and some static before he could hear what he believed to be Luke's voice between distorted crackles. "Logan… Ethan's here… said… Getting Izzy… old church…" Was all Logan could make out. He was surprised that although Luke's voice was filled with urgency, he still sounded relatively calm.

"Church?" Logan said questioningly, hoping now that he would hear him a little clearer, "No, just stay put and I'll meet you there." He said it but Logan understood the need for Luke to get his fiancé with this madness going on. If it were Jen, he'd already be out the door to try and rescue her. Not to mention, the score of brownie points he could potentially earn. "Matt, you there?"

Matt's voice came over as he whispered into the mic, "Help me." Was all he said in such a way that made it sound like he was hiding from something or someone. And with that, the mic went dead. The TV flashed black and an error message appeared on the screen. The internet connection that held them together in the game had been severed. The game screen now sat idly in offline mode.

Logan took the headset off again and slowly placed it down on the table, transfixed on what he heard his brother tell him. Izzy was Luke's fiancé Isabelle and she lived only about a mile from him. Matt was about a mile in the other direction, closer to Logan. And the mention of an old church further confused him. What church and why? He thought for long moments, weighing his options. He was unsure if he was close to making a decision or not when he heard a loud thud behind him, followed by that ominous low growl he recognized from outside.

Without turning he reached for his waistband, hoping to grab his nine-millimeter from its holster and realizing Jen was still upstairs gathering all the guns. He exhaled heavily and slowly turned to see John once again rising to his feet. The wide-open window next to him a clear indication of how he gained entry.

"Seriously?" he all but whispered to himself. Logan's head swiveled from side to side in hopes of his eyes finding a suitable weapon for his hands. On the small table next to him was Jen's treasured orange cat lamp. He grabbed it at the cat's legs and ripped the lampshade off just as John catapulted over the couch straight at him. Logan stepped back and swung the lamp across the side of John's face as his body crashed down into him. There was a loud crunch as John's jaw and cheek exploded with the impact of the fiberglass cat. John's already bent and broken glasses flew from his face as blood spewed from his mouth.

Logan stumbled over and fell with his back against the wall. Before he could gain his footing, John had turned and leapt again, seemingly agitated with his thwarted effort. His arms were outstretched, and his neck extended as his jaw bit down at Logan's face.

Oh my god, I love this cat! is all Logan thought for a second as he thrust the lamp up and caught the mouth of John's incoming bite. He held the lamp firmly in place as John bit down harder, wriggling with the lamp in his mouth but not letting go. Logan could feel his arms tiring and was now kicking at John's midsection, praying it would send him back and give him some much-needed breathing room.

John pushed harder as black saliva and red blood oozed from his mouth onto the lamp where he was clasping down. His stained gums were torn to shreds and some of his teeth were cracking, but he showed no signs of tiring. The flesh at the corners of his mouth ripped and peeled back as they were mere inches from Logan's face. He growled through the unrecognizable lamp and Logan got a whiff of the foulest odor he had ever had the displeasure of having jammed into his olfactory senses. Logan was mesmerized by the red and white pock marks on John's face that pulsated and spewed a sickening yellow-green puss. Dark blue veins bulged from his forehead as he bit down, straining every muscle he could to get just a little closer.

Logan grunted and thought John was just about to break through the lamp and dig into his face when the single shot of a handgun boomed through the house. John's jaw loosened and Logan saw the life in his eyes fade away as the side of his head exploded and expelled bits of bone and brain with blood and other fluids onto the wall.

John's body slumped over, lifeless. Logan looked over wide-eyed and bewildered to see Jen standing in the doorway with a pistol outstretched in her hands. Logan wiped some of the blood spatter from his face as she ran over to him, holstering her weapon.

"You okay hon?" she said with genuine concern in her voice. She cupped her hand around the side of his face and forced him to look at her.

"I…" he stammered, "I'm so sorry…" he said in a defeated tone.

"Oh God, for what?" she said with fear and concern as her eyes scanned his body for wounds she knew would be fatal.

Logan lifted the unrecognizable remains of what was once her favorite lamp. "I broke your cat." He said flatly, almost letting a smirk creep over one side of his mouth.

Jen smiled and let out a small chuckle of relief. "It's okay, you ass. Here." she said as she handed him another handgun from her waistband. Logan took it as he stood and ejected the magazine to get a bullet count.

"Really?" Jen asked indignantly. "You expect me to give you a half-loaded gun or something?" She was arching an eyebrow but there was a joking tone to her question.

"Sorry, force of habit." He said shyly. He closed the window and locked it, pulling the curtain over as another infected person ran by. Logan leaned against the wall, trying to conceal himself further. Jen crept over to a black duffle bag she had dropped at the doorway and pulled out a holster, then threw it to Logan.

As he looped the holster through his belt, he could feel Jen's eyes baring down on him. "What?" he asked.

"What are we doing, Logan?" she said with a soft but worried expression.

"We're arming up," he replied, a little confused at her question.

"No," she said shaking her head at him. "What's our plan? What do we do? Where do we go?" She began to sound nervous and agitated. "I tried calling my parents and my sister but my phones not working. What's going on?" A single tear threatened to push through and run down her cheek. She looked away from Logan and over at John's body on the floor.

"I don't know," he said softly, embracing her gingerly in his arms and pressing her head into his chest. "I don't know, but we'll figure something out. We can stay here if you want to. Border everything up and sit tight. We have enough food for a few weeks and can see if this whole thing blows over." He was going through at least a dozen options of what they should do in his head, but he could tell they clearly needed a minute to take it all in. They also had no clue what exactly was going on outside.

"That gas, or mist, or whatever, did something to him," Jen said still staring at John. "We don't even know if we can go outside." She was right. That mist had changed the people out there. It mutated their neighbors into feral, ill-ridden monsters who seemed to want to consume the flesh of their fellow man.

"Zombies…." Logan said like it was both obvious and a revelation.

Jen pulled away and looked at him like he had said something offensive. "No fucking way." She was in disbelief, and who could blame her?

"You saw what they were doing out there," Logan reasoned, "they were…." He paused as the images ran through is mind again. "They were eating them."

They shared a moment of uncomfortable silence before Jen spoke again. "I don't want to stay here."

"Then we won't," Logan assured her. "But I heard Matt asking for help over the headset before it went dead."

The implication in his voice alarmed her. "So, you want to go get him?" she said with surprise.

"I do, but I'm not going to chance putting you in danger." He replied.

Jen was unbelievably strong with an iron clad will and unwavering resolve. She was no hapless woman with delicate sensibilities. She was a fighter, plain and simple. So, when Logan said he had to get Matt, she knew he would go. And she was going with him.

Matt was Logan and Luke's best friend since high school. They had gotten in a lot of trouble together, faced many of life's teenage perils together, and through it all, their bonds of friendship were strengthened. Over the past few years, they haven't had as many opportunities to meet up as life just, kind of happened. That's why whenever they had the chance between their respective shiftwork and family responsibilities, they would meet in a digital battleground online. They were all and have always been avid video gamers.

"Screw that." Jen said firmly, "You know I'm going with you."

Logan smirked. He knew he wasn't talking her out of it. "Ok. Let's see if we can get any information from the news. We'll watch the windows and doors and stay quiet while we get ready. We'll leave in an hour if we can, get Matt and meet Luke. Then get your sister and parents."

"You make it sound so easy." she said turning on the TV and flipping through the channels for news. "Every station is off."

"That was fast," he responded going into the closet and pulling out two large backpacks. These were their go-bags. They weren't apocalypse preppers or crazy conspiracy theorists, but the idea of some sort of pandemic or nuclear fallout didn't seem unforeseeable, clearly. He moved the curtain over and peered outside. There was far less commotion than earlier. A random person would sprint past the window or across someone's lawn. He could only assume it was in search of food. It was quiet again except for the shrieks and growls of the things running around.

"Fuck, that's terrifying." he said in a low voice to himself. "The fog is gone but I think we should still wear the masks."

"Ok." Jen said taking a bite from a slice of pizza. Logan stared at her a minute with a blank expression but decided it was best not to say anything.

Chapter 2

The next half hour was all business as they packed their car with all the necessities of their trip: weapons, ammo, extra food, some clothes, go-bags comprised of military MREs (meals ready to eat), protein bars, multi-tool/swiss army knives, med kits, sewing kits, gas masks, matches, flashlight with extra batteries, glowsticks, sanitizing wipes, full water bottles, water purification tablets, compressed socks and underwear, ponchos, and a blanket. The go-bags were also equipped with sheaths for machetes which they would just put on their belts for easier access.

Logan's old profession gave him not only a respect and understanding for firearms, but also a love for them. So naturally, he owned a few. He had a Mossberg five-ninety pump action shotgun with two cases of three-inch shells, an AR Fifteen with six spare thirty round magazines of five-five-six ammo, a forty-caliber handgun with eight spare magazines loaded with ten rounds each, and two nine-millimeter handguns with twelve extra magazines, also fully loaded to capacity.

Jen had never given him a hard time about the guns. She had not only been understanding and supportive of him buying them, but also intrigued. She had always had respect for their power and admired how they had both the ability to take a life and safe a life, sometimes simultaneously. Logan had talked about purchasing more firearms from time to time when he would go through phases, and she had talked him out of it several times. If she ever foresaw what happened today, she would've told him to just keep stocking up. As it stands though, they had more firepower than most people in their neighborhood and she would have to hope that it was enough.

They owned two vehicles. And although Logan's SUV was considerably larger with more cargo space, they decided on Jen's Toyota sedan. It wasn't spacious, but it was quaint. Their supplies had only taken up half the trunk space save for the guns they carried up front with them and Jen's go-bag at her feet in the passenger seat. The car was better on gas mileage and they had to plan for the long game. They would never fit as many people in the car as they wanted to, but those were bridges to cross when they would get there. The decision to take the sedan was made easier in part because it was parked in their garage attached to the house, while Logan's SUV sat curbside.

The time they took loading the vehicle with equipment was uneventful. They would shuffle in silence to the garage and back out to fetch more supplies. When someone would run by the house or occasionally bang on the front door or window, Jen and Logan would become statues. They froze in place and fell completely silent. After a few more bangs of the person's fists and a few unsettling shrills, the infected person would become disinterested and run off in search of food elsewhere.

Logan had just closed the trunk when Jen walked up to him handing him a slice of pizza. He removed an offending pepperoni and took a bite. "We should check on Mary," she said with concern.

The past few years they had resided in Willow Valley have been an adjustment for the two. They were used to the hustle and bustle of city life in the neighboring metropolitan of Philadelphia. When they moved into the quiet suburb, they had a small amount of difficulty finding comfort, and Mary's hospitality had been crucial to their integration into small town living. When that first zombie attacked her outside earlier, Logan leapt to her rescue without a second thought. He owed her that.

The two went upstairs into the second bedroom they had converted into an office. Jen worked out of this home office between hospitals and institutes she visited. They slowly slid open the window that faced Mary's adjacent window. Given the cookie cutter layout of the houses, they believed this to be the bedroom of her daughter who was away at college.

They listened for a moment and looked down to the ground. They could hear the heavy footsteps of the "zombies" running through the neighborhood, bellowing their twisted and chilling growls intermittently.

"How do we get her attention?" Logan asked, his words muffled by the gas mask he now donned.

"We could throw something small at the window, like change or something." She responded in the same muffled tone through her own mask.

"Like we don't want her dad knowing we're sneaking her out?" he said amused with himself, his words so distorted by the mask she didn't understand him.

"What?" Jen said, wrinkling her face in confusion behind her mask.

"I said like we don't want her dad knowing we're sneaking her out." he said. But she heard *Weedle water put snowing beeper out?*

Jen shook her head and put her fingers to her ear to communicate that she couldn't understand him. He waved her off and said, "Never mind," which she heard clearly.

Jen was reaching into her pocket in search of change when she saw Logan pulling his arm in and extending it out, as if readying to throw something. "I got this," he said stretching his arm quickly and releasing his grip. Something small and round flew through the air at the closed window. Jen stared as there was a wet *thump* and the small red circle stuck onto the glass.

Jen squinted through her mask at the oily meat adhered to the window. She sighed, not wanting to know where he pulled the pepperoni from. She slapped his shoulder as she opened her hand to reveal seventeen cents in her palm; one dime, one nickel, and two pennies. Logan nodded

Jen lightly tossed the nickel and there was a low ping as it bounced off the pane and fell to the grass below. She waited a few moments and tossed the dime next with the same result. She then threw the first penny slightly harder than the previous coins. There was a louder tap noise that was almost deafening in the stillness. They cringed and waited patiently.

The blinds cracked open and they could see Mary peeking out with trepidation. She was unsure about drawing the blinds when she saw the intimidating masks on their faces. When Logan waved nonchalantly, she visibly sighed with relief as the blinds went up. She went to open the window but stopped to grab a handkerchief from the dresser next to her. She then lifted the window as she covered her mouth and nose with the cloth.

Jen seemed to be saying something through the mask and using hand gestures at Mary who stared blankly, unable to understand what she was saying. She cupped her ear with her free hand and leaned slightly in the, *I can't hear you* gesture.

Logan noticed that the fog had dissipated or "moved on" and although he wasn't eager to take any deep breaths of tainted or infectious air, he lifted his mask slightly above his mouth to make communication easier.

"Are you ok?" Logan said softly with over accentuated lip movement. "Are you armed?"

Mary nodded quickly and reached over to her right, then held up a kitchen knife. The shiny blade was an indication that she hadn't had to use it yet. That was just as much of a good a thing as it was a bad one.

"We have to leave," Jen continued, also using accentuated lip movement. "Will you come with us?"

Mary's eyes widened with fear and she shook her head vigorously. "I have to wait for Becca to get home." she said with alert.

Becca was Mary's daughter and attended Florida State University. None of them were sure how far this catastrophe reached, but if it had hit the rest of the country like it did their little slice of Heaven here, neither Logan nor Jen believed Becca would be making any trek back home.

"Mary," Jen said with her expression softening. "She might be safe in Florida, we don't know. We'll watch after you if you come with us."

Even though Mary thought the two didn't take many things in life seriously, she believed Jen when she said they would keep her safe. The two had strong convictions and Mary knew of some of the intense encounters Logan had been involved in.

"Where are we going?" Mary asked them both.

"Pinegrove," Logan replied pulling his mask up again. "We're going to get our friend Matt first, he's in trouble. Then get my brother Luke."

"I like your brother." Mary said absently with a smile as she thought about the offer. She was safe in her own home for now but couldn't be sure for how long. They could see and hear that more and more of the "zombies" or "infected" were taking to the streets, so it was only a matter of time before they got into her house or she ran out of food.

"Let me leave a note for Becca and grab a few things." she said.

"Okay. I'll have the door open for you in a minute." Logan responded, pointing down to the side door located directly under them. He turned to Jen and continued, "Can you keep an eye out up here while I get her?"

Jen nodded and he went past her, pulling his mask back on completely. He was down the stairs in a few seconds and slowly pulled the door open as he peered through the crack. Although the sounds were unsettling, he couldn't see anyone from his position. He waited for what seemed like a lifetime until he finally saw Mary opening her door cautiously. She came through and closed it, putting her key in to lock it up. She fumbled with the tumbler and stopped to adjust a blue backpack she now donned on her back that kept falling down her shoulder.

Logan rolled his eyes as he waited impatiently. *What is her problem with doors?* He caught himself almost saying the thought out loud. Mary turned and pulled her key out before stepping across the gap towards Logan.

"Psst," they both heard from above and saw Jen pointing over to the left. In the clearing stood their neighbor Brian. Well what was left of him, anyway. The entire right side of his face had been torn off. Matted hair stuck to his blood-soaked skull that peered out from sections of removed flesh. Chunks of skin and bone launched from his head as he jerked from side to side in uncontrollable convulsions. His shirt had been almost completely removed and they could see sections of flesh missing from his neck and chest that were oozing red viscous blood and other unknown fluids. He seemed to be desperately searching for prey through his spastic head movement, but the lack of his right eye was making it difficult.

Mary put her back flat against her closed door and Logan swung his closed softly but left just enough room to keep an eye on Brian, who had begun thrashing his hands in front of himself in frustration. He held his fingers like claws and with each swing, he let out what sounded like a disturbing combination of a shriek and a bark.

Logan chuckled to himself thinking that he almost sounded like a terrier with a voice changer to his mouth. It didn't stop him from shivering at the sight of the blood and saliva Brian spat with every one of his shrieks and disjointed spasms. Regardless of the fear, he was slightly amused.

Brian turned his back to them, and Logan swung the door open, waving Mary over with haste. Without hesitation, she jolted across the grass and into his door. He closed and locked it as soon she cleared the threshold. They both sighed in relief until they heard Brian let out a very different sound then his agitated barking. He let out what seemed like a gurgled war cry, a long guttural shrill that made Mary and Logan's neck hairs stand on end.

What the two hadn't seen is that at the same moment Mary had dodged the pirate-like gaze of Brian, Jen was staring intently at the lone pepperoni Logan had thrown at Mary's window upstairs. The oily sliver of meat had slid off the glass and dropped down, twisting on its descent as if dancing in the wind until... *SPLAT*. The pepperoni landed inside Brian's skull and on his visible, grated brain.

Brian spun around and looked up. Before he could glance at the window that had dropped the accosting meat, his good eye locked on Jen. His neck stuck out and his mouth opened. His lower lip hung down at his chin, since his lingual frenum had been torn away along the side of his face. He let out that ear-splitting cry of hunger as he ran full force into the wall under Jen's window. His fists slammed down on the aluminum siding in fits of rage as he whaled relentlessly.

Jen slammed the window down just as she spotted another infected person coming around the side of the house. "Shit." she said. Brian's temper tantrum was causing a commotion and would undoubtedly draw more unwanted attention. She went downstairs and met Logan and Mary.

Logan was looking out the side window at the crowd of infected that was now forming around their house. "What the hell's getting them all riled up?" he asked to no one in particular, not taking his gaze from outside.

"They seem to share your distaste for pepperoni." Jen said condescendingly.

Logan shot her a genuinely confused look but said nothing. She shook her head and moved past him to get her own look at the undead crowd. Logan went into the closet and pulled out another gas mask then tossed it to Mary.

"Put this on." he told her. "It's better than a handkerchief."

Jen saw Mary struggling with the mask and helped her put it on, then pulled her own back over her face. The three went to the garage to start Jen's car and make their heroic escape. Countless hands were now hammering on the walls and doors to the house. What was once a single unsettling shrill of unrelenting hunger and aggression had now been lost in an ocean of high pitch growls and shrieks of anticipation. They had found food and this house was not going to stop them from acquiring it.

Logan started the car as the white garage door turned black with the silhouettes of at least half a dozen undead bodies clambering against it. They could see the faces of people they didn't know, as well of a few they did, through the glass panes on the garage door. A pale face of a man who appeared to be in his thirties slammed into the glass with his mouth wide open. Blood and flesh bits lined his teeth and lips. The thud drew their attention for a second as Logan and Jen both recognized the man as Samuel Gilbert of the Sams' household.

"Shit. I guess we don't have to go to dinner with them tomorrow." Logan half smiled over at Jen in the passenger seat, hoping she would share his amusement.

She narrowed her eyes at him, not in the least amused by his insensitivity. "Let's go before we ARE dinner for him." she responded.

"You guys ready?" Logan asked them both. He could feel his adrenaline rising. His palms were sweaty on the wheel and his mouth was dry. He licked his lips and noticed his heart threatening to thump out of his chest with this surge of fear and excitement.

The incessant banging combined with the screams and shrieks of the undead crowd was terrifying. The three straightened up in their seats as Logan pressed the button on the garage opener. As the door rose, they could see the feet and legs of at least ten people pressing against it, waiting for access inside. They could hear a loud crash from inside the other room, followed by glass breaking. Just like that, the monsters were inside.

The back door had been smashed in just as several of the undead had simultaneously broken through the living room window. They poured into the house, quickly taking to each room in search of food. The garage door was about halfway up when one of them entered the garage through the foyer at Logan's driver side. A decrepit female slammed into the door. Her thin frame made a surprisingly loud thud against the metallic frame, which made the three sitting inside the vehicle jump with surprise.

They hadn't known her, but there was no denying she was an attractive woman all but a few hours ago. Her long blonde hair that had glistened like the sun now hung as dirty and lifeless as her eyes. That her blouse wasn't even slightly disturbed and there were no visible bite marks was an indication that she was caught outside in that strange white gas like John had.

She pounded on Logan's window as two more infected now entered the foyer. The garage door was only inches away from being open enough to squeeze the car through.

"Why, the fuck, do garage doors open so slowly?!" Logan yelled through gritted teeth as he leaned away from his new girlfriend at the window. The glass began to crack with the impact of several fists until finally, the car window shattered inward. Glass fragments rained inward at Logan's face. He closed his eyes to protect them, even though he still had his mask on.

The next thing he felt were several cold hands pulling on him. Their grips kept slipping as he twisted and ducked in the small confines of the car. Thankfully, they were all trying to reach their heads in the window at the same time and kept bouncing each other into and off of the frame.

"GO!" Jen screamed as the door finally rose above the height of the sedan.

Logan pushed the accelerator to the floor, not bothering to look where he was steering. It sped forward, barreling through the zombies who had finally past the threshold of the garage. There were several thumps and cracks as frail, infected bodies were met with four thousand pounds of fine, Japanese engineering. They had just about cleared the crowd when one of the zombies jumped at the car in motion and managed to gain hold of Logan's door through the busted-out window.

It was Sam Gilbert. Well, Samuel Gilbert. He hissed to show strings of blackened saliva stretching across his blood-laced mouth. Logan swerved the vehicle left, then right, in an attempt to loosen his grip. While doing so, he almost struck down even more infected who littered the streets, seemingly lost and unaware. The screeching of the tires was drawing unwanted attention as sickened, colorless faces turned and joined the chase.

Sam reached a sore covered hand at Logan's face and caught him by the chin. Logan felt the grip on him squeeze and pull as it tried to tear the flesh from his face. When Logan pivoted his face, the gas mask gave way. As Sam pulled it away with his prize, he lost his hold and tumbled to the ground, landing under the back wheel of the speeding vehicle. The three occupants inside were lifted from their seats as the rear tire went up and over Sam, crushing his spine and leaving his mangled corpse behind.

Logan's focus went back to the road as he drove, dodging a few straggling creatures as the horde they had just narrowly escaped slowly faded into the rearview mirror.

Chapter 3

"Logan." Jen said in a quiet but alert tone.

He scanned the road for a threat he wasn't aware of. "What's wrong?" he finally asked when he was sure he wasn't missing something.

"Your mask…." She didn't have to finish the sentence.

Logan's eyes went wide with panic as he put a hand to his face. "Shit…. wait," he said, his expression changing to confusion. "We've been driving for like ten minutes now."

That was all Mary needed to hear. She ripped the mask off hastily. "Good, I can't breathe in that thing." She said catching her breath.

"That doesn't mean there aren't effects of long-term ingestion." Jen said looking back at her.

"Oh great." Logan said sarcastically. "Thanks honey." His face soured.

"Well, we just don't know," she defended herself. "It's a lot thinner than it was earlier."

Logan didn't look over as he spoke, "That's what she said." he replied surly.

Jen did a double take at her husband. It had slightly annoyed her, but she smiled at his adolescent quip. He had an innate ability to find humor in any situation and in most cases, it would cheer her up. This was no exception. She removed her own mask after thinking about it a moment longer and turned to address Mary. "You ever fire a gun before?"

"Once, yes. When I was nine at my uncle's ranch. He had a bunch of guns and I shot one like that Clint Eastwood fellow had," she jabbered. Mary had a habit of talking for extended periods of time when prompted. Jen didn't think she was going to under these circumstances but knew that now, she would just have to sit back and listen.

"A forty-four magnum? Like Dirty Harry?" Logan said with excitement.

Mary paused and scolded him for the interruption, "No, like Clint Eastwood. Anyway, that thing scared the hell out of me, so I've never used one again. I'm more than sure this knife will be sufficient." She said holding the knife up and smiling curtly.

Jen looked at Logan and without a single word she shared her thoughts. He simply shook his head. Bringing Mary might not have been a good idea after all. The drive had gone uninterrupted for the most part. They passed several dozen of infected roaming the streets. Some would turn and give chase to them in the car, only to realize they couldn't keep up, while others just snickered and snarled as the group drove past. And some fed. Small groups sat or kneeled over the bodies of poor souls that were too slow to get away. The monsters would look up with the "food" still stuck in their teeth, disinterested in the passing vehicle.

Matt resided in a small apartment complex in the neighboring rural township of Pinegrove. Luke also lived in this locale but on the opposite side, closer to the city border of Philadelphia. The plan was to get Matt and go right to Luke's. Of course. The complex was five floors of apartments and Matt lived on the fourth.

As they pulled up it actually looked relatively quiet. Logan thought they might have gotten lucky and there would be no infected people here. Then, he remembered Matt's transmission on the headset. He had clearly said, "Help me", before it cut off. And hopefully, it wasn't too late.

After they both did a quick check of their handguns, Logan removed the magazine of his AR and gave it a once over. "You should probably stay here." Logan said to Mary as he slammed the magazine back into the well.

"With that broken window as easy access?" she said pointing her knife at the window next to Logan. "I don't think so. I'm coming with you two."

"You sure you don't want a gun then?" Jen asked her sincerely.

Mary shook her head in the negative, "No thanks dear." And she opened the door and stepped out.

"Does she seem eager to get eaten?" Logan whispered to Jen, who nodded slightly.

They walked up to the door and listened for a second. Nothing. Logan located the bell for Matt's apartment four-twenty-eight and held it for a second.

"If he needs help do you expect him to answer the bell?" Jen asked unsurely.

Logan shrugged and rang it again. Still nothing. "I guess we can try the door," he said pulling on the entryway door handle. It opened and led them to a lobby with an empty reception desk. They both had their firearms out and down, ready to raise them up. Jen had one of the nine millimeters and Logan the forty-caliber. Mary, on the other hand, had her knife lazily at her side.

When they scanned the room and saw no immediate threat, they made their way to the elevator. After pressing the call button a few times, they realized it must have been stuck on a different floor.

"Well, I guess the stairs it is, then", Logan whispered with a sigh as he thought to himself how any decent horror movie has a broken-down elevator and a terrifying ascent up through a monster infested stairwell.

They opened the door to the stairs and cautiously peered up. To use the word 'foul' to describe the odor that invaded their sinuses would be putting it mildly. It reeked of death and sickness. The scent of decaying flesh and human excrement fused in the stale air with the heavy smell of infirmity.

Logan's face soured, and he let out an involuntary cough before covering his mouth. Jen and Mary followed suit, although Mary gasped some inaudible utterance. All three swallowed hard trying to fight off the urge to dry-heave. Within a few minutes the putrid odor had either subsided, or their olfactory senses had adjusted enough for them to simply tolerate it.

"Still not as bad your farts." Jen whispered, wrinkling her face one more time at the smell.

"Still not as bad as your cooking." Logan replied not missing a beat. What he couldn't see was Jen mentally flipping him the finger as they carried on.

Logan stayed in front, with Jen following closely. Both had their weapons drawn and trained at the unknown darkness ahead. Logan angled to clear the stairwell as he moved up while Jen took the steps in a wide arc and covered the landings. So far, so good. They moved with purpose and confidence, but their hearts threatened to punch through their chest cavities like a freighter through tinfoil. Their foreheads were thick with sweat, but their breathing was tempered and controlled. Logan adjusted the choke of his hands on the handgun when he noticed his palms were damp and sweaty.

They cleared the third landing when they heard a single zombie let out a thunderous roar. The only thing more unsettling then the cry it bellowed forth were the echoes that reverberated throughout the stairwell.

They stopped mid-step and waited for the echo to die down so they could try and track the origin of the shrill. Logan looked over at Jen and held up one finger, then pointed up, letting her know it sounded as if it was on the next floor. They proceeded with extreme caution and moved as if they were entrenched in molasses. Each step was methodical and precise.

Jen kept her gun pointed at the two staircases as Logan opened the door to the fourth floor. He closed the door quickly and looked at Jen, who met his gaze.

"Is it clear?" she asked him almost impatiently.

He shook his head. "Not exactly," he replied. "There's a group of four near Matt's door that are crouched over, eating. They look distracted if we can sneak up on them."

Jen took a few deep breaths in preparation. Logan sensed her hesitation and put his hand on her cheek. "Hey, are you ok?"

She gave a fake smile and responded, "Yea it's just... this is terrifying."

"I know," he assured her, "It's fucking nuts, but we got this love." He kissed her forehead. He didn't really know what to tell her right now and hoped that had been enough for now. It was.

Logan opened the door and the three of them crossed through the hallway. Jen felt hot breath on her neck and an invasion of her personal space. She turned to see Mary practically nose to nose with her. She waved her fingers in a shoo motion as if telling her to back up a little. Mary mouthed sorry and created a gap between them.

Logan eyed the doors to make sure there weren't any open ones that would have unwanted guests pouring out at them once they disposed of the four who were enjoying their dinner. Once Logan was satisfied, he nodded over at Jen who stood at the opposite wall of the hallway. This way, there was no chance for friendly fire.

They both aimed down and acquired their target when Logan held up three fingers and counted down slowly. As his final finger closed down and he made a fist they both pulled their respective triggers. Logan blew a hole through the back of the head of a man who looked to be in his mid-twenties. There was a teenage girl who dined with him. She looked up from her meal with a fresh piece of cartilage and muscle dangling from her mouth just in time to have a bullet punch through her eye socket and explode the back of her skull.

Logan only heard his two gunshots and glanced at Jen. She was pulling the trigger but there was no bullet expulsion. "JAM." she shouted at him as she dropped the gun and went for her machete at her side. Although she knew how to clear the weapon's jam, she was short on time and space as undead eyes were now on her.

The two zombies closest to her were now well aware of her presence. The older of the two males jumped to his feet and let out that familiar ear-splitting shriek. He lunged at Jen with his arms outstretched as he was snapped his teeth at her. Logan closed the gap and put his shoulder into the man's sternum, slamming him against the wall and sending him to the floor.

The fourth zombie was an Asian man who had just ran past Logan as he knocked the other one down. Logan dove forward and managed to grab the zombie's ankle as he closed in on Jen. The man went down with a loud thud and his teeth could be heard cracking on impact. He turned and looked at Logan with pure hatred in his white lifeless eyes. He snarled and opened his mouth which allowed Logan to see that he had been right. At least three of his teeth had been knocked out when he fell and torn through his upper lip. Fresh blood poured out from the open wounds. The Asian man started clacking his teeth together and bent over to get closer to Logan.

Jen finally managed to free her machete from the sheathe and drove it down into the man's head. The blade entered his temple and threatened to push his eyeballs from their sockets as she forced it in further. When it was clear that he had stopped moving, she pulled the blade out. The third older zombie was back on his feet and headed right for Logan, who was still on the floor.

Logan turned on his back and placed his feet up as the zombie attempted to dive on top. Logan drove both of his feet into the man's midsection and bent his legs. Rolling backwards slightly he extended his legs and launched the man over him. The zombie flew past Jen and landed hard on his back.

Seemingly unfazed the zombie was back up again in an instant. This time he turned to Mary who was now closest to him. She screamed and closed her eyes as she held her knife up in front of her, hoping he would just kind of run his own head into the pointy end.

Logan was on his knees and brought up his pistol, firing at the man at an angle. The front of his head exploded and caked Mary's face with blood and brain matter. Her eyes were still closed but she jumped with the splatter of the bodily liquids.

Jen sheathed her machete and picked up her pistol to clear the jam while Logan stood. They eyed each other. Another close call.

"We have to get better at this." she said fighting back a tear of emotion.

"We will." he assured her, swallowing down the same urge to cry a little. He never wanted them to be that close to danger again. He massaged his palm to ease his own trembling hands.

They looked over at Mary who was still holding her knife out and squeezing her eyes shut so hard, they wondered if she would go blind.

"Mary," Logan stage whispered to her. When she didn't budge, he repeated, "Mary, you're ok."

She cautiously popped one eye open and had it do a three-sixty scan of the hallway, then opened her other eye. Bringing the knife down she dropped her shoulders and relaxed her posture slightly. "Do you still have that extra gun?" she asked with trepidation.

Logan pulled the extra nine-millimeter from his waist band and held her hand before placing the firearm in her grip. "Trigger safety," he instructed her, "finger stays off the trigger and outside the guard until you shoot. Raise it up, breathe slowly, and squeeze, don't pull." He let go as the weight of the firearm dragged Mary's hand down. She fought to raise it up and took a second to adjust her grip.

"Ok," she responded nervously, "thank you." He squeezed her shoulder gently and ushered her over with them.

The hallway was eerily quiet, and Logan was convinced that the confrontation would draw out more of those things from all over the building if they didn't move quickly. They stepped down and slowed as they approached Matt's apartment.

A cold shiver ran down Logan's spine as he noticed the door was cracked open. His eyes ran along the frame and strike plate, searching for signs of forced entry. There weren't any. The door had just simply been opened. He felt a little better, thinking to himself that it was a good sign no one had exited the apartment during their encounter moments ago. They surely would have been caught off guard and the results could have been fatal.

Logan used the muzzle of his sidearm to delicately push the door open. The creaking it emitted had the effect of nails on a chalkboard as it made his blood run cold with every centimeter it shifted. They stepped through and Logan scanned the living area as Jen covered the hallway attached to it.

Mary closed the door quietly and attempted to connect the latch and secure them inside. The problem was that she still had the gun in one hand and the knife in the other. The clacking of the chain against the door as she was unable to gain hold of it was booming through the silence in the apartment. Logan and Jen looked over and watched Mary switch from her gun hand back to her knife hand a few more times. It then dawned on her to put the knife on the entry table sitting directly next to her. She placed the knife down and successfully attached the latch. Then, she turned to see her audience staring at her as if she were the main attraction at the circus.

When she didn't say anything, Logan spoke to her. "Stay here Mary and watch the door for us? Let us know if you hear anything out there."

She nodded adamantly, and Logan turned back around to Jen, raising his eyebrows and mouthing the word *WOW*.

The two walked down the hallway that hosted the apartment's bathroom and bedroom. They could begin to hear what sounded like a TV coming from the back room. Jen shot Logan a mild look of confusion.

"Horde Z," he smirked. He recognized the sounds of the game and now knew that Matt had been thrust into the madness with no time to turn off his console. That wasn't a good sign.

The bedroom door was closed over much like the front door had been. Again, the door screamed in protest of being inched open by the muzzle of Logan's gun. *Don't they oil any of the doors around here?* he thought to himself as he rolled his eyes.

The lights inside were off but the TV illuminated the room save for a tall man standing directly in front of the screen. Logan drew a deep breath at the unsettling image of the person who was standing in place, facing away from him and transfixed on the TV. The raucous sound effects and sharp graphics of the game were holding his attention. Logan had seen enough horror movies to know that this was not normal human behavior.

The man was the same height as Matt and wore a similar backwards Philadelphia Flyers cap. In fact, Logan noticed, he recognized the hoodie he was wearing. It was dark green with the words 'If you can read this, I just farted' emblazoned on the back.

"Oh fuck," Logan said with worry. "Matt…." He felt his heart sink, fearing the worst.

There was no way he heard Logan over the gunfire and screaming taking place on the TV, so Logan believed he must have felt the presence of someone else in the room. The man turned slowly ala Resident Evil. His white eyes gleamed with the prospect of fresh food and his mouth opened slowly in the fashion of a yawn. Saliva poured over his lower lip in preparation of dining.

When he faced them head on the light from the hallway revealed that the man was in fact, not Matt. Logan exhaled in relief and slacked his gun slightly, looking over at Jen. "Thank God." he told her, managing a half smile.

She looked at him incredulously. "Seriously?" she snapped.

"Well I mean, I'm sorry for this guy…" he back peddled, "but it's not Matt at least, is what I mean. What I wanna know is…." He was cut off when the man half barked and lunged at him, knocking over the small table in his path. Logan hopped back a step and sent two rounds into his midsection to stop his forward momentum, then aimed up and fired into his head. The bullet entered through his nose and sent his cap flying from his head as it exited the back of his skull.

The man's body fell back and dropped to the floor, taking a shelf adorned with knick-knacks down with him. There was a moment of silence when his body stopped moving that was broken by Mary appearing at the doorway.

"You two ok?" she asked, looking into the room but not daring to enter.

"Yea, we're good Mary." Jen said. "Thanks."

Just then the closet door in the room swung open wildly and there stood a tall messy haired man in his boxers and a tank top. He was wearing a microphone headset that almost looked worthy of an NFL play caller. It was Matt.

"Holy shit Logan, am I glad…." He started before a startled Mary gasped and simultaneously brought her pistol up, squeezing the trigger.

The bullet punched a hole in the frame of the closet and spat out splintered wood fragments. They all flinched, but Matt shrieked loudly as he jumped away from where the bullet would have caught him in his chest.

Jen walked over to Mary, who was already holding the firearm out in front of her as if it were a used child's diaper. She took it from Mary and tucked it into the back of her waistband.

"I'll just…. use the knife." Mary said sheepishly.

Logan walked over to Matt, who was gaining his composure, and the two bro-hugged. "Fuck, I'm happy to see you two," he said with elation to Jen and Logan. "And hi there 'Lady who almost shot me.'" He looked at Mary indignantly.

"Sorry about that," she said. "I'm Mary. I never liked guns ever since I shot one when I was a kid and we just… well THEY just had a nasty fight with some of those sick people in the hall and all I had was a knife so I thought it would be a good idea to try a gun again until you jumped out of the closet." She was rambling a mile a minute and speaking as if they weren't all just witness to the incident.

The look of bewilderment on Matt's face amused Logan, who cracked a smile. Mary was about to start up again when Logan got Matt's attention. "What happened, man?"

Matt removed the headset and ran his hand through his dark hair a few times, trying to place the events of the last few hours. "It was crazy, dude. We were online and that weird…. horn went off. I thought my head was gonna explode." He put some pants on as he talked and looked down at the man on the floor for the first time. "Oh shit." he said covering his mouth. He turned back into the closet and vomited.

Mary and Jen took this as their cue to leave the room and left Logan behind to tend to him. A few dry heaves followed Matt's initial lunch expulsion as he was getting back to his feet. "That's gross." Matt said to Logan.

"It happens." Logan reassured him. "What happened after the horn?" he prompted Matt to continue.

"Chaos." he said curtly. "I went out in the hallway with a few of my neighbors and heard a bunch of commotion outside. They started running around out there and killing each other and shit." He shook his head and exhaled a heavy breath as if he was seeing it all over again. "All of a sudden, a bunch of people came running into the hallway and killing my neighbors...they killed Rico, man." His eyes teared up and he swallowed hard as he went on. "But then Rico got up and killed Chan.... And Chan got up and killed Stacy... they chased me back in here and I hid in the closet. I've been in there since."

"You've been in there for four hours?" he said, sympathetically. "Jesus Christ, man."

"Yea," Matt said. "and I had to pee since the third round of Horde Z...."

"Go now then." Logan replied.

"...I went in the closet a few hours ago." he said disgusted. "So gross."

"Oh...." was all Logan could respond with. "So why is this guy wearing your clothes?" He pointed at the lifeless body, changing the subject.

Matt wiped his mouth again and replied. "That's Rico. He had a fight with his lady a few days ago and she burned all his clothes. So, I gave him some of mine. I actually wanted the hoodie back though."

"Yea it's a good hoodie." Logan said glancing down at the wording on it again. "Let's get you cleaned up real quick before we head out."

"Head out?" Matt said in alarm. "I'm not going anywhere."

It always amazed Logan how Matt stood an imposing six-foot and some change and almost two hundred pounds of solid muscle, yet he had the intestinal fortitude of a teddy bear during confrontations. This madness wouldn't be a fight he would be able to steer clear of.

"Dude it's not safe here. And if they heard all those gunshots, those things are gonna be on their way in here soon." Logan explained.

"Shit man, shit." Matt said lowering his head. "This is not like Horde Z, Logan. This is real life. This shit's scary."

"Yea, which is why we have to go." he retorted. "You can use the extra nine-millimeter that almost killed you." Logan said as he smacked him on the shoulder and smiled.

Matt looked up at him and nodded. "Yea, yea." he exclaimed excitedly. "Yea ok, let's do it. Where are we going?"

"There's the Matt I know." Logan cheered with a friendly punch to his friend's arm. "I've been in contact with a close-knit special ops friend," he continued as he deepened his voice. "There's a secure military bunker five clicks west of here that he instructed us to rendezvous at where we'll get new weapons and a sitrep."

"Holy shit dude." Matt said excitedly, looking up from tying his sneaker. "You serious?"

Logan couldn't help but crack a smile. "No, dumbass. We're gonna go get Luke and find a place to lay low. Maybe our parents' old cabin up north, who knows?"

Matt's face dropped. "You are such an asshole." he said shaking his head but letting a smirk spread across his face. "I knew that sounded too good to be true." He stood up and they made their way to the kitchen where Jen and Mary were already raiding through his cabinets.

"Don't cook much, do you?" Jen asked.

"Well I only cook for myself, so I go to the corner market and get fresh stuff every day." He said. "I would be normally getting back about now. I do have a whole cabinet full of protein bars though." He pointed over to the cupboard next to Jen.

When she opened it, she was greeted by the sight of at least a dozen boxes, each containing a dozen protein bars. There may not have been any perishable foods in his kitchen, but high-protein factory sealed meal supplements dominated his pantry.

Matt pretty much lived at the gym. His beach muscles, though lacking in functionality, were impressive sights to behold. He was strong, and Logan knew they would need him.

Matt had been to the range a few times with Logan and had an interest in firearms and their mechanics, but never really understood the point of owning one. *That's what cops are for,* he had told Logan, which was a comment Logan resented at the time.

"Still think cops are the only ones who should have guns?" Logan chided him.

"Well you're the one who came to my rescue so…" he replied, letting his sentence hang.

"Yea good point." Logan said stuffing supplies into a backpack. Matt noticed what he was doing and rummaged through some drawers to add to the Jansport bag he would be carrying. "That should be good, we have to-" The last words of his sentence were lost in a sudden cacophony of otherworldly shrieks and groans.

They all froze to listen as it fell silent again. Only for a moment until one, then a second, then a third roar of the undead echoed forward in a frenzied declaration of hunger. The maddening screams seemed to be coming from the stairwells and were getting noticeably louder. Which was an indication that the monsters were getting closer.

"They're in the stairwells." Logan announced to the group as they all readied up to exit. Then there was a loud knock on the front door that caught everyone's attention.

They all stared, perplexed at the notion that a zombie may have just given them the courtesy of requesting an invitation before feasting on their flesh. After a moment, a soft female voice spoke.

"Hello, Matt? It's Carrie." the female voice said through the door.

Matt's expression became pure elation and he silently fist pumped the air. He looked around and gathered himself before running to the door.

"Hey Carrie, what's up?" he said suavely, as he cracked the door.

"Um," she started nervously, "Hey Matt… I heard all that commotion in the hallway…" she said as she stared at him through the crack of the door.

"Oh yea," he said with a smile, "that was my friends. They kind of just saved me so I'm gonna head out with them."

"Cool," Carrie replied with an unsure nod. "Can we uh…come in? So, we don't get killed in the middle of our conversation?" She shot him a glance like the invitation to come in had been clearly overlooked and she wasn't happy about it. Carrie knew Matt liked her and she would sometimes catch his stares lingering at her while they conversed. Under normal circumstances, she usually found it endearing, but this was hardly the time for puppy love.

Matt just smiled at her for a moment before realizing he still hadn't responded. "Oh God. Yea, yea of course." he said opening the door and letting her in, "Wait, *we*…?" A skinny man with short, blonde hair and a black jacket pushed past Matt right behind Carrie. "Oh," he said, deflated, "you brought Rick."

Matt shut the door and turned to the group. He looked around and did quick introductions, "My neighbors, Carrie and Rick. Why are you guys here?" he asked looking at Carrie. She was short with shoulder length brown hair and dark mascara which was smeared and running. She'd clearly been crying.

"We heard all the fighting in the hallway and saw them enter your apartment. We figured you would have somewhere to go" she said, slightly abashed, digging her hands into her pockets.

"And we gotta get outta here." Rick interjected forcefully, "So, we're going with you." He pointed a wooden baseball bat in his possession at Matt. The tip was stained red as if it were used then scrubbed vigorously with a cleaner.

Logan found himself wondering if it had been stained with blood before the zombie incident. He knew this guy for all but thirty seconds and his shitty disposition was as clear as the sky was blue.

"Ok, but we have to leave now." Logan said to them. "You have supplies?" He glanced back and forth to the newcomers.

"You do. So, now we do too." Rick said as he stepped forward and sized Logan up in a clear show of dominance.

Logan pulled his gun from his holster and casually placed it at his side, never looking away from Rick. Taking one glance down at the firearm, Rick stepped back and smirked defiantly.

"You done?" Logan said intensely. "Cause we gotta move."

Carrie stepped in front of Logan, "I'm sorry." she said holding her hands up in a placating gesture. "He can be a douche until you get to know him."

"What the fuck you just call me?" Rick said angrily as he turned.

Carrie waved him off. "We're ready."

"Jen," Logan said, still eyeing Rick. Logan was all about laughing and joking at inopportune times to create levity and break tensions, but this alpha male had just pissed him off. Now he was stone faced and all business.

Without a response, Jen knew what his prompt was for. She went to the door and drew her gun. She cracked it open slightly and listened. "Maybe sixty seconds, max." She said softly to them.

Logan swung around Jen and took lead as he stepped through the door with his gun up. Jen followed with Mary, Carrie, and Rick behind. Matt was on the end with his gun, looking back.

"We saw the elevator is stuck on this floor," Jen remembered. "Think we can get it to work and just bypass them?"

"Wouldn't want to chance getting stuck," Logan replied. "We'd be like a sardine can for them." They glanced around for a way out as their legs and eyes moved interchangeably. They all silently prayed that they would not have to fight down an entire stairwell of those monsters.

Another sudden set of unnatural human barking filled the hallway as the door behind them swung open and at least six of the infected came into view. They all stopped for a second, their jaws clacking with heavy saliva lubricating their palates. Their necks and hands twitching uncontrollably in quick jerky movements. They looked ravenous.

There was a collective utterance of "Shit" among the group as the zombies sprinted forward at them. Matt took aim and fired at the man in front as they all ran towards what they hoped would lead to an exit. Blood spurted as the rounds punctured the man's chest cavity but did little to slow his momentum.

"Headshots or leg shots." Logan screamed over the gunfire now erupting in the hallway. Before he finished his sentence, Jen was lowering her gun and firing at three pairs of legs that were barreling down the hall at them.

All three of the infected, two men and a woman, went down face first onto the carpeted floor, their leg bones shattered from the bullets. The now nine or ten infected that followed immediately tripped over them. This essentially caused a traffic jam as even more of the infected now couldn't make it through the threshold of the stairwell.

The group rounded a bend in the hall and could spot a fire escape at the end. "See it?" Logan shouted, never breaking stride.

"Fire escape," Matt shouted over everyone, "I completely forgot about that."

An apartment door on to the right creaked opened as they ran past. No one took notice until Carrie crossed the doorway and a tall black man leapt out, grabbing her waist and pulling her down to the floor with him. She screamed and attempted to scramble to her feet as he gained hold of her legs and tried to bite down. She kicked at him wildly, breaking his nose but not stopping his advance.

The man's hands were thrashing at her as he crawled overtop, trying to get at her face. Carrie turned and saw Rick with his bat running right at her attacker. "Help me." she screamed at him as he lifted his bat just before reaching them and then…. jumped completely over them. Carrie's horror filled expression intensified as she screamed again, "Rick, HELP!"

Rick turned after he landed and shook his head at a struggling Carrie before taking back off down the hall. Her scream caught the attention of Logan, Jen and Matt who were just about at the window with the fire escape. They all turned as an exhausted Rick caught up with them.

"You prick." Logan said as he and Matt went off to aid Carrie. Logan holstered his sidearm and slung his rifle around. He brought it up to his eye and unleashed death into the mass of undead pouring around the corner.

Matt stayed low as he ran full speed to Carrie who was crying uncontrollably as she fought to keep the man's teeth from sinking in. As he closed the gap, Matt pulled his right leg up and let go with all the strength he could muster. Upon impact with Matt's boot, the man's head snapped back with a violent crack of his jaw and spine. His foot throbbed from the kick, but he'd have to worry about that later. He pulled Carrie up and pushed her in front of him as he felt a pair of hands swipe at his back.

Matt turned just in time to see the ashen face of an undead inches from him extending its jaw and reaching for his flesh with its decaying, jagged choppers. Before he could reach for his gun, the creature's face exploded with the sound of Logan's rifle fire. As if in slow motion, Matt could see the nasal cavity and eyeball collapse inward as the bullet entered, expelling blood and puss as it traversed through his skull, finally taking refuge in his malformed brain.

Matt and Carrie ran past Logan, who was still firing into mass. The ones they had shot in the legs had done the job. The zombies following directly behind them tripped up and went over in a twisting heap of uncoordinated flesh. As more and more of them flowed in the halls they were slowed by what was seemingly becoming a mountain of bodies. As they scrambled to gain ground and push passed each other, they were met with hot lead that permanently stopped their advances. The now lifeless zombies only added to the fleshy obstacle course. But for all the effort, they were still gaining ground. Slowly, but gaining ground, nonetheless.

Jen glanced out the window and down the fire escape. "It's clear all the way to the car." she shouted when she was satisfied with what she saw.

"Then go!" Logan shouted back at her as his rifle clicked empty. He swung it to his back and pulled his pistol again, knowing there wasn't ample time to reload it just yet.

Jen was ascending the fire escape, clearing two rungs at a time and looking up periodically to check on Mary who was following. She was moving at a noticeably slower pace but the panic she wore on her face told Jen that she was going as fast as her body would allow. Matt helped Carrie out the window and she shot him a glance of admiration on her way down.

When a crawler homed in on Rick, his "tough-guy" façade quickly faded, and his expression flushed with pure terror. He looked at the undead face closing in on him and couldn't help but find himself transfixed by the grotesquery. His thirst for blood and hunger for flesh were heavily reflected in the putridity of his white eyes. His shoulder length hair whipped violently as he dragged his matted beard across the now bloodstained floor. He was letting out a throaty growl as his mouth hung open, spit flooding out. The mass of zombies behind him crashed around the walls like a tidal wave of decaying flesh and snapping bone.

Rick turned and shouldered passed Matt, dropping his bat and diving out the window. He scurried like a rat with its ass on fire down the ladder, almost stepping on Carrie's head as he caught up to her.

Matt stepped through the window and turned, covering Logan as he backed toward the window and inserted a fresh magazine into the well of his gun. Matt started down when Logan had one leg through the window. It was close, but he was comfortable with the mass of bodies in the hall, as that should give them just enough time to escape. By the time he got to ground level, Jen should have the car started and they can take off like a bat out of hell.`

A sudden ding and green light off to the side let Logan know that the elevator that had been stuck previously was now operational. This elevator that had just fixed itself was located between the now slowly advancing horde and Logan who was still sticking halfway out the fire escape. The door hissed as it slid open and a blur of a person bolted out towards Logan. With a split-second glance he could see that it was a young man in his early twenties. He sported a New York Yankees hat and matching shirt. The man looked young enough that the signature red sores of the affliction that lined his forehead and cheeks may have passed for acne only one day prior. Ribbons of flesh hang from his flayed lower lip and dark blood drenched his lower jaw. Missing bottom teeth revealed his smoky pock-lined tongue that danced around the inside of his mouth, flinging crimson droplets carelessly onto his once coveted sports attire.

Logan pushed off the frame just as the Yankee fan rammed into him, not clearing the window. He crashed through the frame and sent glass and wood raining down the ladder. Logan hit the metal landing hard but kept his gaze on his attacker. As a result, his face was cut by the flying debris in several spots. He ignored the pain for now, as the man's upper half was currently on top of him. His arms thrashed violently at Logan as his legs were still hanging through the busted-out window. Logan held the boy's face at arm's length, but it was letting out a flurry of wild punches.

"Ok," Logan yelled as the man pummeled the sides of his face, "So you know I'm a Phillies fan I take it?" The man hit him hard again and Logan could feel the daze setting in from the impact. He couldn't pivot his body in such a way to allow him leverage and he hadn't enough room to reach for a weapon.

"Hold on." Logan heard Matt yell to him and found himself wondering just what Matt was going to do. He hoped, for the love of God, that he wasn't about to attempt a headshot at this distance and angle with just a nine-millimeter. Matt would be just as likely to shoot and kill Logan as he would the attacker.

"Take your time, Matt." Logan shouted as he tried to shield his face from the onslaught of haymakers. "I have him right where I want him."

Logan felt a meaty hand on his leg and before he could look, he was dragged across the landing, almost falling down the ladder chute. Logan glanced at the zombie who was no longer in reaching distance and sighed relief for the momentary reprieve.

Matt had come back up and pulled Logan away from the zombie fixed by the ankles. Before heading back down, Matt chuckled at Logan, "You were just tenderized."

Logan couldn't help but let out a little laugh as he watched the zombie shuffle and twist as it tried to free its trapped legs from the window. Logan assumed he must have broken both knees against the lower frame since they weren't moving amidst his wriggling.

More growls and screams echoed forth through the window as several more undead faces finally reached the opening. Logan was already moving down, practically stepping on Matt's head who was scrambling to reach the ground. He could hear glass shatter and wood splinter as the mass of zombies removed the remains of the window as they pushed through.

The ladder shook violently as the weight of the attackers flooded the fire escape with no regard for their own safety. Logan heard a few pitched barks fade away and caught glimpses of a zombie or two as they fell passed him to the ground. A hand even swiped his pant leg as they tumbled over the gate and down, heads exploding as they met solid concrete.

The loud thuds of boots on metal rungs were an indication that the mechanics of ladder descension were not lost on the undead. There was simply too much mass at the ladder opening and not enough patience among them to each carefully take their time trotting down for dinner. As far as Logan and Matt were concerned, they were fine with the undead thinning their own herd.

Matt was on the ground and opening the front passenger door when he noticed that Jen, Mary, Carrie, and Rick were all crammed in the back. "Why isn't the car started?" he said with panic in his words.

"He has the keys." Jen said pointing over at Logan, who was just now on the bottom rung.

Logan hopped off and ran to the car. He stopped short and jumped when a zombie crashed down onto the hood. The metal caved in under the weight of the obese man, who bounced off like a basketball and rested on the cement several feet away, dead again.

Logan pulled at the passenger door and saw the group of faces staring back him. He looked at the driver door then back at them again. "What the hell?" he uttered with winded breaths.

"You have the keys." Jen repeated to him.

"Shit." he said, reaching into his pocket as the first of the ladder climbing undead touched ground and tumbled over, clearly not coordinated enough to stick the landing. Logan was in and turning the keys in seconds as more and more zombies rained down from the fire escape. Heads and limbs exploded and snapped. Several sit unmoving like nothing more than discarded and ruined children's dolls, their spines crushed from the impact.

The several zombies who made it down the ladder were now regaining their footing and turning to the car while their legs simultaneously ushered them forth. The one in front now had his right femur protruding from his leg but was seemingly unaffected by it as he ran towards them. The wheels screeched and kicked up heavy smoke as the rubber burned hot with the reversing vehicle. The limping zombie went from reaching distance to thirty feet away before being overtaken by the large crowd who were all running with two functional legs.

Logan slammed the brakes and turned the wheel, then cut the opposite direction and slammed back down on the accelerator. Again, the tires shrieked as they gained traction and the car punched forward. The momentary pause of the vehicle was all it took for a single sprinter to get within distance. An athletic teenage boy who was probably on the local track team vaulted through the crowd and landed on the back of the car that was now gaining speed.

"Company." Jen yelled to Logan, who already spotted the intruder in the mirror. He stomped down on the brake so hard that he thought his foot might actually go through the floor. The car skidded and drifted at an angle as the brakes locked, sending the zombie over the top of the car and right down onto the front windshield.

"Shit." Logan said as the young aggressor looked squarely at him and opened his mouth. His sore covered tongue whipped around outside his blackened mouth. A pimple above his eyebrow popped and yellow-green puss erupted out and dripped down his cheek. Logan did his best not to gag at the sight as the zombie then bashed his own head against the glass several times. Spider cracks took shape as the integrity of both the window and the zombie's head were now in question.

Logan hit the accelerator again as the zombie's now completely disfigured face poured blood all over the cracked windshield, further obstructing his view. Logan leaned his head slightly out the shattered driver's window but had to lean back, as the zombie would let go of his hold to reach at his face. Fortunately, the rural street they were speeding down was mostly clear save for a few randomly deserted vehicles along the road.

"Shoot him." Rick screamed in horror as he was being lifted from his seat repeatedly.

"No," Jen hollered back, "We'll all go deaf."

"Deaf is better than dead." Carrie interjected.

"Yea fuck it." Jen said as she rolled her window down and stuck her gun out. "Logan, give me a shot!", she yelled to him as she pulled her gun and leaned out the window.

Logan knew what she wanted to do and he slowed the vehicle to a low enough speed that he could lean further out. When he did, the zombie went for him. He reached his cold pale hand around the window and brought his head over, right into Jen's view. Logan let the zombie grab him and quickly leaned back inside. She steadied her hand as much as she could with the car still moving and let out three shots for good measure.

Several things happened next in quick succession. One of the three bullets Jen fired entered the zombie's temple and exited his skull at an angle, sending brain matter and bone fragments soaring. As this happened, Logan spotted a fast approaching brick wall and once again brought his foot down heavily on the brakes. He jerked the wheel and the vehicle's tail end spun out and came to an abrupt stop. The body of their guest, now lifeless, careened through the air and hit the brick wall with such force that it burst into several fleshy pieces. His already thrashed and glass-infused head was liquefied, and his right arm was thrown from his torso at the shoulder. His left knee made a *POP* sound as it was snapped off and away from his upper leg. The twisted, bloody mass that could no longer be called a body hit the ground with a wet and heavy thud. A large splatter of blood now covered the small section of wall at the impact site. A thick red trail ran like an arrow down to the remains.

They all took a moment to catch their breaths. "Everyone ok?" Logan asked, looking around at the shocked faces.

No one answered and in the awkward silence they could hear the car screaming for help. The engine sputtered and smoke crept up from the sides of the now deformed hood.

"I think…." Mary started in shock, "we need a new car."

Logan nodded in agreement almost robotically. His hands were squeezing the wheel so tight he wondered if his skin would come off when he could finally manage to peel his fingers free. His eyes were staring straight ahead, but he wasn't really looking at anything. He could barely see through the mangled windshield, but when he noticed movement up the road through the fragments of cracked glass, he became alert. He narrowed his eyes, but still wasn't sure what he was seeing.

Matt had a slightly better view from the passenger side and his eyes widened as his sight managed to make sense of what was in front of them. His mouth dropped open and his finger came up. He wiggled it back and forth, pointing at what he saw down the road since his gaping mouth was unable to speak.

Chapter 4

They had crossed into a busy thoroughfare on the border of Philadelphia. Much like the small suburban county of Willow Valley, that strange, white fog had swept through other heavily populated cities mercilessly and produced the same, if not worse, fate for its denizens.

It consumed and killed indiscriminately, then reanimated them with the most unnatural of hungers. It twisted and contorted their bodies and minds and rebirthed them into a malformed incarnation of amalgamated death and disease. They arose as undead cankerous shells of their former selves and fed on the living flesh of their once fellow human beings.

The city street had been heavy with pedestrian and motor vehicle traffic before the event. The hustle and bustle of everyday life had been cut short with the waling of the siren and the release of the gas. Businessmen on lunch and housewives taking their children for a stroll were all caught by surprise. Any witnesses who survived this otherworldly attack would not be foolish enough to wander outside in the streets, unless they were well armed and prepared.

Yet, there they sat in a beaten and battered Toyota sedan that was barely holding on to dear life. It sputtered in place as the engine lamented its abuse and desperation for a tune-up. It sat defeated, mimicking the expressions of its occupants as they faced down a horde of the undead that spanned city blocks.

The zombies were shuffling aimlessly about, much like the slow dead-brained ghouls of the old George Romero films. There was every previous occupation in the crowd, from street vendors, first responders, and mechanics to suits and joggers. God have mercy, as there were even children included in the horde. The ages varied, as some looked to be maybe five or six and others looked as if they were in their mid-teens.

When everyone realized just what they were looking at, the silence was broken by the sound of Matt's automatic window being rolled up. When he noticed Logan and Jen looking at him questionably, he simply shrugged and said, "I don't know."

"Everyone, slowly get out and head for that repair shop next to us." Logan said calmly but lacking confidence. He readied his rifle and opened the driver door. He handed Jen a go-bag before swinging his own onto his back and slinging the weapons sack on his shoulder.

They were walking cautiously towards the door of the auto shop with their weapons up when one of the shamblers about seventy-five yards out turned in their direction. Logan could only tell it was a woman with long hair and what looked like a trench coat … or maybe a man with long hair and trench coat. So, after he thought about it, he realized he could only tell it was a *zombie* with long hair and a trench coat. Regardless, *it* watched their slow walk over to the garage before shuffling a few steps and stopping. It looked up and let out a guttural howl.

This alerted most, if not all, who were seemingly unaware that food had entered their dominion. Hundreds of faces from both ends of the undead spectrum turned. Some appeared to be relatively normal save the sores and skin discoloration. Some were nothing more than skin and bones, as if they had just been unearthed after hundreds of years of rest. And the rest were sad souls who just weren't fast enough to outrun the others. Their faces and unseen areas of their bodies were riddled with bite marks and chunks of missing flesh.

Mary was first at the main door to the shop and pulled on it. It didn't budge. She pulled with heavy heaves and still it would give no ground.

"Move, bitch." Rick said pushing her a little too hard to the side. She stumbled and fell over, letting out an involuntary cry of protest.

"Fucking asshole." Matt said loud enough for Rick to hear as he and Carrie helped Mary to her feet. Rick ignored them and continued to pull at the door that still wouldn't allow them access.

"No pressure, guys." Logan said, bringing his rifle up. The slow shuffle of the crowd steadily turned into a normal walk, followed by a brisk pace, and then, finally, an all-out dash. "Ok," Logan continued, "a little bit of pressure."

Matt walked up with Jen and the two turned the corner of the shop to check if the side of the building was clear. They were about halfway across when Jen tapped Matt on the shoulder who was now passing her.

"Hey, hey," she said eagerly, "look."

Matt turned and saw that the service garage was wide open with a clear view of the main floor. The best part was that it appeared to be clear of any infected inside. They ran inside with their guns aimed at eye level just to be cautious. Looking clear didn't mean that the building *was* clear.

"Somebody get that damn door open!" Logan shouted as he fired a few rounds into the mob that was running at them. He had a little more ground before he had to trade precision shots for the spray-and-pray method.

Rick was pulling on the handle with all his strength when the door finally gave way and he fell back with his own weight, his ass crashing to the ground. On the opposite side of the door was Matt and Jen, who had just pushed the crossbar open for them from the inside.

Rick was rubbing his sore backside and Mary and Carrie were sharing the same, puzzled look. "Service garage." was all Matt said.

"Oh, that's nice." Mary said sweetly as Carrie all but pushed her through the door.

"Logan," Jen yelled over her husband's rifle fire. "Get in."

Logan turned and ran inside. They slammed the metal door shut, once again locking the crossbar over. Logan turned when he entered and saw Matt fighting with one of two large garage doors that were wide open. He rolled his eyes, "Fucking duh." he said to himself before running over to close the second one.

Matt's door was almost fully closed, and he could see Logan struggling with the chain on his door. He ran over to him and took the chain from his grasp. "I'll pull, you shoot." he half yelled with a matter-of-fact tone. These were the roles Logan knew they were meant for. Matt was there to move heavy objects and put foot-to-ass while Logan was to shoot first and ask questions never.

"I would've gotten it eventually." Logan said as he released the chain and took aim with his rifle.

Some of the faster undead were maybe thirty or forty feet from the garage when Logan sent his five-five-six rounds into their faces. Matt finished bringing the second door down and there was enough space that they had finished wrapping the chains when the first of several bodies began slamming into the giant metal doors. The metal bowed at the hinges and pushed inwards and outwards with each impact of the growing horde.

"Keys." Logan exclaimed loudly. "Jen, can you check the office for keys to any of these cars? We need to move them up against the doors."

"Yea, good call." she said, as she turned to head to the office in the back of the service area. She looked around at the group and thought about who to bring with her for backup. Matt was busy helping Logan and she knew she couldn't count on Mary, seeing just how jumpy she was. She couldn't trust Rick and his self-conservationist attitude as far as she could throw him. This left Carrie. She was green behind the ears, but Jen knew she could at least trust her.

"Carrie," Jen said, "Give me a hand?" She took her machete out and extended the handle out to her.

Carrie had an expression of both apprehension and reverence. "Yea sure." she said, taking the long blade.

Jen thrust the office door open and stepped back, aiming her gun inside. The dim light on the wall cast an ominous glow in the vacant room. She stepped in and was greeted with the offensive odor of death.

She was on high alert. Her heart pounded and her brain raced with possibilities of what awaited her. Her breath was heavy and her legs were as shaky as a virgin on prom night, but she exhaled a heavy and controlled breath. *I got this* she thought to herself as she stepped further into the office.

On the far end of the back wall, she spotted a wide-open key box. She went for it. As she got closer, she could see the multiple keys hanging on their hooks with the maintenance tags attached. As she passed the service counter the leather stool resting behind it rolled about a foot out into the clearing. Jen stopped and jumped back a step, aiming her gun at the chair.

That split-second reaction saved her life as before she could even squeeze the trigger, a male in overalls with the name 'Derrick', as shown on his name tag, jumped out from behind the counter. He sent the chair wheeling out across the floor and landed right where Jen would have been standing. Although his body hit down on the hard-concrete floor of the shop, his arms still managed to grab hold of one of Jen's legs.

She aimed down at his head just as his flailing arm struck the gun and sent it sailing across the floor. She spun to evade her attacker, but he was already lifting his legs and standing. The awkward momentum caused his body to push into hers and the two went over, taking a magazine display with them. Jen reached for her machete and realized, when her grip came up empty, that her fate now lied in the hands of the squeamish Carrie.

Shit, she thought as she drove her feet as hard as she could into Derrick's face and chest in a desperate attempt to create distance. She turned and scrambled up the counter, her hand grabbing hold of the first item it could find at the top as she stood. A pen with *Trump Taj Mahal* would be the instrument of her salvation or her demise as she turned to face Derrick.

A lunging Derrick was sent flying to the side as Carrie stood behind him and mercilessly hacked at his back and side with the machete Jen had given her. Blood splattered in every direction with each undisciplined strike to his body. Derrick laid on the ground, his overalls split and barely covering his upper torso, spilling thick, red and black fluids from his multiple wounds as he tried to stand up.

"The head." Jen said, with a heavy breath.

Carrie exhaled a few times and repositioned her grip on the handle of the machete. She raised the blade high in the air and came down like a medieval executioner straight into Derrick's head. She exhaled loud, uncontrolled breaths for a moment as the blade rest in Derrick's skull, fresh blood oozing from the kill site.

"Thanks." Jen said, as a fresh spirt of blood erupted from Derrick's entry wound like a horror-themed water fountain.

Carrie understandably turned and vomited. After a few seconds she held her thumb up at Jen without looking at her. "No problem." she said between bated breaths.

They strode back into the main floor with the key box. "Anything interesting?" Logan said to the women, noticing just how much blood now covered Carrie.

"Nope," Jen said in response, looking at Carrie. She opened the key box and handed it to Logan. "Nothing we couldn't handle."

Chapter 5

Carrie and Jen had come out of the office with about fifteen sets of keys. Fortunately, there were cards in each of the vehicles with numbers that matched the key tags. Logan asked Matt and Mary to move the vehicles. When Mary had almost driven the minivan through the garage door, Carrie stepped in and took over for her. All in all, they relocated two pickup trucks, a minivan, and a small sedan for reinforcements. It didn't go unnoticed that Rick had done nothing during the entire exchange.

Logan and Jen cleared the rest of the garage and found a stairwell to the roof. They went up and peered over the sides at the mass of hundreds of undead who were focused on the building currently occupied by the living. All four of the surrounding walls were three rows deep with the monsters, those in the back fighting for a modicum of space in front. Their endless adrenaline-fueled screams cut through the now twilight sky.

"We are sure as Hell not doing that again." Logan said, taking note of a fire escape on the east side of the building.

Jen shook her head in agreeance, and they went back inside.

Time seemed to slow as the group finally managed an uneasy rest. They ate what they could and sat around, throwing ideas as to what their next move could be between the uncomfortable gaps in small conversation. The garage doors pulsed inward with every hungry fist pounding on them, as hundreds of the undead wait impatiently outside for entry. The chains that secured the giant metal doors clanged loudly. The shrieking and shuffling of the undead, along with the hammering on the doors and rattling of the chains, formed an uneasy orchestra in the otherwise still air.

"I can't take it." Rick shouted after what seemed like an eternity of listening to the unrelenting symphony of death. He jumped up from the seated circle the group formed in the waiting area. "I can't take it anymore, we gotta leave." He gritted his teeth and strained every muscle in his body as he spoke.

"You know we can't do that yet." Matt said, barely phased. "We're at least secure for now." He looked up at Rick, whose veins were bulging from his neck.

"Secure?" he yelled indignantly. "They all know we're in here." He was pacing as he waved his arms around at the garage doors. "They're gonna get in. We should take one of these cars and drive the fuck outta here!"

Logan slammed a magazine on the counter. He and Jen were doing a bullet count and weapons check. "No car in here will get through a crowd like that." He said matter of factly. "We'll stay here tonight and take shifts on lookout. We can brainstorm more in the morning"

"And who the fuck put you in charge?" Rick said, pointing a particularly disrespectful finger at him.

"You did," Logan said, cocking his head to one side, "when you showed us what a chicken shit you were in that hallway."

Carrie looked down at the floor. The words stung her slightly, but she knew Logan was right. Rick left her to die at the hands of that zombie and she knew deep down from the beginning that self-preservation was his prerogative. Regardless, Rick was still her man.

"Fuck you, man!" Rick shouted as he strode towards Logan in an aggressive manner.

"Rick!" Carrie yelled, trying her best to reel him in.

Logan and Matt both jumped up from their seats, not knowing what to expect from the approaching hot-head.

Rick caught a good look at the two men who would clearly take pleasure in making his ass kicking a team effort and began slowing his advance until finally stopping only a few yards from them. "Well, give me a fucking gun and I'll leave." he said holding a hand out to them.

Matt shook his head in the negative. "I'll give you a bullet if you don't sit the hell down." Logan said with a smirk.

Rick's already reddened face was getting darker with anger by the second. "You're not as tough you think you are," he said in a lower voice than his previous holler. "Put that gun away if you're so tough and let's go." The fearful expression on Rick's face betrayed his words, but Logan wasn't going to pass on the opportunity to smack around some bully.

Logan placed his gun down and walked around the counter. Matt's face was also flushed with anger and as much as he hated Rick for the few years that he's known him, he understood that this was now between him and Logan.

Carrie stepped in front of Rick and gently pressed her hands into his shoulders, trying to move him back and away from the confrontation. "Baby, it's ok." she said trying to placate him.

"Don't fucking touch me!" he shouted as he pivoted and grabbed her by the neck, then slammed her to the hard service floor.

She went down with a loud thud but managed to brace her fall and have her shoulder absorb the brunt of the impact. Rick turned and saw Logan within arms-reach, then threw his right fist out at him. But where he should've felt the face of his target, Rick instead only felt air. Logan had ducked under his attackers' fist and twisted his hips. He curled his right hand into a solid brick of fingers and extended it into Rick's abdomen.

Logan thought he would be blown over by the sheer force of air that left Rick's lungs as he fell to his knees. Logan held his fist up and over the collapsed Rick as he prepared to strike again. After watching him try to catch his breath for a moment, he decided against it and slowly lowered his arm.

Matt and Jen were standing with Carrie and looking over a fresh bruise on her eye, compliments of the cement flooring. Mary sit at a café table across the room, eating a pack of peanuts from the vending machine. She had inserted seventy-five cents into it and asked around for the remaining seventy-five cents before Jen noticed why and just broke the glass for her.

"We're done." Logan said as he turned and walked back to Matt, who was shaking his head at him. "What?" he asked.

"I'm jealous," he responded. "And a little disappointed." When Logan shot him a confused look, he elaborated. "You didn't knock him out or break anything. You must hit like a bitch."

Logan chuckled. "Careful, meat-head. You might find out."

Carrie was helping Rick up, who shrugged her off and retreated to a set of chairs against the far wall.

Jen placed a gentle hand on Logan's back. "You take it easy on him, or can't hit as hard as you used to?" She smiled.

Matt laughed, "I knew it." He said.

"Don't you start," he said to Jen, kissing her forehead. "I'll take first watch." He racked the rifle on the table and swung it over his shoulder.

"I'll take first on the roof then." Jen said taking a bite of a protein bar.

"Is that for me?" Matt asked with a twinkle, looking down at the shotgun that still sat unclaimed on the table.

"Sure," Logan replied. "You know how to handle it." He slid over a shell holder with twelve extra slugs resting in their loops.

The first shift on lookout was quiet, save for the incessant banging and waling of the horde's unyielding desire to gain entry. Jen stayed on the roof and watched the streets for any cars or pedestrians. She was able to stay awake with no problem, but was more than disappointed to see that in the course of her shift, there was not one single sign of life amidst the rural cityscape.

Logan woke Matt and sent him up to relieve Jen, then looked over the rest of the group. Mary was fast asleep, and Carrie was curled up with a taut, sleeping Rick. "Shit." he said to himself as Jen walked over to him.

"What's wrong?" She asked trying to wipe exhaustion from her eye.

"Looks like I'll just have to take second watch too." he responded, pointing over at them.

"Just have Mary watch the doors." Jen said wrapping her arms around his waist.

He let out an involuntary laugh, a little louder than he should have. "Doors seem to have some personal vendetta with her or something. So, I don't know if I want her watching any of them for us."

Jen chuckled. "Wake me in a few and I'll take it for you." she said as she smacked him on his ass and walked away.

Logan smirked and watched her as she turned back and winked at him. His man card dictates that he never admits just how much she made his heart flutter.

Chapter 6
Mr. Stone

A suave, middle-aged man walked casually to his private Bombardier jet that rested in a small hangar in Istanbul. He adjusted his Dolce and Gabbana eye-glasses and picked a single piece of lint from his navy blue Kiton suit jacket before reaching in his pocket and removing his cellphone.

"Yes sir." the male voice on the other side of the call said.

"We're ahead of schedule. There's only a few of *them* left." Mr. Stone emphasized to his subordinate.

"I'm an hour or so outside of Pennsylvania, sir." he responded.

"Contact me when you're done." He said imperiously as he stepped up and into his ride. He took a seat and looked at his Rolex Submariner watch. "The first trumpet sounds in seventy-five minutes."

"Yes sir." the other voice said before it disconnected.

He slid his phone back into his pocket, then reached over and poured a glass of his vintage whiskey from his diamond cut decanter. He swirled the glass and took a deep breath. His eyes involuntarily closed as he was lost in the invigorating aroma of aged oak and honey notes that made love to his olfactory receptors.

"We're ready to go, Mr. Stone." a voice came over the intercom above him.

There was a loud gulp in the quiet of the jet as he downed the golden liquid almost too quickly to taste it. He looked out the window at his entourage of vehicles and soldiers who would be staying behind. They had work to do here.

"Then, let's go." Mr. Stone said pushing in the intercom button. He couldn't help but let a serpent-like smile creep onto his face. After countless years of preparation, everything was finally coming together. He had been brash and uncalculating in his prior years. He acted with arrogance and reacted with haste, and it had cost him so much time. This time, he had grown wiser, more cunning. The careful stages of his endgame had all gone perfectly now. The pieces that were in play on his board were being steadily removed, thus his opposition was dwindling.

He lifted a clipboard from the table that contained a list of names on it. Clicking a pen from his lapel, he ran his eyes down the paper until it rested on the name he searched for. He drew a single line through the name and flipped over to a page labeled "Legacies."

Written on the number eight and nine spots were Logan and Luke Matthews, complete with addresses and detailed, personal information regarding their lives, bank accounts, investments, family members, careers, and personal interests.

Mr. Stone chuckled as he tossed the clipboard back on the table and the jet took off, carrying him to his next destination.

Chapter 7

Luke stared intensely at the TV screen as Matt's avatar pulled off amazing feats of combat. After single-handedly wiping out the other team, he had leveled the playing field and made it a one-on-one in the digital arena. Luke's ass was literally hanging off the edge of his couch cushion.

"Luke's down. But there's only one threat left." He heard Logan say through the mic. Luke put his controller down without taking his eyes from the screen.

That's when he heard it. That's when the deafening, thunderous waling began to sound. He shot up from his seat and winced as the noise entered his eardrums and pounded his brain like a bass. He looked frantically around his living room as if the source was in plain sight.

"You guys hear that?" he yelled into his mic, knowing he wouldn't even be able to hear a response. Removing his headset, he walked out of the living room and into the kitchen. What he hadn't seen as he stepped passed his front door was that it was slowly opening inward. Any creaking or cries of warning from the hinges were blanketed by the continuous scream of the horn.

A tall man in his late twenties who looked of European decent stepped through the door wearing a black suit and red tie. He locked onto Luke, whose back was facing him, and closed the door softly. The ear-splitting waling seemed to be of no bother to the man, who reached into his jacket and pulled out a firearm. He worked quickly as he screwed a silencer onto the barrel, hoping Luke wouldn't turn to face him.

Luke was staring out the window in hopes that something outside might explain the source of his temporary misery. When he felt the floor shift under his right leg, he was taken back to a conversation he had with his fiancé, Izzy, one too many times about fixing the loose floor tile in the kitchen. He remembered how she would be standing where he is right now, facing the window, and he would enter the kitchen, stepping on the unbalanced tile. She would think she was alone but as soon as the tile moved, it caused a chain reaction that ran the length of the entire room and shifted her weight ever so slightly so that it would startle her.

This all ran through Luke's mind in a single instant until he realized that it had to mean that someone had just walked up behind him. He knew Izzy wasn't supposed to be home for a few more hours. His eyes went wide as his heart began to race. He turned and instinctively dove to the side counter towards his knife block.

The man in the suit fired his gun once and missed as his target evaded to the side. He swiveled and went to squeeze the trigger again. The round went into the ceiling as another man entered and grabbed the attacker's wrist, quickly pushing up just as the trigger was squeezed. The defender drove his knee into the man's stomach, making him bend forward at the waist. Then drove his elbow straight back into his face, shattering his nose. The attacker reeled back and his grip on the gun faltered, sending it to the ceramic floor.

The attacker pulled a knife from his belt and shook his head, expelling the pain of his broken nose and sending blood droplets onto Luke's clean countertops. He held the blade out and dove at the defender, going for his sternum. The defending man pivoted and grabbed hold of the knife hand, then turned his body and drove his forearm into the back of the man's elbow as hard as he could. The audible snapping of his arm being broken in three places cracked through the siren wale like thunder through a rainstorm.

The man cried out in pain and reached over with his good arm as if to give it comfort. The defender reached down and picked up the gun from the floor and aimed it at the broken man's head as he sat there on his knees.

Luke could see the lips moving on both men as they were now having a brief conversation through the still boisterous blaring, though he couldn't make out any words. Then... he shot him. Red mist sprayed from the broken attacker's head and his body flew backwards against the cabinets.

The defender tucked the gun into his waistband and adjusted his shirt before looking over at Luke, who was still fumbling with his knife block for a weapon. The pitching of the siren finally died down, and all that could be heard in the silence that followed was Luke struggling with cutlery atop his granite countertops. The clanging of metal molded with the scratching of compressed igneous rock until he finally gained hold of a handle and held it out in front of him like he had just pulled Excalibur from the stone.

"Luke." the man said presumptuously, raising his eyebrows.

"Oh shit." Luke said, gaining his composure. "What the hell, Ethan?" He looked back and forth between the two men with a look horror mixed with confusion, and appreciation.

"I can explain." Ethan said, still catching his breath. His brown skin was glistening with sweat and he had red dots of the other man's blood splattered across his face.

"Uh, yea, please?" Luke said still holding out the knife.

"Can you lower that?" Ethan asked, extending his hand outward.

"Oh, yeah, I guess." Luke replied, lowering the knife but not loosening his grip. "I think you just saved my life, so… thanks?"

"I did," Ethan said, sticking his chest out. "But we don't have a lot of time. That horn means something really bad is happening right now and we need to leave."

"Like what? A riot or something?" Luke asked, raising an eyebrow.

"Something like that." he replied. "Where's Izzy?"

"She's at the library. What's going on?"

"Are your doors all locked?" he asked, as he bent down and went through the dead man's pockets.

"Well, they were until you guys broke in, remember?" he said with a hint of derision.

"Right," Ethan said, placing something in his pocket. "Look out the window and whatever you do… don't scream or draw attention to us." His voice was low and his tone deadly serious.

Luke's expression dropped from confusion to caution. He turned back to the large kitchen window as Ethan secured the front door he had entered. Before his eyes even met the outside, he began to hear screaming coming from his neighbors. There was a thick, white mist covering the streets outside. People were running frantically. Some ran to their houses or cars, while others ran away from their neighbors and family.

Luke spotted his neighbor, Karen, just standing idly in the middle of the street. She was facing his direction but couldn't see him through the window. He could tell something was wrong by the way she was just, standing there. Her skin looked pale, and dark green veins protruded across her face and along the cleavage of her low-cut shirt. He'd always thought she was attractive and loved when she wore revealing shirts. He could see red dots lining her arms as her body began to twitch, almost like a nervous tick at first. Then, her head jerked uncontrollably, sending her blonde hair to and from like a tarp in the wind.

Another man Luke knew from down the street, Rob or Ronnie or something to that effect, ran up to her and began yelling at her. He grabbed her shoulder and shook her gently, trying to bring her out of whatever daze she was in. In one quick movement, she turned and sunk her teeth into his neck. He screamed in terror and betrayal as she brought him down to the ground. He pushed up at her, but it was no use. She was biting into him repeatedly, removing chunks of flesh and sinew coated with blood. She tore through his neck until his clavicle and vertebra were visible. Blood and muscle dripped from her mouth as she chewed and swallowed, then rinsed and repeated.

"What...? The fuck?" Luke said in disbelief, not looking away from the gruesome sight. The only thing more disturbing than what he had just witnessed was what happened next. Luke began shaking his head bewilderedly, "No, no, no… no no no…." was all he could say as he watched Karen stand with bits of RobRonnie still in her mouth. Then she simply ran off down the street, shrieking and growling like a rabid animal. He followed her with his eyes for a moment until she was out of view and his attention was brought back to the body in the street.

RobRonnie had begun to stir. A finger twitch here, a head twist there, until his whole body was moving again. Like a newborn baby, he shuffled on the ground awkwardly trying to gain control of his different body parts and create a single, unified movement. He stood, his head now hanging down and to the left as a result of Karen making his neck and trapezial her dinner. His mouth opened, but with a half-eaten voice box, whatever sound he was attempting to make came out as nothing more than a gurgled moan.

Although what he just witnessed was terrifying beyond all comprehension, Luke almost wanted to chuckle at the sound RobRonnie was emitting. Until he finally realized what exactly it was he just witnessed - a real-life zombie attack.

"We have to get Izzy." He said to Ethan without looking away from the window.

Chapter 8

Ethan was Luke and Izzy's next-door neighbor. He had bought his house and moved in exactly a week after Luke and Izzy had moved into the neighborhood. Although they weren't exactly sure what he did for a living, he would leave his house at all sorts of odd hours. During small talk with the other nosey residents, he would just state that he was away on business trips. Again, no one seemed to know where he was going or who he even worked for, but he was by far one of the nicest neighbors on the block. Even went as far as hosting the "Turtle Street Game Night" every other month.

Ethan had no pictures of family or friends in his house and, although everyone thought it strange, no one dared question him. His quiet life was his to live. In the several years that followed Luke and Ethan became good friends. They hit the bars together, watched Sunday football together, and even became friends with his brother, Logan. Luke eventually began to wonder if Ethan even had anyone else in his life. He would often go with or take a woman home during their escapades and just when Luke thought Ethan might have a potential girlfriend, he would call it off. He was just a "no strings attached" kind of guy.

This is why so many questions were racing through Luke's mind right now, and he wasn't sure which ones to start with, so he had to play it cool.

"So…" Luke started tactfully, "What the fuck?" Yup, nailed it.

"What the fuck, what?" Ethan repeated back to him as the two were packing provisions.

"Well, let's start with the whole Jason Bourne shit in my kitchen, then get into how you know about that smoke outside. Is this a chemical attack? Oh my God, are we being invaded by terrorists? Or aliens?" His mind was flooding with possibilities even faster than his mouth could verbalize them.

"Whoa, whoa, man," Ethan said, putting his hands up. "Aliens? That sounds a little ridiculous, don't you think?"

Luke just stared at him with his mouth open in disbelief. "As opposed to fucking zombies?" he said, in a whisper-yell.

Ethan sighed. "Listen, I can explain a lot of it later, but we have to move first. I have a group of people who are equipped for this at the old church just on the border of the city limits."

"You have people who are equipped for zombies?" he said, with even more disbelief.

"They're technically called *plaguers*, not zombies," he responded. "The term *zombie* is a more modern verbiage for them. When they first showed up in the fourteenth century, they…."

Luke cut him off, "Fourteenth century?! You're serious?"

"Afraid so, now you wanna let me talk while we move or just keep interrupting me?" His eyes tensed. He was clearly getting a little annoyed.

Luke gave a sheepish look. "Sorry, go on."

"In the fourteenth century," he continued as he loaded rounds into an extra magazine for his nine-millimeter, "they were called plaguers. They became afflicted with almost every and any disease known to man. It would alter their brain as fast as it changed their bodies." He tapped the magazine on his temple for dramatic effect. "Then they would spread their disease by attacking and biting other people. Its transferrable by their saliva."

Ethan thought that was a good place to stop talking until he looked at Luke who had stopped loading the extra backpack for Izzy.

Ethan sighed again and continued, "There was a group of soldiers at the time who managed to successfully stop the outbreak."

"No way," Luke said, shaking his head. "That wouldn't go unnoticed. The whole world would know about that. It would be everywhere."

"And you do know about it." Ethan said certainly. "You know the version of the Bubonic Plague that was written by these soldiers. One of the world's biggest cover-ups."

Luke stared blankly. He was dumfounded. Ethan hadn't given him any answers so much as he gave him more questions to ask. "But…" was all he could stammer out.

"More later," Ethan cut him off. "Time to move."

"What about Logan? If…" he suddenly remembered they might still be online. "Shit, hold on." He ran back into his living room and put his headset on. There was a lot of white noise and nothing else. "Anyone there? Matt? Logan?"

Seconds felt like minutes which felt like hours as he hoped for some sign that his brother and friend were ok. Finally, there was a crack in the static.

"Matt? Luke?" He could hear his brother. "Matt? Luke? You guys ok?"

"Thank God," Luke said, looking up to the skies passed his ceiling. "Hey Logan, Ethan's here and he has an idea about what's going on. We're getting Izzy and heading to the old church at the city limits. Copy?"

The static intensified but Logan's voice cracked through. "Church…" was all he said before the line went out.

Luke sat for a second and removed the headset again. He held it in his hand and just stared at it, worrying for his brother now more than he ever had before. *You better make it there*, he thought to himself, just as Ethan entered the room.

"I'm supposed to get him after I get you to the church." he said. "So, we need to get Izzy now."

"Wait, what do you mean *supposed* to get us?" he turned, his face showing suspicion.

"When we get your brother, I'll explain more." He turned and left the room.

Ethan drove a supercharged Chevrolet Suburban. It always looked suspiciously like a government vehicle, so when he insisted that they take it, Luke's suspicion only increased.

"Do you work for the CIA or something?" Luke asked flatly. "Are you going to kill me when we get near a bridge or something..."

Ethan stopped in his tracks and stared at him in total astonishment. "Man, get your white ass in the car and stop with all the stupid questions. No, I don't work for the damn government." His tone was finally reflecting his level of agitation with Luke.

Luke had that effect on people. He could make a Hare Krishna want to punch a baby out of pure frustration. Most times, he would be amused by his own innate ability to piss others off. He wasn't willing to take the chance during a zombie…er, *plaguer* apocalypse with Ethan, his neighbor of six years, with whom he just found out knows martial arts, how to use guns, drives a government vehicle, and apparently has inside information about said apocalypse.

"Ok, ok, damn." Luke said as they got ready to open the front door.

"Wait," Ethan said, "I know you like the forty, but all I have is an extra twenty-two." He pulled out a small handgun and extra magazine and handed them to Luke, who checked them over.

They had been to the range before with Logan. Luke wasn't the best shot, but he was no slouch either. When the three of them had gone together Ethan was by far the worst shot. He could barely hit any part of the paper target. Now, Luke found himself wondering if it had just been a front.

"So, do you shoot better than that time we went to the range?" Luke asked.

"I can hit the tip of a match at twenty yards." He said, confidently.

"Son of a bitch. We bought you drinks that night because of how bad you were."

"Yea, best buzz I ever had, too." He said smiling. "There's more gear we're going to need in the back of my SUV. We can go through it when we get somewhere quieter."

Ethan cracked the door open slightly and the sounds of madness punched through like a bull horn. Luke winced at the loud shrieks and shrills of hunger that came from the denizens in the street who searched for food like wild animals.

"It's on your left and it's unlocked," Ethan said quietly, "Get your ass right in the passenger seat, I'll cover you."

Luke nodded a not-too-reassuring nod and took three deep breaths. They threw the door open soundlessly and Luke darted out. He stopped at the edge of the sidewalk as two of his neighbors turned to greet him.

They were teenage brothers Carl and Cal. They weren't twins, as Carl was two years older than his brother. More than likely, their parents were just lazy and didn't expect to have another child. So, what would be the easy way to name him? Drop a letter off the older one's name. Now you have Cal.

They resembled each other as much as brothers born two years apart could. Both had similar brown hair and the same mop-top hairstyle. They had nearly identical facial structures that were only discernable by Cal's prescription glasses. And, if it wasn't for Carl being six inches taller, everyone would probably think they were twins.

They looked ill. Open sores and green veins littered their ashen skin and emphasized their sickly appearance. They opened their mouths in unison and Luke saw up close for the first time the hunger that permeated their undead faces. They both snarled at Luke, who froze for a brief second before going to raise his gun. His hands shook as he took aim. They lunged forward but were punched back as two deafening gunshots rang out. Carl's head exploded and, before his body could hit the ground, Cal followed suit.

Luke turned and saw Ethan with his gun extended, the barrel still smoking from his insanely accurate shots. "Move, damn it!" Ethan shouted.

Luke turned right and took three large strides up the street before he was stopped by Ethan's yelling at him again.

"Your other left asshole!" Ethan roared as he fired more shots at a few of the undead closing in on Luke.

"Ah, shit," Luke grumbled as he turned on his heels and went the other way, passing Ethan again, who was just stepping onto the sidewalk from the landing. The door to the SUV was in reach, but as he went to pull on the handle, an undead face came around the front and leapt up at him. Luke let out a shriek as the middle-aged woman gripped his shoulders and pushed into him, taking them both down with her on top.

Luke managed to get his arm across her neck as his back hit the ground. Her broken jagged teeth snapped inches from his face as blackened saliva flung wildly from her flailing tongue. He turned his head and sealed his lips as tight as possible to avoid the spittle, then fired several shots into her midsection. Her body shook as the bullets entered her abdomen and exited her back, but she was completely unaffected. He turned his wrist slightly and attempted a headshot. The bullet exited her chin and blew jaw fragments and teeth outward.

Luke's arm was fatiguing fast, and he could hear Ethan's gunshots from behind him get louder as he approached closer. The woman on top of him now oozed dark blood and black fluids from the fresh hole in her face. A single tooth sat in the thick stream of crimson syrup that slowly dripped from her shattered, lower jaw.

Luke's eyes locked onto the tooth before momentarily fixating on her now more than revealing cleavage. Disturbed as he was by the woman's current state, it wasn't lost on him that she was blessed in the chest area. He caught himself staring almost too long when another undead racing up the sidewalk at him stole his attention. He was already exhausted and pinned down and the athletic looking young man was gaining ground fast.

Luke pushed the woman over slightly just as the athletic man jumped down at him. He was now using the woman as a plaguer shield. "Ethan!" he screamed through gritted teeth.

Ethan had finally backed up to the SUV. He popped a fresh magazine into his gun and racked the slide, chambering a round. Without missing a beat, he fired two more times, and two more threats dropped. He turned and kicked the athlete square across his face. The plaguer scrambled but before he could gain footing, Ethan put one in his brain. He aimed the gun down at the female on top of Luke.

"Aww," he said, moving his gun off to the side. "She just wants a kiss, man." He chuckled.

"Not...my...type." Luke managed to get out between bated breaths.

"Yea, too clingy." He responded bringing his gun back over and shooting her head at an angle. She collapsed next to Luke, who was already clambering to his feet.

Another collection of boisterous supernatural shrills from decaying throats prompted the two men to keep moving. The gunfire was attracting more plaguers from both sides of the street and they were all sprinting full-speed at Ethan and Luke.

Before Ethan could round the front of his SUV, Luke was in the passenger seat and buckled in. The car started and peeled out before the mobs could close in on them. The SUV swerved and snaked between and around the bodies that ran at the vehicle head-on with a clear lack of self-preservation.

The few plaguers clipped by the sides of the vehicle were of no consequence with the speed at which Ethan and Luke were driving. When they made a left turn down a particularly small street only a few blocks from the library, the density of the plaguers seemed to increase.

Small dents and dings began to form as the knees, heads, torsos, and other appendages bounced off the moving SUV. The right headlight burst when a rather obese plaguer tried to jump on the hood and failed miserably, flattening his face in the process and landing under the tire. The all-wheel drive vehicle made quick work of the large body as it climbed over the man's stomach and came down hard, bouncing with Ethan and Luke inside.

"This car is not gonna make it dude." Luke said stressfully.

"The frames getting a little banged up, but the glass will hold. It's bullet proof." He assured him just as three plaguers simultaneously struck his driver's window, cracking the glass before being pulled down and away from the car. He stared at the window as if it had just betrayed him then looked back at Luke. "We'll make it. It's only a few more blocks."

Gunfire rang out from all directions outside the vehicle as survivors fought for their lives against the hordes of undead in and around the surrounding buildings. Scattered groups were either pushing through the plaguers and towards a destination or attempting to flee in search of sanctuary. This did help to pull some of the attackers away from the car, which they were grateful for, as messed up as that sounded.

A small explosion ahead of them sent survivors and plaguers alike soaring through the air like thrown toys. Limbs and other body parts rained down on the streets. Tormented screams of victims and war cries of those fighting were mixed with the cascade of gunshots and destruction. They were driving through a war zone.

A severed arm landed on the windshield of their moving SUV. They both jumped and their eyes lingered on it for a minute. Luke cringed in disgust as Ethan turned on the windshield wiper. It hit the arm and went back down, smearing blood but not moving the appendage from the window.

"You're making it… you … you just made it worse." Luke pointed out.

"Yea, I know." Ethan said, spraying fluid on the window before running the wipers again. The blood and fluids thickened and turned from dark to a lighter pasty red. It covered even more of the glass now.

"That didn't… that didn't help either." Luke said, apprehensively.

"No shit, Sherlock," Ethan said, obviously annoyed, "now shut the hell up." He had a small window of vision and jerked the wheel left to go around a group of huddled plaguers. The arm flew off the glass and smacked one of them in the face just as it turned in their direction.

Luke couldn't help but chuckle. "You threw a punch." He paused for a second to see Ethan's reaction. When he didn't even look over in his direction he spoke again. "I said, you…"

"I heard you," he barked, "I'm trying to drive." He was turning the wheel hard and switching between the accelerator and brake as he navigated a highway littered with obstacles of flesh and metal. Although the hordes began to thin slightly as they traveled, the sounds of fighting continued to run rampant throughout the streets.

About a block away, they could see a crowd of plaguers pounding on the large entry doors of the historical library. Ethan was unable to slow the vehicle for long with so many threats in such close proximity to their objective. They needed a plan.

He circled a large warehouse while a crowd of plaguers followed their vehicle. On the west side of the library, they spotted yellow school buses and some scaffolding that fortuitously led to a second floor window.

"You see that?" Ethan asked as the SUV turned the corner again, moving the buses out of view.

"No," Luke responded, looking out his window frantically, "what?"

"The buses on the side of the library." He saw a blank expression on Luke's face. "You don't know what a goddamn school bus is?"

"I know what a bus is, asshole. What about it?" he shouted back.

"We'll go around one more time then pull up next to them. Get on top of the SUV, hop on the bus and up that scaffold." Ethan said with determination.

"Ok." Luke nodded firmly.

"Climb in the back and grab my duffle bag." he more said than asked as the vehicle rocked to the side again, bouncing a plaguer off the front quarter panel.

Luke climbed over the seats and was tossed about the back by the intense driving and constant collision of bodies against the frame. He reached for the bag but a sudden pump on the brakes thrust him backwards. He flew through the front seats and slammed his back into the front console, expelling air from his lungs upon impact. In the process, Luke's back inadvertently turned on the CD player and music suddenly blasted through the vehicle's speakers.

"Put your hand in my hand baby, don't ever look back. Let the world around us just fall apart, baby we can make it if we're heart to heart...."

Luke couldn't stop a smile from creeping onto his face as he scrambled to get back to the rear hatch. "Didn't take you for a Starship fan." he mused over the music.

"Shut up," Ethan snapped, jerking the wheel again. "Good music is good music."

Luke continued to be thrown around the back of the car when the side window exploded inward and an undead hand reached in at him. Luke put his foot against the door and braced as the vehicle made another loop around the building. He was surprised by his own thought process as he watched the school buses pass by his view through the broken window and the decaying hand that thrashed at him. He wondered who the hell takes school trips to a library anymore with the advancements in modern technology. Then, he began to wonder if any of the kids would know who Starship was.

He was brought back when the car jerked again, and he was forced closer to the plaguer. It grabbed hold of his shoulder and stretched his rotten canines out at him. The spastic movement of the car saved Luke's face from becoming food as the plaguer's teeth chomped down on air. He twisted and pulled as the SUV swerved and he was tossed to the other side of the rear, away from the ravenous undead.

"....*nothing's gonna stop us now. And if this world runs out of lovers....*"

"Shit." Ethan yelled as another plaguer gained hold of his door and began punching at the already cracked window. His foot went down on the brakes again for only a second, then immediately back to the gas. The action had the desired effect of causing the creature to lose his grip and tumble back into the crowd. It was subsequently crushed by the tidal wave of stampeding plaguers that still pursued the car.

"Ethan," Luke shouted over the still playing music. "You want me to get the damn bag or what?" He was practically under the rear seats, the hitchhiking plaguer now half in the window.

"My bad," Ethan shouted. "Shoot the damn thing."

Luke raised his gun in an unsteady hand and fired. The bullet missed with no indication of where it went or what it struck. The boom was deafening in the small confines of the SUV and his ears began to ring. He shook his head and took his time as he aimed again, then fired. The plaguer's body was pushed back and out the window. He may not be able to tell if he struck the thing's head, but at least it was off the car.

The crowd was seemingly unaware of what Luke and Ethan were doing. Instead of the plaguers stopping and just waiting for the SUV to come around the corner of the building again, they endlessly and tirelessly followed behind it. Fortunate as it was, it still did not allow the ability to stop or even slow the vehicle for very long, if at all.

The SUV was making its sixth lap around the warehouse, windows broken out and plaguers in hot pursuit with Starship booming through the afternoon sky.

"....take it to the good times, see it through the bad times..."

Luke finally came back up front with the bag and turned the knob down to an imperceptible volume.

"Ok, see the side pocket?" Ethan asked with hasted words.

"Yea." Luke replied as he unzipped it.

"There's a plastic bag with some bandages in it. Wrap one of them around your arm," he ordered. "Quickly man, we gotta go."

Luke looked at his arms as if he missed something. "I don't have any wounds."

"Just do it, damn it, I'll explain later."

Luke didn't question again. He wrapped the torn cloth on his forearm and pulled his hoodie sleeve back over it. Instead of making a seventh lap, the SUV turned off, heading for the parked buses.

"You ready?" Ethan said more to psych him up then actually asking.

"Fuck no." Luke said pulling over his safety belt and clicking it in.

Ethan followed suit and buckled up, then punched the gas. The car snaked through more of the undead when Ethan began repeatedly stomping his foot down.

"What are you doing?" Luke asked in a near panic.

"Brakes," he yelled back. "brakes are out!"

"Well fuck." was all Luke could say as he stared at the yellow buses that were getting closer.

The SUV crossed the threshold of the parking lot and went up and over a concrete bumper at such high speed that the front bounced up and down violently. The passenger tires became airborne and the SUV sped uncontrollably on two wheels. Ethan turned the drivers' wheel with such force he could feel his shoulders strain in protest. It had the opposite of desired effect, as the vehicle went over onto its driver side and scraped across the concrete. Waling steel tore away as the vehicle slid towards the bus. It kicked up asphalt and sparks from the street as well as flesh from plaguers that were unable to escape the path of the twisted, runaway death machine.

The vehicle began to slow from the multiple obstructions until it finally came to rest against the side of the desired yellow school bus. The loud bang of the front end of the SUV colliding with the side of the bus was misleading, as the impact was barely even hard enough to jerk Ethan and Luke, who were undoubtedly dazed.

Luke was shaking his head in an attempt to remove the fuzziness that was briefly affecting his vision and hearing. He strained to see as he moved his head around. It was obvious his body was off center, but he just couldn't place how or where he was. There was a faint ringing that he couldn't be sure was in his head or from an external source. He could hear someone's muffled speech. He glanced to his left and saw Ethan. His mouth was moving as if to overemphasize what he was saying, but the words were too cloudy and unclear.

Ethan was yelling to get Luke's attention but the distant stare in his eyes was an indication that he was shaken up and possibly had a concussion. Ethan undid his belt and shuffled around until he could manage himself into a low a crouch with his face only inches from Luke's.

"Luke," he yelled with authority and this time caught his gaze. Ethan raised a hand and shook his shoulder lightly, reeling him in. "We gotta go right now, man."

Luke nodded slowly at first then again, a little quicker. His senses were slowly coming back to him. He stretched his achy arm and shoulder over and unbuckled his seat belt. Ethan helped him by catching his weight so that he wouldn't just fall on top of him.

"The window," Ethan said pointing his chin at the busted passenger window now above Luke. "Climb up and get on the bus."

Ethan turned and let Luke step off his shoulder, who used his hoodie to grip the frame of the window which was now covered with broken glass. He was up and reaching down to grab Ethan within seconds. They could hear countless plaguers snarling and screeching with their cries of undying hunger as they closed in around the crashed SUV. They gained their footing and looked at the carnage that surrounded them.

Fires engulfed concrete buildings and the twisted metal of crashed vehicles littered the street, their own included. The bodies of once every day, loving citizens now lay as unrecognizable heaps of shredded and bloodied meat. Limbs and innards accented the apocalyptic backdrop of the destroyed city streets and sidewalks.

The first of the encroaching plaguers slammed against the now overturned roof of the vehicle. Its ravenous stare was locked on Ethan and Luke as it repeatedly drove bloodied fists into the vehicle. It began to punch into the metal harder and harder with aggravation that its food was high out of reach. Several more of the undead follow suit by mindlessly driving their bodies into the large obstacle, then vainly attempting to simply punch through it.

"At least we know they can't climb." Luke said with relief as he turned and pulled himself up the side of the bus. The scaffolding was about five feet higher than the top of the bus which made it a simple traversal to the second story window, which was left slightly ajar.

The sunlight did little to reveal anything in the room as Ethan peered into the blackness. He had his gun raised and his bag on his side. Luke was watching the scaffolding in the event that any of the plaguers below suddenly gained advanced traversal abilities.

Ethan cautiously placed one leg inside, keeping his weapon trained into the darkness of the room. He was in and moving his hand along the wall in search of a light switch. He turned quickly and had both hands back on his gun when a loud crashing of books and wood boomed through the silent dark.

"Sorry, sorry." Luke said, standing back up and brisk fully wiping his shirt off. "I tripped coming in." He said, slightly embarrassed. Although he couldn't see Ethan's face, he was more than sure of the shade of red that coated over it.

"Be quiet, dipshit." Ethan admonished him. "We don't know what's in here."

"Yea, you're right. My bad." Luke replied as he adjusted what felt like a globe with a wooden stand that he had knocked over.

The door at the end of the room opened inward and bright light from the massive hall it led into shined in. Ethan again redirected his gun at the open door towards the two figures that now stand in it. Although the details of their features were barely visible, he could tell the one was a curvy young woman and the other was a medium built man.

"Was that you two blasting that song from that eighties movie?" A female voice asked.

"Mannequin." Luke said throwing his hands to the air in surrender.

"What?" the female asked confused.

"Mannequin." Luke repeated. "Nothing's Gonna Stop us by Starship was the main track in the movie Mannequin starring Andrew McCarthy and Kim Catrall in nine-teen eighty-seven." There was an awkward silence that followed this response, but he could tell that everyone was looking at him. Possibly like he had lost his damn mind.

"Sure," the woman said impassively. "I always hated that song." She flipped a switch to her right and a single light bulb in the middle of the ceiling all but blinded Ethan and Luke. They shielded their eyes for a moment and adjusted.

The woman was short with a slightly sun-kissed skin tone and dark, black hair with blonde highlights. Her tight long sleeve shirt complimented her thin frame and accentuated her curves. She could have easily been mistaken for a Brazilian super model.

"We're looking for his fiancé." Ethan said, nodding over to Luke. "You know if Izzy is here?"

"She thought that was you out there," she said looking over. "Luke right?"

"Yea," he said moving in for a handshake. "She's ok?"

"I'm Nelly, this is Tom," she pointed to the large man next to her, who was holding a fire axe at his side. He was tall and stocky, as if he had been on the high school football team and his best days were behind him. "We're in Izzy's study group. She's downstairs." Nelly took Luke's still extended hand and shook weakly.

Tom gave a lazy wave of his free hand then also shook Luke's hand, "What's up?" he said nonchalantly.

Ethan nodded as he put his gun back into his waistband. "Ethan." he said, more cautious then friendly.

The four exited the room into a massive hallway with elaborate gold and green flooring reminiscent of a regal, European statehouse. The hallways looked to be an old pine wood that had been well taken care of throughout the years, if its' waxed surface was any indication. The hall led them to one side of an imperial staircase. The hall on the opposite side mirrored the one from which they just came. Above the landing of the staircase, the coffered ceiling was adorned with two large antique chandeliers. In all, the building had a very Victorian-feel to it. Its appearance grandiose to some, a bit ostentatious for a library to others.

The sounds of fists hammering on wood and the endless shrills of the flesh-starved undead reverberated off the high ceiling and filled every crevasse of the library. Nelly and Tom led Ethan and Luke down the staircase, not a care in the world as they descended each step.

"Those big-ass wooden doors are bolted," Nelly said. "So are the ones in the back. They can't seem to get through and fortunately for us, they're too stupid to climb."

"They'll find a way in eventually." Ethan said.

"Well we didn't plan on staying much longer," Tom responded. "We don't really have any food or anything. We caught a little information on a radio before it went dark. This is everywhere."

"Yea. It's worldwide." Ethan said matter-of-factly.

They had come to a large room separated from the main hall with a low ceiling that joined at the second-story balcony. The walls were lined with large, glass panes, almost as thick as the wood. Etched on the one side were the words "Quiet Room 1." Luke pondered why a library would need a quiet room but decided to leave the question unasked.

Nelly pushed the door open and stepped aside. Inside there were four more people sitting around a large wooden table. Luke's eyes instantly locked onto his fiancé's gentle face. She had been looking down at the artwork she just graffitied onto the table with her red pen. A rather cartoony plaguer's face winced in pain as a warped and jagged spear entered through its left eye and protruded through the back of its head. Her dark, pixie cut hair hung down over her right eye as she scribbled.

Luke couldn't help but allow the world's cheesiest smile to spread across his face. He had hated that haircut and, on many occasions, tried talking her into growing her hair out again. Right now, he thought it was the most beautiful thing he had ever seen.

"Izzy!" Luke shouted with elation.

Izzy looked up and took a second to focus on her fiancé. Without saying a word, she dropped her pen and jumped around the table. They embraced each other so tightly, they almost looked as if they would melt into one person. Izzy had tears of joy and relief flowing down her cheeks and onto Luke's shoulders.

"Oh God," she said in a light sob, "I was so scared… but I knew you'd come for me."

"Of course I would, Iz," Luke said, gently caressing the back of her head. "And now that I'm here…" he smirked. "Nothing's gonna stop us now."

Izzy pulled away and looked at him with red, watery eyes before letting out a much needed laugh. "Yea I thought that was you."

"Fun fact," Luke said pointing at Ethan who was walking past. "It was *his* CD."

"Mother fu-" Ethan started to say before getting cut off by Izzy.

"Ethan." she exclaimed, happy to see their friend with them. "Come here, you beautiful chocolate man." She laughed as she hugged him briefly and went back to Luke.

"How ya holding up, kid?" Ethan asked sincerely.

"Better now that you guys are here." she said.

"This reunion's great and all," a preppy looking, dirty-blonde man said from the table, "but did you guys bring us some supplies or a way out of here?"

Ethan's face flashed with resentment. "Do I look like fucking Santa Clause to you?" he said enraged as he stepped closer to the young man who now looked like he regretted the words he chose.

"No, no, no." the prep said, putting his hands up to deflect the anger now aimed at him. His voice went from pompous to shaky in an instant. "I was just wondering if you two gentlemen had any idea or plans that we could help with. You know, so we can all get out of here alive."

Ethan was amused by the twerps stammering. "You and your argyle sweater haven't come up with any ideas for the past few hours you've been sitting here?"

The young man bowed his head in shame. He was self-aware that he had always felt entitled. He believed that other people should go out of their way to help him and solve his problems. That's the whole reason he even joined this study group. He knew they would do all the work and he would just coast through this semester. What he wasn't used to was being talked to the way Ethan just had. And honestly, it scared the hell out of him.

"That is Chad." Izzy said with disappointment. "He's also in our group."

"Oh," Luke said with his face lighting up. "You're Chad?" Chad perked up slightly with the prospect that Izzy had mentioned him before. "I heard you were a dick, and now, I know." Chad sank back into his seat again.

"That's Betty, one of the librarians," Izzy said, gesturing to a woman who looked to be in her mid-fifties sitting a few chairs down from Chad. Silver roots peered out from under a head of mostly neon pink hair. "And that's Shane." She motioned again to a man in overalls who was maybe in his thirties. He wore a backwards baseball cap and had a biker-like goatee, which did give him a rather hardened appearance.

"Maintenance." the man named Shane said with a nod.

"So, two questions," Ethan said, placing his bag on the table. "Firstly, who the hell still goes to the library?" he said, shrugging his shoulders. When his question was met with silence, he continued. "Secondly, like I asked Fred from the Scooby-gang over there, what have you guys been doing to get out of here?"

They all shot unsure glances at each other when Nelly finally spoke up. "Like everyone else, we were kind of caught off-guard here. Some of those things got in and a lot of people just ran out the front door." She paused for a second and shook her head. "They were torn apart as soon as they got outside. The rest of us and a few others who didn't make it hunkered down and managed to lock a bunch of them in the basement. Now, we're just waiting for the rescue teams."

"Rescue teams?" Ethan said with an arched eyebrow.

"Well, yea," Tom interjected unsurely. "There has to be military response or state-wide evacuation, right?"

Ethan shook his head in the negative. "I'm pretty sure our government doesn't even know what's going on." He said in no uncertain terms.

"Sure they do," Shane spoke up. "You saw that gas, right? That's a chemical attack, like biological warfare."

"No," Ethan said, bluntly. "That's not what's going on." Again, an awkward silence passed as everyone exchanged confused looks.

"You care to elaborate on that?" Chad asked cautiously. "Um…sir."

Ethan sighed and looked over at Luke with an uncertain gaze. "I came to here to get Izzy for Luke so we could head to St. Andrew Church just outside of Philadelphia. I have people there with some… answers. Given the circumstances, you are all welcome to join."

More befuddled looks and skeptical stares. "How would a church be more defendable than this library?" Tom asked.

"There's a bunker underground," Ethan replied. "It's reinforced and has emergency exits. There's weapons and plenty of food."

"Wait," Luke added, "there's a bunker under that old church? Like a fallout shelter? What the hell for?"

Ethan placed his hand out and waved around the room with a *duh* expression plastered on his face.

"You're saying the church was expecting this?" Luke inquired.

"Yes and no," Ethan said before placing his hands up to cut off the rest of the conversation. "Look, I know everyone has questions, but we really need to get going. I have to check in there and make sure since Luke is here, that his brother is safe, too."

Luke shook his head adamantly. "No man, I need a few answers, now," he said, a little heated. "I'm worried as hell about my brother, but how do you know he'll be heading for the church? I tried telling him over the headset and I hope he does, but how do we know?"

"Just like it's my job to watch you, he has someone watching him." Ethan assured him. "He'll be fine."

Izzy looked up at Luke in bewilderment. "What the hell are you two talking about?"

"Like Ethan said, I'll explain later," Luke told her as he kissed her forehead. "Mainly because I still have no goddamn clue and he won't tell me anything."

"So." Ethan said changing the subject, "Anyone have a car big enough to fit us all?"

"I rode my bike," Chad said first.

"I took the train with Tom." Nelly responded.

"I have a beat-up pickup truck." Shane said, shaking his head.

"Oh no," Betty said last. "All I have is my motorcycle."

"Damn, so we got no…" Ethan paused a second and did a double take at the unassuming older woman. "Hell yea, momma." he said giving her a wink and a half smile. She blushed and he continued. "We got no car to get outta here, and there's eight of us here. Maybe we could…" his sentence trailed off with nowhere to go.

"Hold up, dude," Luke said excitedly. "The damn buses in the lot. There's like four of them out there."

"Good thinking," Izzy said as everyone began to pep up slightly. Her face sank when she came to a realization that they all overlooked. "We need keys."

"Anyone have keys for the bus?" Chad said in a wise-ass tone.

"Yea," Tom said nodding. "The bus driver does."

"…and he would be?..." Ethan asked, with the half information.

"In the basement." Tom said. They all groaned in the negative and a few even muttered a few, choice swear words.

"How many?" Luke asked.

"Let's see," Nelly said, looking up, knowing what he was asking. "There was already a bus here with some high school kids down there, couple employees, three drivers…" She moved her head back and forth as if doing mental math and counting faces she remembered seeing. "Maybe twenty or twenty-five."

"Fuck that." Luke said, looking over to Ethan for confirmation that it was clearly suicide.

Ethan unzipped his large duffel bag and pulled out a small cloth binder held shut with velcro. He undid the straps and opened it to reveal twelve glinting knives of various sizes. Each ideal combat knife had a sleek black leather handle and a carbon steel blade. The groups eyes were instantly transfixed on the impressive weapons. Until he began to pull various handguns and preloaded magazines from the bag.

"I'm sorry, who are you?" Nelly asked him as he loaded one of the forty caliber pistols and racked the slide.

Ethan ignored her as he slammed magazines into pistols and racked their slides, placing the readied weapons on the table.

"Why do you have hacky-sacks in a weapons bag?" Luke asked as he reached into the duffle bag and pulled out a palm-sized, brown knapsack. He tossed it in the air slightly and it was intercepted by Ethan.

"It's not a damn hacky-sack and don't touch it." He said, forcing it back in to the bag and motioning for Luke to hand over the little twenty-two he had been using. Luke removed the magazine and counted the bullets. He took a few fresh mags from the table and inserted one before handing it to Izzy instead.

"She's got it." Luke said to him. He turned to his fiancé who looked at the gun like it was a used band aid. "You'll be fine," he assured her. "Just like the range. You have eleven shots in total. When it locks to the back, reload. Easy peasy." He walked back to the table and took one of the forty cals for himself along with a few extra magazines.

"Anyone here ever handle one of these?" Ethan asked the crowd.

"Yea I can use 'em." Shane said walking over to the table.

Ethan held a nine-millimeter out to him. "There's one in the chamber already." He said.

"You got a forty-five?" he asked, looking at the handgun like it had just offended his mother.

"Really?" Ethan said incredulously. When all Shane did was nod at him, Ethan deferred and handed him the only extra forty-five. "Don't lose that, it's my favorite." He told him.

"I'm good with this." Tom said, choking the shoulder of his axe.

"What about me?" Chad asked indignantly as he stood up.

"What the fuck about you, boy?" Ethan said harshly. Chad shut up and immediately fell back into his chair.

Ethan zipped up his bag when they finished their preparations. It would be Ethan, Luke, Shane, and Tom going into the basement to locate the undead bus driver.

"Alright," Luke said, nodding with adrenaline. "Let's go get them keys. GO TEAM!"

Ethan and Tom were shaking their heads at him. "Dude," Shane said, "you just made it weird."

Chapter 9

"There's a service elevator in the West hall that goes from the second floor down to the basement," Nelly said, pointing to a corridor opposite to them, then moving her arm over to a closer metallic door, "and that's the stairwell."

"Is there a blueprint of the basement or something?" Ethan asked her. "Don't want us to get stuck down there."

Nelly slid her notebook in front of them and picked up Izzy's previously dropped red pen. "No, but I've been coming here since I was a kid. I can draw one." She drew a crude sketch of the basement layout, but they could get the gist of it. There was a L-shaped corridor connected to an open, rectangular room with a small, uneven square labeled "door."

"Gonna have to take the stairs." Ethan said. "Elevator ding would draw attention."

"Well, we could use that to create a distraction." Nelly said, folding her arms.

"We're listening." Luke nudged her to continue.

"We send the elevator down with something that will rile them up and draw them away while you guys creep down the stairs and find one of the three drivers." She said as if it were the simplest plan in the world.

"Or bang on the door and we take the elevator down." Luke suggested.

"No way." Chad interjected with his voice cracking. "Then they'll break through the door."

"They won't," Nelly blew him off. "That door is reinforced steel. This library was built during World War II with worse case scenarios in mind."

"I don't know about THIS worst-case scenario." Luke said questioningly.

"Yea, he's got a point." Izzy agreed.

"Look," Ethan said, putting his hand up like a blade to stop any further seeds of doubt from being planted. "It's not perfect, but it's the best plan we have right now. We need those keys." He looked around the room at all the faces that housed obvious skepticism. "We send the elevator down."

A few minutes later and they were all in position. In front of the six-inch, reinforced steel door with their firearms at the ready were Ethan, Luke, and Shane. Tom stood behind them, nervously choking the wooden handle of his axe as Betty stood to the side, tasked with securing the door upon their entrance and exit. Nelly was at the elevator with her cellphone displaying a video that was waiting to be played from its internal video gallery. Izzy and Chad waited in the middle of the west hall that separated the basement entrances, ready to relay communication between the two groups.

The plan was relatively simple in theory. Send the elevator down with the phone playing a loud, recorded video and when the doors opened the plaguers would swarm it. Cellphone communications and data towers were already down, so it was basically a glorified techy looking paperweight. Drawing some of the undead to the elevator would give them a chance to sneak down the stairs, hopefully unnoticed, and pick out one of the drivers. They would eliminate him quietly and take the keys, making their way back up to the group. If the drivers were all massed in with the group at the elevator, they would have to be ready to plant as many headshots as they could and cover each other as they each reloaded their weapons. Tom's axe notwithstanding.

"Ready." Nelly half yelled with a nod.

Izzy relayed the message to Luke. "They're ready."

Luke nodded and all four men tensed, waiting for their final verbal cue to go forward.

Nelly opened the elevator which had been locked on this floor. She pressed the screen of her phone as a seven-minute video began to play and placed it on the center of the elevator's steel floor. Then, pressing the basement floor button, she stepped out and watched the display as it descended. It beeped moments later when it met the desired level of the building and its doors slid open. When she could hear the violent shrills of a few plaguers through the elevator shaft seconds later, she turned her head down the hall again.

"They're going for it." she said at the same volume as before.

"She said it's good." Chad reiterated to the four at the door with Izzy nodding next to him.

"Ok, gentlemen," Ethan said, "here we go."

The hinges lamented as they pried the door open ever so slowly. All four men winced and temporarily froze as if they had all just gotten caught simultaneously with their hands in the cookie jar. When they heard a culmination of shrieks and heavy footsteps getting slightly more distant, they pulled the door open a few feet further.

Ethan stepped onto the top landing and, with a military walk, he began descending the stairs, his pistol aimed downward. Halfway down, he turned to Luke directly behind and motioned his left hand at him. He gave him the thumbs up followed by pointing his index finger to the left of the stairwell. Luke stared at him blankly. Ethan repeated the gesture. When he saw the same, dumfounded look still on Luke's face, he turned to him.

"I'm gonna go on the right of the stairwell," he said with a whisper that suspiciously wanted to sound like a yell, "You go to the left."

Luke knew what the gestures meant and wasn't sure why Ethan felt the need to turn and explain it to him, but he let it go. "Ok." was all he said.

Ethan swept right, keeping his back to what little cover the railing of the staircase provided. Luke mirrored his movements on the left. As if they had rehearsed the move a thousand times before, Shane went right after Ethan and leapfrogged him, stepping behind the closest concrete column. Tom copied his movement and moved quickly to the column opposite Shane.

They all held their positions and extended their ears outward, listening for their enemy's movement. More and more violent footsteps boomed forward in microsecond intervals, then retreated into the distance. The diversion was working.

The lighting in the basement was not ideal by any standard, but they were fortunate to have electricity at all. Two of the three small lightbulbs with tin shade covers swung ominously from the low-hang ceiling. The light danced around the room, revealing small details that were only lost in the overpowering darkness seconds later. Plaguers darted forward from all directions, their movement hidden in the constant shifting of the shadows.

One particularly nasty looking plaguer dove forward, inches from Luke's face. He instantly placed his back flat against the staircase railing and held his breath. The plaguer fell on his knees as he dove, and Luke could see the exposed brain that protruded from the top rear of his skull. The right side of his face had been torn off but somehow, his glasses sit unperturbed on his face. He was wearing a sweater that was all too similar to Chad's and Luke couldn't help but ponder if Poindexter here was just as big of an asshole too.

The plaguer sat there on all fours and extended his neck outward. The shrill it emitted temporarily deafened Luke. He slammed his blood covered hands into the cement floor in frustration and shot up almost superhumanly, then took off like a bullet back into the darkness.

Luke let out a silent sigh of relief and saw Ethan looking in his direction. He gave a grim nod to Luke and motioned for him to move up. He couldn't help but quietly wonder how Ethan knew so much about what was going on or why he trusted Luke to be right next to him in all of this.

Ethan stepped forward again and stopped as he pressed against the next column. There were five plaguers standing in the open room that were seemingly uninterested in the commotion at the elevator. Two were facing a large bookshelf to the left, their bodies tremoring uncontrollably.

The woman in the center of the floor was sitting on her knees and holding something. Her head dipped down into her hands and twisted, then jerked up violently before spasming and going back down again. It appeared she might be feasting on something, possibly a rat that was too slow to escape her grasp.

Luke watched as the two plaguers on the right both stood with their knees bent in an aggressive stance and faced each other. One would shriek and twitch and the other would respond with similar sounds and flailed spastic movement. Amusing as it may have looked, them appearing to have some sort of disagreement with each other may elude to them being able to communicate.

Luke shook the disconcerting thought from his head for the time being and focused on the clothing the one bickering plaguer was wearing: Navy blue slacks and a light blue button up shirt. *Jackpot,* he thought to himself as he motioned over to Ethan, who was already nodding firmly.

"Guns away." Ethan mouthed to them all as he made a display of holstering his firearm and pulled a knife from his pocket. He turned it over in his hand a few times, allowing the blade to glint in the wild light it caught. He had given each of them a knife to use for close quarters against the undead. And in order for them to be stealthy, they would have to get close.

Ethan stepped ahead of Shane, tapping him on the shoulder and prompting him to follow as he passed. They stopped feet from the plaguers who were concentrating on the spines of classic books that lined the eight-foot high shelf.

Luke and Tom moved over to the arguing plaguers, pressing their backs against a shelf that jutted out and hid them from view. The more aggressive of the two men was facing them and they ran the risk of being spotted if they just ran up on them. They needed to turn him around. The problem was that there was already what sounded like a house party going on in the area behind them and if that didn't draw his attention away, nothing would.

Luke glanced over at Ethan who was shaking his head no at him. Luke held up three fingers and counted down to two. Ethan continued shaking his head in the negative. Luke nodded and dropped his index finger, leaving his middle digit up for his one count.

Cute, Ethan thought to himself as he stopped shaking his head and brought his knife up. He wasn't going to convince Luke to wait, so what the hell?

Luke jumped forward with his knife out. Before the bus driver could turn, he had six inches of steel imbedded into the side of his skull. As the blade went in with a wet slop noise, he extended his right leg out and spartan kicked the second plaguer square in his chest. It flew back and hit the ground where it met a bookshelf adorned with countless pieces of literature. Some of which came tumbling down. It was almost comical, watching Ernest Hemingway clock a plaguer on the top of its head.

Ethan pressed up against his target and slammed its head into the wood of the shelf it was facing while simultaneously driving his knife into the base of its skull. Shane was next to him almost copying his exact moves. He struggled slightly as he pushed his blade further into the things head until it could no longer move.

Tom was at the plaguer who was feeding and brought his axe up over his head. His bulkier footsteps alerted the woman to his presence, who turned quickly as he approached. Before he could bring the axe down, she reached out and grabbed hold of his ankle. In one quick move she leaned in and sunk her teeth into his shin.

He screamed in pain and the swing of his weapon faltered, driving the bit of the axe awkwardly into her shoulder. It had no effect as she bit down even harder into his leg, making him scream louder than before.

Ethan lunged over and drove the still blood-soaked blade of his knife into her once silky, brunette hair and through her now rotted brain. Tom fell over with the plaguer's mouth still very much attached to his leg.

Ethan was switching between trying to cover Tom's mouth to stop his howls of pain and prying the woman's jaws from him. A river of blood flowed from the wound and every attempt to pry her jaws from him would result in even louder screams of anguish.

Luke had just removed his knife from the head of the man he had kicked to the floor when he turned to see the commotion. He stared hard at Ethan who wore the same *Oh Shit* expression on his face.

"Get the keys." he said forcefully to Luke as he tried again to minimize Tom's tormented sobbing.

Luke was moving before Ethan finished his sentence. He rolled the driver over who had fallen onto his face. He frantically checked the dead man's shirt pockets and came up empty. Reaching into his pants pocket he could feel small metallic objects and circular ring. He pulled out the item and held it to his face. Three keys dangle from a large key ring with a large yellow plastic tag.

"Got it," he said with elation. "I got it."

Ethan could barely hear him over Tom's waling but saw his excitement as he dangled keys in front of his face.

A single plaguer emerged from the bend in the corridor. His eyes darted around the room and his head jerked like a pigeon. When he realized food had entered his domicile, he opened his mouth and let out a low pitch shriek.

Ethan went to draw his gun and fire before it alerted the rest of the basement dwellers. Before he could get a shot off, the things head exploded and it fell to the floor, dead again.

They looked over and saw Shane extending the forty-five Ethan had given him. "Now they know we're here." He said in an all-business tone.

Glad I gave him that gun, Ethan thought as the woman's teeth were finally separated from Tom's leg. He cried a sigh of relief as tears poured down his face. "Tom," he said to him, cradling his face. "You need to be quiet man. You're drawing them back."

Tom was full on boo-hooing and couldn't hear a word that was said to him. Shane leaned down and punched him once across the chin. It wasn't hard enough to knock him out, but it definitely got his attention. Tom stopped sobbing and his watery eyes flashed with anger as he looked up at the man who just assaulted him.

"Get your shit together," Shane said with vehemence. "We get out, we get you fixed. You good?"

Tom held a blood covered hand to his cheek, momentarily forgetting that he was just a zombie chew toy. He nodded sheepishly and swallowed hard. Determination flashed across his face and he nodded firmly. "Yea, let's go." he said with tears still streaming down his cheeks.

Two more plaguers turned the corner in a curious sprint and entered the room. Their eyes darted around quizzically like the first plaguer's had. One shook its head wildly and barked a wet, guttural bark. The other took off at them, running full-speed before tripping over the dead body of the one who had alerted them to the trespassers. It fell and slammed its face into the concrete floor. The audible crack of its jaw breaking was accompanied by the sight of at least half a dozen teeth flying through the air and a pool of the blood forming on the floor at the sight of the impact.

Shane put a bullet in its head before it could even attempt to regain its footing. When the second one finally looked over at Luke, it took two running steps and jumped over the body at him. Luke had his pistol out and fired twice, catching his assailant twice in its head. He stepped to the side as forward momentum brought the plaguer crashing down where he would have been standing.

Ethan lifted Tom to his feet, and they were moving back to the stairwell. "Let's go." he shouted back to them.

The hallway was now filling with the remaining plaguers. Another of the bus drivers could be seen in the small crowd behind what looked to be a few teenagers who were ravaged by the undead. Like a dinner bell that had just been rung, they all ran full tilt at their potential meal.

Shane and Luke were firing as they retreated. Some of the undead fell backwards, colliding with those behind them and slowing their advance. Some of the faster plaguers would hurl themselves over the falling bodies only to be gunned down mid-air. Bodies cascaded the floor as copper bullets met undead flesh and bone, but the encroaching horde was closing the gap.

Ethan pushed Tom up the first step when a muscular plaguer turned the wall of the stairwell. It pushed with all of its body weight as it grabbed at Tom, sending the three of them to the cold floor. Ethan rolled to the side and pointed his gun in time to see the monster drive its decaying teeth into Tom's head. You could hear the loud crack of his skull as it bit down, and covered Tom's horrified eyes with blood.

Ethan pulled the trigger and the plaguer's head exploded. A chunk of Tom's hair covered in flesh and bone fell from its mouth as its body tumbled lifelessly to the side. Tom wasn't making any noises, but his fingers and feet twitched. Ethan knew what was next. He did the only thing he was trained to do in these situations. He shot the already expired body in the head.

"Sorry Tom." he said softly. He turned to see Shane and Luke running at him. Shane was slamming a fresh magazine into the well of his gun and racking the slide. He turned and darted up the stairs as if his life depended on it... which it kind of did.

"Betty!" He screamed at the top of his lungs as he neared the door. "Open up."

Luke and Shane were firing down the stairs as the plaguers would rush up the steps and fall back down once they caught a few bullets. Not all shots were kill-shots, but given the confined space they were fighting in, that wasn't a problem. A well placed round or two into the stomach or chest was enough to send one reeling back down the stairs and into any other flesh starved monstrosity behind it.

The stairwell was flooded with the undead. They were scratching and clawing over the dead and injured bodies that fell, gaining precious inches.

"Betty!" Ethan shouted again in a deep commanding voice. "Open this fucking..."

There was a sudden metallic clunk and the door swung open. They pushed through with all the strength they could muster and turned, pressing it closed with their bodies against it. The image of a starved plaguer reaching hopelessly up at Luke with saddened eyes as the large reinforced metal door slammed shut and encased him in darkness wasn't something he would be able to shake from his mind.

'Sorry," Betty stammered. "The bolt was stuck."

"It's ok." Luke said breathing heavily. They were all winded and trying to catch their breaths.

"Tom?" Nelly asked, glancing from them to the door and back again.

Shane and Luke stared at the floor. Ethan shook his head slowly. "He didn't make it." he said sincerely.

Her eyes began to water, and her lips quivered. It was clear she was putting up a dam to prevent the waterworks from spilling over. No one said anything for a moment as she turned and sat at one of the desks across the room. She put her head into her hands and began to weep as Izzy sat down next to her.

Several thuds on the opposite side of the door and the muffled groaning of the horde led Luke, Ethan and Shane to reflect on just how close they had come to death down there. Their plan had worked, but it cost Tom his life.

"I hate to say it," Ethan whispered to them, "but I told him to use his knife." When no one commented, he turned directly to Luke. "And you need to think before you do some dumb shit like that again."

Luke looked at him indignantly. "Are you blaming me for Tom dying?"

"No, I'm not," he said taking the defensive. "I need you to make smarter decisions because I need you alive."

"Well then why the hell did you let me go down there in the first place?" he said, shrugging his shoulders.

"If I had told you to stay up here, would you?"

Luke thought for a second. "Nah, you're right."

"Damn right I'm right." Ethan said almost sanctimoniously. "'And you would've come down there half-cocked and done God knows what."

"I probably would've saved your ass." Luke exclaimed with certainty.

"Yea, right." Ethan replied, taking a seat.

"It's getting late," Izzy said, walking up to them with her arms crossed. "And she's a mess right now." She pointed back at Nelly with her head.

"Yea," Ethan said softly, knowing what she was asking. "We'll get some rest and go in a few hours. That ok with everyone?"

Everyone nodded or uttered a word in agreement. Chad was already fast asleep on one of the tables.

Luke embraced Izzy and looked over at Ethan. "Go." Ethan said. "I'll get first watch."

Chapter 10

A few hours passed and what was once an eerie silence seemed to evolve into a sinister one. Ethan paced around the old wooden tables and desks that furnished the grandiose main hall of the historical library. His first watch was uneventful, and Shane and Luke have since each taken a watch. When anymore sleep eluded him, Ethan relieved him early and took a second shift.

"It's too fucking quiet," he grumbled to himself. There were no noises coming from outside. No screaming or sounds of fighting, no plaguers making creepy ass plaguer noises. And even odder still, was the thumping on the basement door had stopped. He had thought about opening the door to take a peek down there, but decided that he didn't want to be the first person who falls for a zombie's trap.

"That would be some shit Luke does." he laughed at his own quip. The silence was beginning to unnerve him when he spotted a maintenance ladder in the corner by a bathroom. He set it up under one of the large mosaic windows and climbed up to peer out.

The sun had begun to rise and revealed the destruction at the hands of the plaguers from the night before. When he didn't see anyone outside, he was satisfied and began to descend the ladder. He stopped when he realized what he had just seen and clambered back up to do a double take. Sure enough, there was no one out there.

"What…the…fuck?" Was all he could manage to get out. He saw what he was sure were a few random plaguers, but they were behaving differently. They were all walking calmly, not running, past the library. Almost as if they were headed to a specific destination. A few more entered his line of vision and he watched as they simply shuffled by.

"Where the hell are you…?" The words trailed off as a single thought crossed his mind. "Logan." He said to himself. Within seconds he was off the ladder and heading to the second floor with his binoculars. He ran into the room they had first entered through the previous day and stepped out onto the scaffolding.

Plaguers from a mile in every direction seemed to be converging on one area. He watched as hundreds of them shuffled slowly in the same direction as if being compelled. He increased his scope and followed the thickening trail of the undead. His head and arms snaked as he zig-zagged, traveling with them to their destination until…. he saw them.

"Holy shit." he exclaimed as he lowered the binoculars. He smiled in mild disbelief and then, just like that, it turned into a frown. "Fuck, I have to get him," he realized with a twinge of exhaustion. He went back inside to wake the others.

Ethan grabbed the closest book he could as he ran past a return cart, which happened to be a hardback copy of *The Call of Cthulhu* by H.P. Lovecraft. He began banging the book on the wooden tables and shelves. "Let's go guys." he shouted as he moved from area to area attempting to wake his sleeping comrades.

"What's wrong?" Luke asked, already awake and well alert.

"The plaguers are leaving," he said, zipping up his equipment bag. He looked at the Lovecraft book and unzipped his bag again, putting the book inside before closing it again.

"Leaving? Where are they going?" Luke asked as everyone was now gathering.

"They're going after Logan," he said hurriedly. "So, we have to go get him first."

"Logan?!" Luke said with surprise. He smiled until he realized just how dire this was. "Where?"

"Mechanic shop, about a mile and a half from here."

"No offense," Chad said, putting his hand up, "but why do we have to risk our lives getting *his* brother?"

"You don't," Ethan said with a smirk. "Your white-privileged ass can stay right here and read Twilight to your undead roomies 'til the end of time for all I care."

Chad's mouth dropped with the insult. "No," he started, desperately. "I'll go with you."

"I don't know if we can set them off or not, so we should leave the same way Luke and I came in," Ethan explained to them. Izzy brought a distraught Nelly over and brought her up to speed. She nodded weakly.

It was a short trip out the window and to the ground. Luke and Shane helped Betty, Izzy, Nelly, and Chad down from the roof of the bus while Ethan went inside to start it. They all stepped inside and took a seat, except for Luke, who crouched next to Ethan.

"It won't start." Ethan said irritated.

"Are you using the right key?" Luke asked him.

Ethan turned his head slowly to stare at Luke with laser eyes. "Yea it's the right goddamned key."

Luke watched as Ethan struggled with the ignition that refused to turn over for him.

"Let me…" Luke said, reaching over.

"I will fucking cut you, dude." Ethan said, swatting his hand away.

"Um," Luke pointed a finger at the key ring, "what's the number three for?"

Ethan lifted the key ring and for the first time, took notice of the yellow tag dangling from it. Stamped dead center on it was the number three. Luke stepped off the bus cautiously and checked the front grill for any series of numbers. Ethan watched him as he crept over to the other two buses and did the same, then came back to Ethan.

"Well?" Ethan inquired, impatiently.

"So," he said trying to plan his words carefully. "This is bus four."

"Which one is bus three?"

"Well… there isn't one here." he said, scratching his head. "That's one and two, respectfully." He pointed to the other remaining buses.

Ethan's cold stare intensified, and his nostrils flared as his body went rigid.

"You don't have to brain scan me, dude." Luke said.

"What's the hold up?" Shane said, crossing the yellow line.

"We got the wrong key and Ethan's having a stroke. Get behind the line, dude." Luke said, without missing a beat.

"Seriously?" Shane said, as he unconsciously stepped back behind the yellow line.

"This is fucking unreal," Ethan stated angrily. "Well I'm not going back in that mother fucking basement. Stupid ass yellow buses should have universal stupid ass yellow bus keys. And if the fucking…"

Shane reached up and opened the sun visor. A key with an identical yellow tag with the number four on it fell into his waiting hand. He held it in front of Ethan, who only stared for a second. He was debating on finishing his little tirade but decided against it.

"You're damn right." He said as he snatched the key and started the bus. As the engine turned over, he stopped for a second and looked back at Nelly, who was staring down in her seat. "Tom…" he said, disheartened, as he turned back to Luke.

Luke and Shane's expression went grim as they picked up on his unspoken meaning. Tom had died for a key that they hadn't needed, to a bus that wasn't even there. They let his spoken name hang in the air with the sound of the idling engine.

Shane placed a hand on Ethan's shoulder. "I drove trucks for a couple years. I got this." he told him as they switched spots.

"The mechanic shop is a mile and change out. That's our first stop," he said. The bus reversed and pulled out the lot, mowing down several disinterested plaguers who wandered mindlessly towards the same destination.

Chapter 11
Mr. Stone

An impatient Mr. Stone was pacing the length of his large, agarwood desk. The heartwood furniture gave off a naturally occurring aroma that in most cases, would assist in calming a stressed Mr. Stone. Two of his subordinates stood at the ready with their automatic rifles in their hands. They were exchanging nervous glances when their boss finally stopped between them.

"Still no word from Mathias?" he asked sharply to neither soldier in particular.

Bailey, according to his name tag, spoke up. "No sir. The team's been in position awaiting his arrival." He spoke nervously to his boss. He knew all too well of Mr. Stone's proclivity to overreact at the slightest modicum of bad news.

Mr. Stone was shaking his head furiously. Mathias' job was simple; eliminate two measly Legacies and meet his team for the assault on one of the Order of Four's American bases. He was essential to the operation, as he was their mole on the inside. Without him, precious resources would have to be diverted and their progress would be slowed.

"Billy," Mr. Stone barked.

"It's Bailey sir." Bailey corrected him. Mr. Stone looked at him as if he would flay his skin for the indiscretion. "I, mean yes sir, Billy...sir." He stammered.

Mr. Stone turned to the other soldier. "Gun." was all he said as the soldier handed his sidearm to his employer. Mr. Stone lifted it up without hesitation and fired, putting a bullet square between Bailey's eyes. The other soldier winced from the bang of the gunshot in the close confines as his comrade's lifeless body hit the hard, metallic floor.

The soldier stared down at Bailey's body in horror until he saw Mr. Stone handing the firearm back to him. His shaky hand took the gun and holstered it back up safely.

"What I need you to do," Mr. Stone paused to look at the standing soldier's nametag only to see Tzchevsky. He rolled his eyes and turned towards his desk. "...son, is to tell Suthers to standby. I'll be bringing Gol over."

The soldier's eyes widened. He had heard rumors since he entered this organization about the legendary Gol and his exploits in combat. His fear and trepidation were suddenly replaced by the anticipation of a child expecting candy.

"Yes, sir," the soldier said as he turned to exit the room.

"Excuse me." Mr. Stone said, turning the soldier on his heels mid-stride. The soldier stood at attention and shifted his gaze from side to side, unsure what his commander wanted. Mr. Stone pointed an ominous finger down and wiggled it at the lifeless body on the floor. "Take *that* with you."

"Yes, sir." Tzchevsky replied, robotically. He reached down and grabbed Bailey by his stiffened arms and pulled, dragging him along the floor as he scurried backwards out the door.

Mr. Stone took a seat at his desk and looked over his clipboard. He went to the page labeled "Legacies" again and ran his finger down the side of the list under the "Agents" column. When he found Matthias' name, he looked over at the two targets assigned to him.

Luke and Logan Matthews ... brothers, he thought to himself. Placing the clipboard down, he opened the top drawer of his desk and removed a single manila envelope labeled "Matthias." He fingered through the contents of the dossier, passing by several photos of targets with the word "Disposed" stamped across their faces. He stopped when he came to Luke's file.

"Who are you born from?" he said to himself as his eyes locked on the bold lettering of **Descendants of: Unknown.** "What?" he said moving his face closer to the page, hoping to reveal more words he may have missed. He pulled Logan's file and looked down to see the same disposition.

His eyes narrowed in anger and confusion as he glanced back and forth between the two pages in disbelief. "That's not possible." he growled to the empty room. He slammed the folder closed as a sudden unfamiliar feeling crept into the pit of his stomach. It was doubt. How did he not notice this before? Why was it not brought to his attention when he clearly overlooked it?

His mind scrambled as he recounted too many recent occurrences that were too specific to be coincidental. The relic he had acquired had went missing at a very inopportune time. His best agent and understudy had not checked in and was presumed dead. And now, he finds that two if not more Legacies have either had their information altered or erased. The thought of a mole in his own operation infuriated and frustrated him.

Mr. Stone had agents everywhere and, even though he still had a strong ally within the Order, he didn't particularly trust him. Much to his dismay, he would have to reach out to him after the more pressing matter at hand was dealt with. First, he would need to contact his own overseer.

The prospect of him not knowing the lineage of a single Legacy was a danger to his plans. The fact that there were two currently unaccounted for could prove disastrous with the relic missing. He began unconsciously tapping his finger on his desk, weighing his options. He pondered on his "business arrangement" with his partner. He most certainly did not want to get him involved, but the two threats had to be found. There was always the distinct possibility that the plaguers would just take care of them for him. No harm, no foul. Likely as it could be, he would not be able to leave such a loose end to chance. Especially if the brothers were aided by a Sentinel.

Sentinels were the most skilled fighters in the Order of Four and their sole responsibility laid with the protection of their Legacy. Rare as they were in the Order, Sentinels were only assigned to the most promising or important Legacies. They were hard to track and even harder to kill, since they were even blessed with a touch of arcane knowledge.

Mr. Stone pulled an old concrete bowl from a cupboard and placed it on his desk. He leaned over it and stared intently at the ingredients already resting within. Petals of a white lily flower line the inside of the bowl and a three-inch cut of a thorny shrub sit atop them. A torn strip of cloth and chunk of iron ore rest lazily next to a scrap of worn leather. Mr. Stone had used these items almost regularly as of late, and they had an almost blackened hue to them as a result.

He opened his left hand and held it over the bowl almost ceremoniously. Then pulling a knife from his waist he ran the blade across his open palm. A single thick rivulet of his crimson sacrifice ran down his hand and dripped gracefully into the bowl, covering the contents inside.

"Acciri equitibus Plaga," he said in a loud authoritative voice. His head began to ring, and his vision blurred. Any and all thoughts occupying his mind were erased and replaced with a vast, calming emptiness. The ringing stopped and his sight adjusted to match the absence in his mind. A white film covered his eyes and gave them the similar appearance of the plaguers' undead stare. A low growl crept through his mind and echoed in his ears. He was now in open communication with the real head honcho.

"We might have a problem." he said aloud with more irritation than concern.

Chapter 12

Logan had gotten a few restless hours of broken sleep between shifts in the auto body shop. He, Jen, and Matt had rotated between a couple hours on watch in the main garage area and the roof. One would rest while the other two kept lookouts. He paced around the beat-up pickup truck they had pressed against the garage door to reinforce it, his AR-15 at the ready.

Mary had been sound asleep the moment she laid on the worn-down leather couch in the lobby. Carrie and Rick would alternate between inaudible conversation and low arguing for several hours before finally falling asleep.

Logan looked over at Jen who was spread across several of the padded armless chairs that usually accommodated customers awaiting their vehicle's repairs. Before any of this even happened, he was amazed by her strength and ability to fight on any front for what she believed in. Now, she had proven that she was an all-out soldier. He was completely blown away by her. He smiled at her back and turned away.

Logan's smile faded as he took another step around the truck and listened for a moment. Silence. The screaming steel of bending garage doors being pounded and pressed incessantly by the countless bodies of the plaguers outside had suddenly stopped, along with their moans and shrills that had been piercing the night sky. The only sound left was the unnerving rattling of the chains used to open and close the bay doors.

His eyes darted around nervously. He saw Mary turning over on the couch, her hard sleep disturbed by the sudden quiet that broke through the racket.

"Hey, Logan," Matt shouted down through the vent that connected to the rooftop he was posted at. "You might wanna come up here."

Jen was already at Logan's side, rubbing sleep away from her eyes. "Go." she said, "We're good here." She pulled the gun from her holster and checked the magazine.

Logan nodded and headed to the stairwell. He pushed the door open and saw Matt with the shotgun down at his side, staring over the edge of the roof in a daze. "What's up?" Logan asked, a little more winded than he felt he should be.

"They just…. stopped." Matt replied absently.

Logan joined his friend and peered over the side. The plaguers were standing as still as mannequins, their eyes locked on the two figures on the roof staring back at them.

"What the hell?" Logan whispered, more to himself than to Matt. Movement up the street caught his glance and he could see more of the undead slowly shuffling towards the building from all directions. He pointed lazily at them, "They're just…walking. Like old school, horror movie zombies."

"Yea, but why are they walking towards us specifically? And why are those ones frozen?" Matt was as confused as he was concerned.

"I don't know." Logan said lifting his rifle and locking his sights on an easy target. He squeezed the trigger and the rifle kicked back with a bang as the projectile flew forward and dropped a tall infected that stood out to him. It fell to the ground and was lost in the sea of undead bodies that hadn't so much as flinched. Logan brought his rifle back down.

Ominous clouds began to form in the morning light a few blocks from the auto shop and cast the city streets below in a premature dusk. Logan and Matt were transfixed as the dark swirls slowly enveloped the morning sky. Unnatural lightening crackled through the dim and dense clouds and illuminated the lifeless features of the undead.

An unsettling howl of wind emanated from the malformed windstorm before them. Its howl elongated and contorted into a high pitch whale that broke with a deafening boom of thunder. The sound swept across the rooftop like a sonic boom and almost knocked Matt and Logan over.

The howl returned as the otherworldly white mist that infected the many citizens with the undead plague took center stage underneath this unannounced maelstrom. It danced and snaked into the shape of a large mountain rivaling the buildings it rested between.

The mist lowered slightly and extended, taking on the shape of some sort of distorted quadruped. In one quick and fluid movement, the mist expanded as if there was internal explosion. It shot out at incredible speeds across the sky and landscape, dissipating with distance until there was none left. The howl that accompanied the mist lowered into what sounded like the unmistakable neigh of a horse. The sound died down with the expulsion of the mist and left a thunderous silence in its wake.

Logan and Matt stood with their mouths gaped open in shock and awe as they stared out into the street in total disbelief at what they had just witnessed. Even stranger was that, where the mist had just disappeared from, now stood a single solitary man.

Although the details of his features were unclear from this distance, they could see firstly that he was abnormally tall, as he was standing what had to be an imposing eight or nine feet. They could see he was wearing a stained, tattered, and torn white cloth that hung from his waist but remained topless. They could also tell that he was so thin that he appeared to be ill stricken and sickly. If his sudden and otherworldly arrival was any indication, however, they knew that wasn't the case.

The large humanoid creature turned his head to the right and slowly rotated up and around to the left, taking in his current surroundings. He turned his gaze up and onto Logan and Matt ahead of him and then tilted his head to the side, almost as if confused. He took in such a deep breath of air they could feel the oxygen around them thin slightly on the roof of the mechanic shop.

Logan would never forget the terrifying smile that spread across the monster's nightmare-infused face as it held its deeply inhaled breath and stared almost longingly at him. It had sharp and blackened teeth that were visible because of ripped and missing flaps of ashen skin where lips should be.

It let out the air as it bellowed a single word in a supernatural growl that echoed and shook everything within earshot. "Caaaiiiinnnn," it said, taking its time to annunciate each letter. Suddenly, the idle mass of the undead came back to unlife. They let out a unified shriek of anger upwards toward the roof.

Logan broke his glance from the large monster and looked down to see the plaguers in an all-out frenzy as their assault on the building began anew. That strange white mist was now being emitted from their eyes and mouths as they pounded mercilessly on the garage doors. This time, there was an unsettling screaming of metal coming from the garage doors with the impacts.

Logan moved hurriedly to the other side of the building and looked down at the heavy steel entry door. He listened as he heard the integrity of the massive bolt securing the entrance becoming compromised.

Logan turned and headed for the stairs. "We have to get them up here." he told Matt, who was close behind him.

Jen tensed as she heard the crackling of lightening and boom of thunder. She stood next to a pickup truck they parked in front of one of the garage doors for extra security. She glanced back at Mary who was visibly shaken by the sudden thunderstorm. Rick sat on a nearby chair and tapped his foot nervously. Jen wasn't sure if he was afraid or just needed a hit of some recreational drug. Probably both.

Carrie walked up to Jen's side with caution. "What's going on?" She asked.

"I don't' know," Jen replied, checking her magazine and reinserting it. "But I don't like it."

"Caaaiiiinnnn!" she heard cut through the garage like a revving engine with a bullhorn placed up to it. The hanging lights swayed to and from, and the parked cars creaked as their heavy still frames were shaken.

"What the...?" she said to no one and moved closer to a small glass portion of the garage door that was too small to even be a window. Her eyes got about six inches from it as she tried to peer out before the mist-covered eyes and nose of a plaguer slammed into it. She jumped back and let out a small involuntary gasp.

They shrieked and shrilled their undead war cry and brought their hardened, rotted fists to cold steel with the strength of a battering ram. The side of the garage door bent inward as the rest of it began receiving hand sized dents. The sudden increase in their strength threatened to cave the door inward and allow the ravenous creatures inside.

"Holy shit," Jen exclaimed in horror as a single crusty hand reached over the bent corner of the door and pried it down further. The metal cried as it bent, and the plaguer poked his tattered head through to catch a glance at its food. It barked as it laid its foggy eyes on Jen, who brought her handgun up and sent two rounds into its head. There was no blood as its head exploded. Instead, that damned white mist was sent spewing from its head as it tumbled back and into the crowd.

A loud clank and ear-pitching wale to her side caught her attention. She turned to see the security door down to the halfway point where it met the roof of the sedan sitting against it. A thin plaguer, reminiscent of a drug addict in build and frame, catapulted through the new opening. Before it landed over the roof of the car, another undead was pulling himself into the garage. He was slightly stockier than the first and moved through noticeably slower as a result.

"Get upstairs!" Jen yelled to the others as she retreated back and fired at the thin plaguer who was running at her. It lunged with arms outstretched and gained purchase as it grabbed her shoulders and tumbled to the ground on top of her. She was firing wildly into its chest, hoping that one of the random bullets would be enough to at least drive it back.

Rick was backing up slowly with pure terror plastered across his face as he looked back and forth at the entrances that now birthed several of the zombies. He turned and ran for the steps, knocking over an almost hysterical Mary and leaving Carrie behind.

"You pussy!" Carrie screamed as she pulled the firearm Jen had given her. Her inexperience was evident as she tried to adjust her grip quickly, sacrificing necessary time in the process. She cried as she brought the weapon up and aimed at the plaguer snapping its teeth inches from Jen's face. A single shot rang out and the dead attacker fell to the side, a large hole in the side of its head.

Logan stood on the stairwell with his rifle at eye level, smoke coming from the tip of the barrel. It was a risky shot, but he didn't have time to try and close the gap. He swiveled as he came down a step and fired into the torso of another plaguer who was running at Mary. It sprawled backwards and slammed into a shelf which came down on top of it, a container of oil covering its rotted face.

"Get to the roof," Logan shouted in his best drill instructor voice as Rick hopped up two of the stairs. Logan squeezed the trigger again right by Rick's ear as he attempted to squeeze passed him. Logan shifted over and blocked his path. "You go last, asshole." he said to him as he pushed him in the chest and temporarily trained his rifle on him.

Rick stared at him with a combination of horror and anger. His gaze remained on Logan as Mary squeezed passed them both and through the door at the top of the stairwell. Carrie gave Rick a glance of disdain as she slipped through the space Logan allowed her.

"Go," he said again to him as he bladed his body and continued to fire at the encroaching undead. Rick ran like a rat with its ass on fire.

Jen was up and limping as she ran to Logan, firing behind her with half glances. A female plaguer was on her heels and lashing at her blind spot. Logan jumped down to ground level when he was convinced his wife wouldn't make it. He ran and grabbed Jen with his one arm and swung her around. As if in slow motion they turned and the barrel of his rifle extended outward, pressing directly into the flesh flayed face of the young woman. He fired as the bridge of her nose collapsed like a sink hole and drug her already sunken eyes in with it. The bullet traveled up and out the back of her skull, sending brain fragments and hair careening through the air as she flew backwards.

They slammed against the wall together and Jen looked at him intensely. "That was hot." She said bluntly.

Logan cracked a half-smile before realizing the ground level of the garage was only seconds from being overrun with the new and improved undead. "Let's go." He said hastily, as he fired two body shots to drive the closest threats back. His rifle clicked empty and he went to join his wife who was already at the top.

They had set up various chairs and furniture at the top of the stairwell the day before with this exact possibility in mind. Well, not exactly. They knew there was the chance the undead would get in their makeshift domicile. What none of them could have expected or even imagined was that there would be some giant, uber zombie appearing out of nowhere and pissing the lesser zombies off to the point of what could only be described as a frenzied hunger, granting them super human strength in the process.

The idea was that the last person to the top would push the heavy desk and filing cabinets down the stairwell, which would take the chairs and the rest of the debris down with them. This would at least buy them some time and best-case scenario, if the zombies outside flooded into the garage, a path could open up for their escape.

Matt joined Logan and the two heaved with all their strength. The scraping of the large metallic items halted for a moment as they tilted from the landing. They were rewarded for their effort with several large bangs and thuds reverberating through the stairwell as the cabinets, desk, and chairs bounced down, crushing the five or so undead who were unable to evade them.

The echoes of the deadly tumbling furniture seemed to last forever. They stood, staring down at their work as the plaguers didn't hesitate in traversing the collapsed furniture. It would take some time, but they would get through, and more than likely it would be sooner than later.

Logan backed through the threshold and Matt brought the roof door closed, fishing the large bolt through the lock catch and jumping back as if it would burst into flames.

They all stood, looking in the distance at the large afflicted man. "Wha…what is that?" Mary said in near panic.

"That's the guy who pissed them all of." Logan said, putting his hand on Jen's shoulder.

"Now what?" Matt said to anyone who would answer.

They were all glancing in different directions, hoping that some unseen salvation would materialize before their very eyes.

"I guess…" Logan started as he inserted a fresh preloaded magazine into his AR15 and racked it, "we just try to stay alive as long as we can." His voice wavered with a lack of confidence or conviction as he knew just how dire the situation was. He couldn't help but feel completely responsible for their current predicament. It was his decision to recruit his all-too caring neighbor Mary who could still be waiting at her secure house for her only daughter. For all any of them knew, her daughter could've had the means and know how to take her mother and anyone who was willing to follow to safety. Or at least, a zombie-free existence.

Logan's "what if?" scenarios were cut short when the large humanoid creature in the street took one monstrous step forward. The thunderous boom of cement cracking under his supernaturally heavy weight coming down demanded attention. The thing had an indifferent expression as it towered forward, one behemoth step at a time.

After six or seven advancing steps, the creature stopped. It tilted its bald head to the side in curiosity again. Then with its brows furrowed, it reached its right hand up at them, palm open.

"Rise." it said in an echoed growl that threatened to shake the sky as he closed his open hand. The first line of the undead that were already gaining entrance to the floor level of the garage stopped their advance. Craning their necks almost defiantly at the human survivors gathered on the roof, they stared directly and collectively bent their knees to get down on all fours.

As if it had been rehearsed by the undead cheer squad at the local high school, the second line of plaguers clambered forward and onto the backs of the first line. They moved with a previously unseen coordination amongst their decayed and rigor mortis-infused numbers as the line behind the stacking group would move forward with discipline to fill the ranks. They would then climb the makeshift human ladder and kneel on the back of their cohort, forming another undead rung for the next plaguer to ascend. All the while never looking away from their awestricken food at the top.

Like disposed and putrid puppets, they continued their ascent as their master commanded. They climbed with emotionless expressions and white mist drifting outward from their soulless eyes. Although the stench they emitted threatened to burn through the groups' collective sinus cavities, it was overshadowed by the fear they instilled with every determined movement.

The groups' faces turned from shock to sheer panic as they watched the stack reach the height of four grown men and counting. At this rate, they would be able to traverse the shop's walls within minutes.

Logan turned and saw everyone had been looking at him, possibly for a solution. Except Rick, who had been covering his ears with his hands and shaking his head violently back and forth. Logan let his mouth drop with no real words of solace to offer the group who looked at him for leadership.

"Just…shoot…" he said at first with defeat. "Just…. fucking shoot." He said again as anger began to well within him. He was convinced that they were all dead at this point, but God be damned if he wasn't going to take as many of the flesh-eating bastards as he could to Hell with him.

They all fired indiscriminately over the side of the building. Gunshots tore through the early morning sky as undead flesh fell back and down into the mass of plaguers like drops of sand into the desert. Countless decaying hands overwhelmed the survivors resolve as they gained purchase to the rooftop's clearing, forcing the group to retreat further into the center.

Like a world class pole vaulter, one leapt from the shoulders of its reanimated human stepladder and cleared the landing. It never slowed or broke stride as its right foot touched down and forward momentum carried it like a torpedo towards Matt. It cut through the air as it closed in, eagerly snapping its chompers.

Matt pumped the twelve gage Logan had given him and squeezed the trigger at the fastly approaching zombie. The three-inch slug punched a fist-sized hole through its heart and stopped its forward movement. It hit the ground and slid back slightly, pushing its legs out and turning to gain its footing before ever coming to a complete stop. Logan turned and put one in its head as it strode forward again, putting it down for good this time.

Another biter came at Matt from a blind spot behind the roof access. Her arms were stretched out at him and her shriveled hands grabbed at the air greedily as she approached. He pumped his shotgun again and fired, blowing off a section of her shoulder and making her body twist mid-stride. She swung her body straight and Matt tried to fire again. The weapon clicked empty as the woman slammed into him. He turned his shotgun and thrust it up and under her chin. He could feel her throat shatter as she pressed it against the forend of his weapon in an attempt to sink her teeth into his face.

Jen turned and shot the woman in the cranium, who crumpled over lifeless. "Reload." she yelled at Matt, who began frantically inserting more rounds into his shotgun.

Bodies upon bodies began flooding the rooftop. Some ran and jumped over the carcasses of their comrades, while others stepped purposefully with a heavy-footed walk. The sounds of varying caliber weapons rang out in a cacophony of gunfire.

Logan continued pivoting as he fired, taking as many headshots as quickly as he could but settling for body shots that would drive the threats back. His slide locked to the rear and he pressed the magazine release, slamming one of the few fresh ones he had left into the well.

Mary stood skewed from Jen and cried hysterically as she held her kitchen knife out and thrashed wildly at the air in front of her. She knew it wouldn't kill anything that came passed it, but she prayed it would be enough to make any monster think twice before coming in at her. But it wouldn't.

Carrie's unproficiency with firearms was again evident as she held her nine-millimeter with two loose wrists and pulled the trigger with an angry, jerky finger. She winced and squealed with each shot as the bullets flew wildly through the air. Gravel from the rooftop sprayed up as the projectiles went low and wide. Only a few targets were actually struck, and only in spots that seemed to have no effect on their advance.

Rick was pacing in small, panicked steps from one end of the group's defensive circle to the other. His hands were clasped on his ears in a vain attempt to block out the chaos around him. He spun on his heels and only saw death closing in on them from all directions. His mind began to unravel, and anger came to the front. He hated Logan for placing them in this predicament. If it weren't for him, he would still be in his apartment getting high and verbally abusing Carrie in a fashion that would make her feel responsible for his displeasure. She would apologize adamantly and throw herself at him, which he would take full advantage of in both a sexual and otherwise nature.

Rick's eyes focused on the spare handgun tucked in Logan's rear waist. His face scrunched as he hastily pulled it free and pointed it at Logan's head. They all turned inward to face his maddening gaze. His teeth clenched and the small caliber weapon shook uncontrollably in his trembling hands.

"This is all your fucking fault." he screamed with his voice cracking and spittle flying from his lips.

"This is not the time, fuckstick." Matt said looking over, but still firing into the massing crowd.

"Fuck you." Rick said, seething with anger as he turned the gun in Matt's direction. Logan saw the opportunity and took it. He lunged in and swatted the handgun out of Rick's delicate grasp with his rifle, then brought the butt of it back and straight into Rick's face, crushing his nose.

The impact sent him stumbling several yards until his back smacked right into someone who had been standing idle. He turned slowly and froze in awe and terror as what would have normally been a beautiful young woman with brown hair stood before him.

Had it not been for the boils and pockmarks that currently covered her otherwise flawless twenty-something year old skin, he would've been instantly smitten with her. Time slowed for the briefest of seconds as she almost seemed to smile at him. Rick let out a half nervous chuckle at the woman before realizing he had made a fatal mistake.

The woman's mouth opened wide and a low hum could be heard as the deadly white mist that reanimated the dead spewed out like projectile vomit, covering Rick's head. He let out a blood curdling scream as his sight went blank and his hearing mute from the mist entering every orifice of his terror-stricken face. As if he had just gazed upon the sacred Ark of the Covent, the flesh on his face began to melt away from his bone.

Outer layers of what formed details on his face caved in on themselves. His lower lip fell forward and, with no chin for it to grab hold of, seemingly fell away. Blood poured from his sunken eye sockets as hair follicles dissolved with rapidly liquefying skin and fat cells. A small, diamond cut stud earring that clasped to his left earlobe plummeted to the floor as the cartilage bent and twisted into the side of his skull before disappearing entirely.

Rick's hands shot up to his face, more out of instinct than to offer any type of assistance. His head jerked from side to side, as if to throw the pain off like a bull does its rider at the rodeo. He turned, still howling in agony, and ran with all the speed he could muster. With no sight and in a full panic, he darted for the far end of the roof, pushing through countless undead who did nothing to stop him. Everyone watched as he went straight over the edge and almost seemed to stop in midair for the briefest of seconds.

Rick's body landed on top of the climbing plaguers who instantly began tearing him apart. His weakened head was ripped from his body by a strong pair of teeth taking purchase in his skull. It was a feeding frenzy as several ravenous undead bit into his stomach and legs. His torso split down the middle and peeled open like a fileted steak as bloodstained hands reached in for whatever organs they could claim. His liver, heart, intestines and all other manner of his unmentionables were devoured in seconds until there was no trace of Rick ever having been on the Earth.

"Oh no," Matt whispered to himself in pseudo concern. "They killed Rick."

With no time to react to Rick's indiscretions, the group kept pushing back. Even Carrie seemed unfazed at the moment by her boyfriend's gruesome demise. It wasn't hard to understand why. Survival was at the forefront of their minds right now. It was all that mattered. Besides, they all knew Rick was a dick anyway.

A clearing in the corner to which they were retreating opened up and they pushed towards it. Logan unsheathed his machete as his rifle clicked empty and he had no time or space to reload his final magazine. *Waste of bullets,* he thought to himself as he swung wholeheartedly at any encroaching undead. His sharpened blade sent fingers, arms, and even heads that got too close to him careening across the rooftop as he slashed with a wild proficiency.

Jen's last round was spent, and the slide of her primary weapon locked to the rear. She holstered it as quickly as she could and pulled her own machete. She looked over at her husband who was hacking away mercilessly at their pursuers with a look of desperation and fear. Her eyes welled with tears and she screamed with unrelenting anger and disdain as she drove her blade down into the skull of a middle-aged man that approached her.

They were overwhelmed and penned into the corner like cattle. Air evaded their lungs as their chests heaved and hearts pummeled against their ribs. They were completely fatigued. With no fight left, they barely managed to even lift any of their weapons. They were pressed close against the corner edge of the building.

The eyes of the undead horde observed their exhaustion and seemed to report the information back to their master. And with it, the horde stopped their advance. The dead, diseased faces stared at the group from only feet away. The mist emitting from their eyes acting as a leash and holding them back from tearing them apart. A few snarled, clearly displeased that they were so close to food and were unable to take a taste.

"Why'd they stop again?" Carrie asked with a crackling voice riddled with fear. Jen shook her head, unable to provide an answer.

There was a loud cracking of concrete as the building tremored. Followed by the same sound and quake a few seconds later, this time louder and closer. Then again. Until finally a large deformed hand reached over the opposite side of the roof's clearing. The plaguers separated like the Red Sea for Moses as the large creature from the street rose into view and stepped a massive foot onto the rooftop.

The groups eyes grew wide as they laid sight on the giant before them. His visage was that of a grotesque marvel. Much like that of a train wreck, he was a true sight of carnage to behold, if your stomach could withstand it.

Blisters and spots of discoloration littered his bare chest and arms and continued up his neck in no real pattern. His flat, indifferent face held two deep chasms for eye sockets with the blackest of abysses within them. The geyser where his nose should be pulsated and spewed mucus and puss with each heavy breath he took. An elongated, asphalt colored tongue swept across the area where lips should be and lapped up the discharge from his lone nostril. Saliva strung across his open mouth and plaque-encrusted teeth and gums.

The large creature halved the distance of the group and stopped. "Legacy," it shrilled in a growl that ripped through the uncomfortable silence like thunder, "step forward." Unrecognizable black fluid shot out from his mouth as he spoke.

The survivors traded questioning glances. Their primordial fear being temporarily replaced with confusion. Logan slightly jumped back when the creature pointed a rather sinister looking index finger out at him.

"Legacy," it bellowed much more demanding this time. "Step-"

His sentence was cut off by screeching tires and gunshots as a large yellow school bus turned the corner and came into view, mowing down plaguers in the street. Bodies exploded by the impact of the heavy metal death machine on wheels.

"...Dooooon't you remember? We built this city. We built this city on rock and rolllll..."

The hordes of undead didn't turn or make any attempt to identify the source of the commotion. But their master was all too curious as he pivoted and looked over the side of the building.

Logan smirked and let out a light chuckle. He felt his energy replenishing and fresh adrenaline beginning to course through his veins.

Jen looked over at him like he had lost his mind. "What the fuck is so funny?" she whisper-yelled at him.

He turned to face her, his small grin now becoming a shit eating grin that spread from ear-to-ear. "It's Luke." He said plainly.

The group didn't seem to share his enthusiasm as they just stared at him blankly, failing to see not only how he would know this, but the relevance it bared.

"There's only one person who is equal parts stupid and ballsy enough to attempt to rescue us in a school bus while blasting a shitty band like Starship. It's Luke," He reiterated, "and he has to have back up."

Jen pepped up slightly and gripped her machete even tighter. Matt pumped his shotgun, feeding a slug into the chamber. Logan slammed his last magazine into his rifle and racked it. Even Carrie managed to load her final magazine and bring her handgun up.

The brakes on the bus whaled as it fishtailed and came to a stop along the wall the group was congregated above. The herd of undead was thinned at ground level by the majority occupying the inside of the garage or surrounding it and being used as a human pyramid. They had easily taken out at least twenty of them upon arrival.

"What the fuck is THAT?!" Shane said as he slammed his foot so hard on the brake, he thought it would go through the floor.

"No," Ethan whispered to himself. "It's him." He turned to Izzy who was finishing up with tying the end of a rope. "You done?" he asked her. She nodded and handed it to him who in turn passed it to Shane. "Change of plans." he said as Shane unsurely took the rope.

"Hey Logan." Luke shouted upwards as he pushed open the emergency hatch on the roof of the bus. "How ya' doing?"

Logan laughed again as he squeezed the trigger and let out short controlled bursts of lead, separating heads from necks. "Well I have a higher KDR now than I did in Horde Z, so pretty good I guess."

"You're still not gonna catch up to me." He shouted back.

"You gonna help or just bust my balls?" Logan replied, trying to push him along.

"I can do both. A rope's coming up. Tie it off and get down here." he said as he headed back down.

Shane came up with the rope and allowed about three feet of slack to dangle to the side. Spinning it like a lasso, he locked his eyes on the roof and aimed, readying his throw. The rest of the group on the bus were firing their weapons from the windows, eliminating any of the plaguers who closed in on them. Their primary target was clearly those on the roof, as they only seemed to attract stragglers.

The creature on the roof roared and began a destructive advance towards those on the other end. He effortlessly tossed plaguers aside as he swung his elongated arms with every step, sending them raining down to the streets below. Logan fired his rifle and let out a three-shot burst straight into the monsters' face.

It reeled back as black fluid cascaded out the rear of his skull and the dark canyon of his right eye exploded. It stepped forward again almost immediately and Logan could see the tainted flesh being sewn back together before his very eyes. The creature growled again as it marched, shaking the building with every colossal step.

Matt turned and pointed his shotgun straight up to the monster's malformed face as it came within arm's length and let loose. Black mist sprayed up as its head all but disintegrated from the three-inch slug bursting forward at such close range. The creature's headless body flew back and down, crushing two zombies underneath its massive frame.

Matt and Logan turned back and saw Carrie and Mary tying off the rope to some sort of duct that should surely hold. A few good tugs to ensure their safety and Mary was on her way down. Carrie followed almost immediately.

"Go Jen." Logan said as the last of his rifle ammo finally ran out. He swung it on his back and again drew his still blood-soaked machete.

"I'm not leaving you here, dickhead." She said with vehemence.

"I'll be right behind you. Go damn it." He responded forcefully.

"Yea, I'm here too," Matt interjected. "I'll go." With that, he fired one more shotgun blast and shuffled down the rope.

The dead bodies that littered the rooftop were once again proving advantageous as they presented an obstacle that the approaching plaguers would have to traverse. The runners were being funneled into a section of rooftop that was closing in on itself fast.

"Mine!" A booming voice declared with otherworldly rage. Logan froze as the last few zombies stopped their assault again and the large creature stepped forward, its head completely healed back to its original disfigured and wretched form.

It reached out with its large slimy hand and wrapped its eel like fingers around Logan's throat, lifting him several feet from his footing. His feet dangled uselessly as he flailed his machete at the creature's arm. He watched as the slices of flesh the blade made disappeared as quickly as they formed. His weapon wasn't just ineffective against this thing, it was completely useless.

"No." Jen shouted stepping back onto the rooftop and releasing the rope she was about to descend. She grabbed the handgun Rick dropped to the floor and fired every round in the magazine at the monster's face. Her accuracy was impressive as every round struck home at its intended target, ripping small holes into his head, face and chest as he held Logan out like his play-thing. But it proved futile as the rounds had absolutely no effect on the beast. She dropped the empty gun and pulled her machete again, staring hard at the monstrosity. It snarled at her and opened its lipless mouth wide, letting the evil plague mist flow freely out in her direction.

"Jen…" Logan shouted as loud as he could with the pressure being applied to his throat.

Down below Ethan clambered through the hatch and stood on the roof of the bus with Shane as he leaned backwards and thrust the rope up to the roof with all of his strength.

"Cover them," Ethan told him. "This will take me a minute." He pulled the little cloth bag that Luke identified earlier as a hacky sack from his jacket pocket. He held it up by the tied end with two fingers and began speaking a language that Shane couldn't understand. Shane looked over at him in bewilderment until the movement of someone coming down the rope caught his attention.

It was a middle-aged woman who looked like she had never climbed a rope before. She wasn't so much as climbing down as she was falling in increments. Shane reached up when she was in arms-length and helped her down gently. Mary was already entering the bus when Shane was again reaching up to assist Carrie who was next.

Shane took a step back as a tall muscular man came down with the confidence of an athlete. The man looked down when he was a few feet from the bus roof and let go of the rope. He landed and stood, facing Shane.

"Thanks, man." Matt told him as he swung his shotgun over and fired off the side of the bus. Another plaguer hit the ground dead. He looked over and saw Ethan dangling something in front of him and speaking indistinctly. "Ethan, what are you…?"

Shane put his hand on Matt's shoulder and shook his head, "Don't interrupt him. He said he's doing something important. Just cover him." Matt nodded at him. "Anyone else up there?"

"Yea, two more." Matt replied. "Logan and Jen."

They observed Jen grab the rope and begin to let her weight carry her backwards. Before she fully descended, she pulled herself back up. They could see why as whatever the giant creature was now had Logan by the throat. She was firing everything she had at it, but it just wasn't enough.

"Um," Matt stammered, "whatever he's doing, now would be the time to do it."

Ethan's low speech became louder and louder until it was normal conversation tone and again as it turned into a low yell. He increased his volume yet again and shouted his last two words at the top of his lungs, "...ADOLEBITQUE IMMORTUOS!"

The bag he held out in front began to emit a faint blue light. It intensified and darkened until a slight fizzle could be heard. As if under an open flame the bag ignited, and a blue fire danced from the bottom of the cloth material to the top. The fizzle turned into an audible *whoosh* as the bag disintegrated and the blue flame exploded forward and dissipated only several feet away.

The same blue light that enveloped the bag formed on and around each member of the undead horde. It snaked around their bodies and covered them completely, then swirled with the white mist that emanated from their eye sockets before crossing through the doorways to their skulls. Their reanimated bodies began to flicker with a blue haze, until finally they burst into flames all at once. The collection of departed eyes remained unfazed by the fire that devoured their already ravaged bodies.

The creature holding Logan let out a guttural roar as the mist he was spewing towards Jen ignited and swam like a shark back to its source. It threw itself into his open mouth and thrust him back, losing his grip on his prey and dropping him to the ground. The fire engulfed the monster, who could only stare down at Logan with the purest of hatreds as he was locked in place.

The surrounding plaguers burst simultaneously into individual clouds of blue flame and, like a spectacular fireworks display, fizzled into absolute nothingness. Jen ran to Logan and knelt at his side as they watched small collections of ash either fall to the ground or get whisked away with what now seemed to be a gentle, morning breeze.

They looked back at the uber zombie who seemed to be fighting the fire that was eating him alive. They clambered to their feet together and stepped back, unsure just what was happening or what would be next. Logan met his adversary's abysmal, onyx eyes and was frozen in place by the depths of disdain he felt beaming from them.

"Who are you?" Logan asked with a low, shaky voice.

The creature's skeleton like mouth widened into a humored grin. The blue hue darkened as the fire intensified from the flap of shredded skin above his missing lip and spread like a wave over his face and body. In the same fashion as his minions, the flame swept skyward and he disappeared. Unlike the zombies however, there were no ashes or dust. There was nothing. No trace of the creature whatsoever.

Logan looked at his wife for the first time, who was almost in a full cry. "You ok?" he asked her, putting his hand to her face.

"Am I ok?" She asked with a chuckle. "You just got fucking manhandled by Mumm Ra. Are *you* ok?"

Logan hugged her and kissed her forehead, "Nice name drop." The two laughed for a moment and finally found some much needed levity to break the tension of the past twenty minutes.

"You guys ok up there?" they could hear Matt shout from the side of the building.

They had completely forgotten about the rope and their group waiting below. Logan ushered Jen over and the two were down in a few minutes. They glanced around at the ash that rained down around them and covered the streets like dirty snow. There wasn't a reanimated corpse in sight.

"What was that?" Logan asked, astonished, as Matt helped him and Jen down the hatch.

"That was him." Luke said, nodding at an exhausted Ethan as he gently helped him to a seat.

"You just… Thanos-snapped all the zombies." Logan said, snapping his fingers.

"Plaguers." Luke corrected him, as he approached with his arms open.

Logan gave him the bro-est of bro-hugs and slapped his back, fighting away tears of joy. "What?" he asked, furrowing a brow.

"They're called plaguers, not zombies, technically." Luke reiterated as he pulled away. "Ethan can explain later."

"That was our one and only purification bomb," Ethan grunted from his seat. "Killed every dead thing in a half mile radius."

"What are you doing with a bomb?" Logan asked, quizzically.

"Like he said," Ethan responded with a motion towards Luke that seemed to zap him of any remaining energy. "I'll explain later." And with that, he passed out, resting his head on the window.

Logan let it hang in the air for the moment as he redirected his attention back on Luke, a smile spreading on his face. "Glad to see you're alright, man."

"You too, dickhead." Luke said.

"Logan, right?" Shane asked walking up from the driver's seat.

"Yea." Logan extended his hand to him. "Thanks for the assist…"

"Shane," he said after he caught himself staring longer than he should have been. He took Logan's hand and shook cautiously. "Do I know you from somewhere?"

Logan's face contorted slightly, and he shook his head as he brought his hand back to his side. "Not that I know of."

Shane nodded unsurely, "Just one of those faces I guess." He got back into his driver's seat and turned the key in the ignition, bringing the yellow behemoth back to life.

"Yea, I guess." Logan muttered to himself as he turned to join in the rest of the introductions. Normal pleasantries were exchanged between them as if they were all simply chaperoning a field trip for school.

Shortly after, there would be a respite from conversation as the bus fell silent, allowing each of them the opportunity to try and wrap their thoughts around recent events. The buses' windshield wipers swept from side to side, clearing the ash that had formerly been a horde of flesh-eating undead from Shane's view as they turned the corner and headed to St. Andrew Church.

Chapter 13

The majority of the drive to St. Andrew Church had been uneventful. The further they drove from the mechanic shop, the less ash could be seen littering the streets and buildings. Plaguers' footsteps disturbed fallen ash as several of them lightly jogged and frantically strode through, unaware they had just dodged certain death and were now kicking up the remains of their fellow undead.

Little by little, the asphalt on the highway became more visible as the survivors traveled closer to the invisible border of the spell that had saved their lives. The plaguers moved past them in disinterested strides and never gave a second glance.

Shane kept the bus slow and steady as he maneuvered through the increasing numbers of wandering corpses on the street and took the on ramp to I-95 South. Only a few deserted vehicles littered the highway and for the moment, not a single plaguer.

Ethan woke slowly and shifted in his seat. He rubbed his eyes and took a deep breath, feeling infinitely better. The spell he casted had worked. It gave them the time and space to make a daring escape, but had left him completely drained of energy. He glanced the bus and saw that everyone was either resting or interacting with one another.

Luke and Izzy sat across from Logan and Jen, catching each other up on their challenges and adventures that led them to the current location. The brothers told their stories to each other with a humorous intensity. The severity and danger of every event was stressed, but the words were spoken to each other with a mutual respect and sympathetic tone. The other listened intently when prompted, inserting light-hearted jokes at the speaker's expense and making the four of them crack a smile for the moment and sometimes, even a laugh or two.

Silver and pink-haired Betty was resting against the window, with a snoring Mary fast asleep on her shoulder. Drool hung from her open mouth and threatened to coat Betty's leather jacket.

Chad sat by himself with his feet on the chair. His head was down across his arms which in turn rested on his bent knees. His body language was sad and off-standish, but whether he wanted to be isolated or felt cast aside was anybody's guess.

Carrie chatted softly with Matt a few rows behind the rest. A slight twinkle in her eye as he made her laugh and feel warmth to which she wasn't normally accustomed. Her carefree conversation temporarily blocked out the carnage and negativity around them. Not a single thought of Rick and the abuse he unjustly doled out to her hindered her emotional reprieve.

Nelly slept on her side across from them. She looked the part to the others at least. Her eyes were kept weakly closed and she breathed steadily, but she was anything but asleep. Memories of her high school love flooded her thoughts as she feigned unconsciousness. Unable to cry, she lay there, feeling empty and just pretend that Tom was sitting with her for the time being.

"You're bleeding." Luke said as he pointed down to a small pool of blood by Jen's foot, interrupting her story. She rolled her pant leg up slightly and they could all see the red trail that run down from a gash on the side of her leg.

Jen winced in pain as she had just realized the severity of the wound that she had previously been ignoring. A jagged five inch tear in her flesh zigged and zagged like a drunk lightning bolt up her ankle.

"It's from when I got knocked down in the shop." Jen said as she gingerly touched the surrounding area to gauge its tenderness.

Concern flashed across Logan's face, and he realized for the first time that he didn't have either of their go-bags. He noticed a small black duffle under Luke and Izzy's seat. "Is there a med-kit in there?" he asked as he pointed to it.

"It's Ethan's, so there's mostly weapons in it, but I saw some stuff earlier." Luke said as he shuffled items around. He handed Logan an alcohol bottle, cotton balls, and some anti-bacterial.

Logan made quick work of cleaning the wound. "No gauze?"

"No, I don't...oh it's on the side." He remembered Ethan making him bandage his own arm earlier for some unknown reason. Luke unzipped the small freezer bag and removed a rather odd colored strip of gauze.

Logan looked at it sideways as he took it from his brother and delicately wrapped his wife's wound. A single piece of medical tape held it in place as she carefully slid her pant leg back down.

"Hopefully, we can get that stitched at the church." Logan said to her.

"Thanks, hon." she said and kissed him softly on the cheek.

"So, where'd you get the Starship CD?" Logan asked Luke, changing the subject.

"From Ethan's car." he replied amused. "Did I forget to mention the part where he forced me to listen to that at max volume for our entire trip?"

They all laughed a hearty and whole laugh. "Didn't take him for a fan." Logan said, looking over at Ethan, who was now slowly approaching them from the aisle.

"Ha, ha." He said with blatant sarcasm. "Nothing wrong with good classic rock."

"I agree with Ethan." Izzy inserted. "There is nothing wrong with good, classic rock."

"Thank you, Izzy," Ethan said with a nod as he took a seat in front of them.

"Well I didn't say Starship was *good classic rock*." She added with a chuckle.

Everyone but Ethan laughed again. "Whatever. Go ahead, gang up on the token black dude." He said, now smirking.

"Wouldn't know it by your taste in music." Logan added.

"Now you know damn well that my favorite band is the Beatles." Ethan defended himself.

"Now *that* is excellent music." Jen agreed.

It was good for them all to find a few minutes of levity amidst such devastation. Logan observed the number of plaguers slowly increasing along the interstate as he turned to stare out the window. Their laughter was dying down when he decided to speak again.

"Who are you Ethan?" Logan asked with a serious tone as he looked his "friend" in the eye. "Really?"

Ethan sighed heavily and drew in a deep breath, thinking over just how much information to offer up. "I work for a religious group called The Order of Four." He glanced around at his audience who shared unsure expressions but said nothing, which prompted him to continue. "They have several sects within their organization, each with various tasks. They observe people of interest, protect specific religious artifacts, and eliminate large scale threats. Simply put, the bulk of their responsibilities can be summed up into the prevention of the apocalypse."

"Well, they kinda suck at their job, then." Luke said, in no uncertain terms.

Ethan gave a weak nod of agreement before going on. "The Order spent centuries preparing for this, but it wasn't supposed to happen in our lifetime. My Order was attacked, and someone pulled the trigger early."

"How?" Logan asked with genuine concern.

"I don't know." Ethan said bluntly. "That's why we're heading to St. Andrew. The high priest of the North American base is housed there. He'll have more answers."

"Well, why were you watching over me?" Luke asked him.

"I'm a Sentinel," He told him simply. "All Sentinels are tasked with protecting a Legacy. Which you both are." He pointed between Luke and Logan.

Jen shifted anxiously in her seat as Luke shared a bewildered expression with Izzy. "That's what that creature on the roof called me." Logan said. "What is a Legacy?"

"A Legacy is a direct descendant of a prophet from the Bible." He stared hard at Logan, then at Luke and back again. The group fell silent, trying to make sense of the words he just spoke. "The thing is, we're not sure which prophet you two are descended from."

"Prophet?" Luke said in bewilderment. "Like Moses or Joshua?"

"Yes, exactly like Moses or Joshua." Ethan replied.

"If we're both Legacies," Logan shot out, "why was Luke only assigned a bodyguard?"

"You did have one assigned to you." Ethan said, as he looked over at Jen with an accusatory glance.

Logan's mouth opened wide in shock as he slowly turned his gaze to his wife. "You?" he stammered out, with both betrayal and gratefulness.

Jen raised an eyebrow and smacked her lips. "Not me, you ass." She said resisting the urge to smack him upside his head.

Ethan laughed so hard he started to cry. "I'm sorry," he coughed out between chuckles. "I had to do that. No, seriously though. You were assigned a married couple. Samuel and Samantha Gilbert."

"The Sams?!" He said with a hint of slight. "Of course. No wonder they were always trying to be my friend."

"I told you to be nice to them." Jen scolded him. "And this is why."

"Oh, you just knew that they would have been our secretly assigned guardians in the event of a zombie apocalypse?" Logan asked mockingly.

"Yea, jackass." she replied with a shrug, "I'm your wife, I know everything."

Logan diverted his attention to Ethan again. "Makes sense why I thought they were kind of weird."

"No," Ethan said with a slight shake of his head, "I don't mean to talk ill of the dead, but we all thought they were a little weird too."

"Hmm…" Logan said, followed by a momentary awkward silence.

"So, you're supposed to protect us?" Luke said, putting everyone back on track. "From the plaguers?"

"Yes and no," Ethan responded. "Like I said, my organization keeps tabs on all Legacies. Before the outbreak, we had eyes on over two hundred of them worldwide. Normally the Order keeps a distance as to not draw attention to them. Other times, they assign people like me to guard them from any threat, supernatural or other."

"Like the guy who broke into my house." Luke said with validation.

"Exactly. That was Mathias." Ethan's expression hardened a bit. "He was supposed to be working for my organization, but I don't know what happened. Someone must have gotten to him and made him turn sides."

"Well, who would want Legacies dead?" Jen asked.

Ethan chuckled. "There's a shorter list of people who *wouldn't* want them dead."

Luke shook his head fervently. "No, none of this makes sense. If people were trying to kill us our whole lives, we probably would have known about it." He was clearly annoyed at the notion of being watched his whole life without ever knowing about it. "And if we were some goddamn biblical all-stars, we wouldn't be pushing regular nine-to-five jobs."

Ethan held up a placating hand. This is why he didn't want to have this conversation until they got to the church. He had just told his friends of several years that he was an undercover bodyguard working for a religious order run like a military group and was tasked with protecting them at all costs because they could be essential to fixing a biblical cataclysm. Of course, they would be upset.

"Listen," Ethan tried to reel him back in. "I know, it sounds... nuts. But my superior at the church can explain more. We'll have somewhere to rest and collect ourselves."

Luke scoffed and sat back in his beat. Izzy rubbed his arm while staring at the floor, thinking over all the information they were just given.

Logan had one more question that was gnawing at him and frankly, he was surprised no one else asked it yet. "Who was he?" he said plainly.

Ethan looked at him with a softened expression somewhere between fear and hopelessness. "You mean who *IS* he? He's not dead."

They all shared the same incredulous expression. "He's not dead?" Logan repeated softly.

"Nope," Ethan said with defeat, "and he is the beginning of our end."

"I need more than that," Logan retorted, as he leaned forward, inches from Ethan's face. "That... uber-plaguer, why does he want to destroy the world?"

Ethan shook his head slightly, as if offended by the question. "He doesn't want to destroy our world. He wants to pave the way for those that follow after him." he said.

More awkward silence as Logan's stare bore into his friend's eyes. He wanted more answers but could tell by the exhaustion Ethan wore on his face that he was done providing them for the time being.

"I see the church." Shane yelled from the driver seat as the bus approached the quarter mile marker for the desired exit. "Ten o'clock."

"It's eleven-thirty." Chad shouted as he checked his watch.

Nelly and Izzy both gave Chad sideways glances while everyone else blatantly ignored what was either his lame attempt at a joke or a clear indication that he had no idea what was going on.

Betty shook her shoulder and woke the slumbering Mary, who smacked her lips together and rubbed her eyes before noticing she had drooled on the leather jacket she was resting on. "Sorry," she said with a sheepish smile as she looked from the puddle of saliva to Betty, and back again.

The streets below them were littered with the undead. Runners moved quickly through the crowds, pushing through the slower shuffling plaguers in a vain attempt to find food that could be hiding somewhere amidst their own. Bodies pressed and pounded on the doors and windows at almost every building within eyesight.

Any plaguer who would wander within twenty feet of the church fences would immediately turn and run off in another direction. Not one reanimated cadaver would cross through what appeared to be some sort of invisible barrier. This left the entire perimeter of the church untouched and clear of any zombified invaders.

"Do you see that?" Shane asked, as he slowed the ride slightly.

"Yea," Logan answered him, pushing his face closer to the glass. "It's like a barrier or something."

"They don't see the church." Ethan interjected. "The Order has a spell up to hide it from the plaguers. Anything undead doesn't even know it's there."

"It's hidden?" Carrie reiterated with surprise. "With real magic?"

Ethan nodded firmly at the many faces who seemed to be aiming confused looks at him. "Once we pass that threshold, we'll be safe."

"Well shit," was all Luke could manage to say as Shane crept the bus down the off-ramp and stepped on the accelerator slightly.

It didn't take long for the loud rumble of the bus's diesel engine to draw attention from the otherwise unfocused and aimlessly wandering masses. Only a few turned their flesh-starved gaze to the yellow behemoth at first. But as news of approaching food spread with their shrieks and shrills of hunger, a platoon of plaguers converged on the vehicle in what seemed like a matter of seconds.

"Hold on." Shane shouted as he pushed the accelerator to the floor. All twenty-five thousand pounds punched forward with the might of two hundred and twenty horses and decimated any adversary brazen enough to step in front of the yellow beast.

The sound of bodies popping and bones crushing into powder filled the cabin of the bus as they mowed down wave after wave of the undead indiscriminately. They took a wide left turn at high speed and the bus lifted off the driver side wheels, threatening to tumble onto its right side. The tires screeched as they gripped the concrete with all their rigid elasticity in an attempt to keep the bus from going over.

Shane corrected the turn and the bus slammed back down, bouncing off another plaguer who managed to run under the undercarriage just before being flattened by its weight. The putrid odor of the rotting corpses may have flooded the group's noses, but the relief they felt when the church came into view was more overwhelming.

"Yes, there it is." Nelly shouted with elation, just as the engine of the bus began to putter. What was a roar just moments prior flittered and fizzled into nothing more than the sound of a balloon with a slow leak.

"Nonononono." Shane said as he smacked the wheel with frustration and kicked at the gas pedal to no avail. The bus would've simply coasted safely into the parking lot of the church, carrying the entire group through the magic barrier that would protect them once across.

The problem was that, even though they were mowing down countless cadavers, the speed of the bus was being drastically slowed by them. With a few final bounces over a couple self-sacrificing plaguers and three more puts of the engine, the bus came to its final rest.

They all stared in collective disbelief as their salvation sit all but thirty feet from them. It might as well have been miles away with the number of infected that fill the space between them and the church. The flesh-lorn mouths of the undead hung open in a mocking anticipation as they impatiently waited for the group to step into the street.

"You have got to be shitting me." Logan said.

"Ok." Ethan said pulling a large blade from God knows where. "If one or two of us can get across we can bring help back."

"Alright." Logan answered unsnapping his sheathe, "Luke, you coming?"

"Hell no." Ethan, Jen, and Izzy all said in unison. They glared at Logan with incredulity, not even acknowledging the grin that formed on his face.

"Jinx," he said humorously as he glanced between their unyieldingly sober expressions.

"You and Luke have to wait here." Ethan said stone-faced. "I'll go. Matt you're with me."

Matt swallowed hard and his muscles tensed noticeably as he gripped the empty shotgun in his hands. It was nothing more than a heavy club right now and he was in no rush to go back out into such madness ill-prepared. "I don't have any ammo." He said blankly.

Logan unsheathed his machete and extended it to him, handle out. Matt breathed heavily and strapped the shotgun around his back, taking Logan's blade with apprehension. They locked eyes for a second and Logan could see that his friend was terrified.

The bus rocked violently from the growing numbers of bodies pushing their, pardon the expression, dead weight, against it. Their shrills reached almost deafening decibels that shook Matt to his core and chilled him to the bone. Images off the past day raced through his mind like a horror focused highlight reel.

Carrie squeezed Matt's arm gently and stole his gaze from Logan. Her dark mascara intensified the hurt he could see in her eyes. She didn't want him to go out there anymore than he didn't want to go himself.

"…Matt." Logan snapped his fingers in front of his face, bringing him back from wherever he was mind walking to.

"Sorry," Matt said, shaking his head. He stared at the machete in his shaky grasp and held it back out to Logan as he took a retreating step. "I…I can't. Not now."

"We don't have time for this." Ethan barked. "We're thirty feet from safety. Pull yourself together."

When Logan realized Matt was in no shape to go outside and crush skulls, he took his machete back and sheathed it. If anything, he sympathized with his friend. He patted Matt on the arm and nodded solemnly at him.

"We might need a distract…" Shane started, until he was interrupted by the sound of shattering glass. The bus continued to rock violently as the front door was forced inward from the outside. Metal bent and splintered as the joints of the mechanical bi-fold door gave way. A single plaguer was pushed through with the door and fell up the steps with all the weight of his ghoulish cohorts pushing behind him.

"The hatch?!" Izzy shouted almost in question as she moved over to it.

"No." Ethan said holding up a hand to stop her progression. "They'll just knock us over and we'll be torn apart." He glanced around and cursed himself for their current predicament.

They watched as the vile thing that fell in shrieked in frustration at his food being just out of reach. Its legs were pinned down by a mass of the plaguers who were literally stuck in the doorway. The wet flopping sound of twisting flesh and organs danced with the audible snapping of bone and bending metal as the oversized mass was desperately attempting to force itself through a tiny opening. Like trying to fit a square peg into a round hole.

"Shane," Ethan barked at him, catching a strange look in his eye and snapping him out of a daze as he backed away from the driver wheel. "Be ready to fight."

They stood, closely huddled in the aisle of the bus, anxious of the certain death that crept centimeter by centimeter across the threshold and into their haven. Their hearts raced and pounded against their chests as the plaguer sounds seemed to almost take on a more excited cry. As if they knew that their food was trapped with no avenue of escape and that soon, very soon, they would finally eat.

Suddenly, the crying and wailing halted. No more shrieks of hunger or lamenting moans. They just simply stopped. Luke shook his finger in his ear thinking some unknown obstruction might be temporarily impeding his hearing. He looked at his friends who shared equal looks of confusion and clearly couldn't hear the plaguers anymore either.

The only sound punching through the awkward silence was the metallic rattling of the giant yellow bus as it slowly settled back into a still position. Ethan stretched his neck and peered out a window only to spot that the plaguers were frozen in place.

"That's not good, right?" Betty asked no one in particular. "Does that mean that *thing* is back?"

"No." Ethan responded with a slight shake of his head. "They're stuck, not entranced. It's magic." He sounded hopeful as he walked up to the mass breaking through the door and knelt, face-to-face with the grotesque man sprawling on the floor with an outstretched arm.

The thing's eyes did not follow Ethan's movements, nor did it reach or turn in any direction. It was seemingly frozen in place.

"Best not to dawdle," a voice from outside bellowed over a bullhorn. "They only stay frozen a few minutes and we don't have another one readily available."

Ethan pushed a window down leaned his head out. "Gideon, that you?" He couldn't see anyone but assumed that there was an outlook positioned in a high window of the church.

"Ethan? Well I'll be damned. Get your ass in here." The slight British accent expressed genuine excitement and concern for his friend. "We'll thin some of the herd for you," he said just as the racking of several rifles could be heard.

The sudden gunfire still caught the group off-guard as shots rang out and the plaguers surrounding the rear of the bus began dropping in troves. They all winced and went low out of instinct with the first few shots before adjusting to the ear-splitting booms.

"Friends of yours?" Luke asked Ethan as he stood.

"Be thankful," he said as they moved to the rear of the bus, "They're trained soldiers." Ethan pushed the door open and casually began moving the plaguers that blocked their path. Many were forced to their final resting spots on the asphalt by the shooters inside the church, but those that the bullets could not find a home in were easily brushed aside or struck down.

Ethan had made a clearing about ten feet into the crowd when he realized he was the only one progressing. He turned and saw his groups bewildered faces staring at him from the beyond the open door. Not a one had followed him.

"You guys coming?" he asked impatiently.

Logan nodded unsurely and Luke held back the urge to gag. They were amazed with the level of ease their longtime friend had just simply pushing dead and rotted flesh away with his bare hands. It looked as if he was doing nothing more than moving old storage bins in his garage to get to the holiday decorations that were always placed furthest in the back.

"After you." Luke said to Logan extending his hand outward like an usher.

"Gee thanks," he replied sarcastically as he hopped down while holding Jen's hand.

They navigated through the serpentine of fleshy mannequins for what seemed like an eternity, Ethan leading the way and Shane at the rear. As they slowly closed the gap to the church, the supporting fire began to slow up. The shooters were now facing the survivors directly and a wild or misfired bullet could just as likely strike an unintended target.

"Hurry up now," the voice from the second story window pressed. "I'm beginning to see some of them twitch."

"Shit." Ethan said as he hacked and pushed furiously at anything in his path.

Not wanting to be swinging a weapon wildly in such close proximity to Ethan, Logan opted to leave his machete sheathed and instead began ramming and kicking aside any unfriendly face he could see.

A familiar moan and throaty growl could be heard in the crowd to their left. Chad and Izzy glanced in the general direction but saw no movement. The sound only urged the members up front to heave and thrust with even more haste.

Another wet shriek to the right. Then, more cries just ahead. Finally, ravenous shrills to their rear. Shane spun and saw the frozen face of a middle aged plaguer only a foot away. It howled that god-awful scream of undying hunger. Its eyes raced around in its head like a caged animal, trying to break its body free from its frozen state. It was clearly not only frustrated that it was unable to reach out at its food, but it was completely enraged.

Shane cautiously stepped back and, before turning completely back around, could see the plaguer's right index finger slowly begin to wiggle. "How much further?" he shouted up front, barely managing to refrain from sounding in a full panic.

Ethan cut down one more undead barrier and kicked it to the side as Logan body pressed a smaller man away to the left. In front of them was a clear path to the church entrance.

"Got it!" Ethan declared as he stepped through and into the clear street before picking up the pace into a slight jog.

"Thank God." Chad said as he was pushing Mary forward from her back.

"Young man," Mary said, slightly turning her head but not slowing her stride, "I can't go any faster, so would you please stop pushing me?"

"Well…" Chad responded just as he saw one of the undead mannequins break free and spring forward with incredible speed at Mary's exposed side. As it reached its fat, sore-ridden arm out at her, Chad bladed his body against Mary's back, pushing her slightly ahead and allowing the monster to grab at him instead.

Chad cried out as the plaguer's nails swiped across his back and gained hold of his shirt. He waited for the searing pain of the thing's teeth sinking into his flesh but, after a moment, he realized the creature must not have all of its mobility back yet. He shook and flailed in attempt to loosen its grip, but its undead fingers clasped down like a clamp.

Mary was now pulling on Chad's hand but every time she yanked, the plaguer's grip on his back would tear even more skin. Shane stepped forward and raised a machete over his head in a sacrificial stance.

Chad's eyes grew wide as he watched the blade reach upward, blocking out part of the sun. Chad shook his head adamantly in the negative out of pure primal fear. "No, no, no…dude." He stammered, just as Shane brought the machete down with all of his strength.

Chad winced and closed his eyes as he felt a tug at his back and heard the wet chopping noise of a blade seeking purchase in flesh.

"Let's go, damn it." Shane said as he pulled the shaken Chad ahead of him. Chad opened his eyes to see the plaguer who had just grabbed him now rested on the ground, sporting a cleaved forehead.

"Oh," Chad said to himself as he quickly regained his composure and continued pushing forward.

Ethan managed to break through the threshold and enter the safety of the "magic bubble." He turned and urged the rest forward.

Logan was now falling slightly back to help Jen, who although she was fighting it tooth and nail, was clearly feeling impeded by her leg injury. The rest of the group was now sprinting past them across the open street.

All at once, the mass of undead punched forward at full speed, as if they were already midstride before being frozen in place. The sound of hundreds of fast approaching footsteps could be heard from behind, though no one stopped to look back.

One by one and milliseconds apart, they crossed like runners crossing the finish line. Luke turned to see Shane enter just as Logan and Jen were about to enter. A single plaguer who had clearly been an athlete in life if his blue basketball uniform was any indication, had gained ground and reached an outstretched arm at them as they ran ahead. It thrashed and swiped as it ran, and at the last possible second, gained a hold on Logan's arm that was around Jen.

As if in slow motion, they crossed the threshold of the church and spun together. Instead of releasing its grip, it lurched its canines forward and bit down. It was rewarded with a decent size chunk of shoulder meat for its effort. It pulled back, ripping its prize free and chewed methodically.

There was a loud scream as Logan tumbled on the ground and attempted to regain his footing. "No," he said softly as he could see the athlete plaguer sitting atop Jen, slowly enjoying his first bite. "No," he said again. "NOOOOOO!" he screamed and was on his feet heading at the undead son of bitch who had just bitten his wife.

The entire group were still putting the scene together when all they saw was Logan charge into the plaguer with all of his weight, lifting it from the ground with almost superhuman strength and slamming it into a tree. He pinned it against the trunk with his forearm pressed into the thing's throat.

The plaguer gnarled and bit the air in front of his face. Logan growled and screamed in blinding anger right back at it as tears flowed from his eyes. He slowly bawled his right hand into a trembling fist and squeezed it so tight, he almost dug his fingers in. Any man staring directly at this rage infused face would know that they had little time left on this Earth. This plaguer was lucky, that if for nothing else, it didn't know fear.

Logan brought his fist into the side of the plaguer's head with such force, it shut the damn thing up for a moment. The neck bent to the side with the impact and there was an audible crunch of cheekbone being splintered. Logan brought his fist up again, hitting the thing's face even harder and caving the entire side of its face inward.

It attempted to let out a growl but came out as nothing more than a murmur. Broken teeth spew out of its mouth in a sea of red as Logan hit it again. And again. And again. His fist moved with the speed and power of a locomotive as he crushed the plaguer's head and face into a red pulpy mess of unidentifiable flesh and bone bits.

The thing had been long dead as Logan continued to unleash his rage. He had lost all feeling in his hand and still, he lashed out at it. He screamed again, spittle flying from his mouth as he took what was left of the plaguer's head and leaned back with it in one hand, then drove it forward with all his might and anger, splattering it against the trunk of the tree.

Brain matter and skull fragments flew outward freely, entangled with rotted flesh and chunky coagulated blood. It fell against the tree, an athlete's body with a mangled mess of bloodied meat where a head should be.

Logan's chest heaved as he stared down at the once living man he had just completely destroyed with his bare hands. He exhaled, his red face slowly regaining color. "Jen," he said, sobbing, as he turned back to see Ethan, Betty, and Izzy already working to aid his wife.

"Fucccckkkk that hurts!" Jen yelled as Ethan pressed against the fresh bite wound on her shoulder. Betty and Izzy each got under an arm and helped her to her feet.

"Babe, I'm so sorry," Logan said, running up to her and cradling her face in his bloodied hands.

Jen chuckled weakly. "Why? You didn't bite me."

Logan let out a cry-filled laugh. He knew what it meant now that she was bit, and he had no idea what to do about it.

"We have to get her inside." Ethan said, nodding to an entourage of men who appeared at the doorway of the church.

"Whoa, whoa, whoa," a voice among the unknown males said, halting any movement. "Ethan, you know we can't let an afflicted in here."

Ethan knew the voice but didn't see the man it belonged to. "Grandmaster, please? I know we can at least…"

"Absolutely not." The voice said sternly as a man who appeared to be in his late forties stepped forward and down a few steps. He had a long, brown goatee, with salt and pepper hair brushed through at the sides. His features and tone reflected a suave and debonair persona, which made the tactical BDUs and para-military ensemble look like he was just playing the part of a soldier.

No one was sure what to do or what to say. There was a group of armed men who knew magic denying them access to a safe haven in a church. This battle was all Ethan's.

"You can either go back out there," the bearded man said, pointing at the group of plaguers who seemed to already forget about them and were back to wandering the streets aimlessly. "Or we can kill her and let you in."

"Fuck you," Logan said, stepping in front of Jen and pointing his red finger over at the plaguer he killed. "Touch her and that'll look like mercy compared to what I do to you, fuckboy."

The man smirked and took another step down. "Logan, you are such a hothead."

"Can it, dickhead," Logan interrupted him. "You don't know me."

The man recoiled, slightly insulted. "I know everything about you and Luke. You are the two most interesting Legacies we keep an eye on." He waved up at three of the men with rifles to join him.

Logan shared an uneasy glance with Ethan and his brother. "If we're Legacies," Luke whispered to them, "they won't kill us, right?"

"Well no. They won't." Ethan replied. "but they'll kill everyone else here."

Luke shook his head. "Dude, your employers are dicks." Logan nodded in agreement.

The three men with rifles stopped one step ahead of their boss and aimed their weapons downward at the group.

"Hey, Ethan," an older gentleman said. The voice matched the one that had been laying down cover fire from the window. He appeared older than one would've pictured, with premature wrinkles and receding hairline. His dirty blonde hair was already turning gray and showed that whatever life he had been living, wasn't very kind to him.

"Hey, Gideon," Ethan replied. "How's this going down?"

"Well you know the rules, my friend," he said with sincerity. "You and the Legacies come inside. The others are welcome, but only if the afflicted is dealt with."

"Her name is Jen," Ethan said, defiantly. "And you know Logan won't go if she doesn't."

Gideon shrugged at his boss. "Sir…"

The man in charge shook his head. "We can't."

Logan reached his arms back at Jen's sides, shielding her slightly more as Gideon aimed down his sights. He noticed blood trickling down Jen's right leg that was slightly to the side of her husband. A strip of yellow hued bandage dangled from her torn and disheveled pant leg. At first it wasn't worth a second glance until his finger hovered over the trigger of his semi-automatic rifle. A slight glint from the cloth caught his eye.

"Ethan?" he asked, lowering his gun again.

"What?" he replied with agitation through gritted teeth. The entire group was now inching closer together.

"How many times was she bitten?" Gideon asked. "I see a wound on her leg."

Ethan glanced over at Jen's leg with the question, unsure what he would see.

"That's not a bite," Logan snapped. "And I wrapped and disinfected it before she got bit."

Gideon smiled and let out a sigh of relief as Ethan finally let his shoulders relax ever so slightly. "Was it from my bag?" he asked Logan with enthusiasm. "The bandage? Was it from my bag?"

Logan glanced back and forth between what he thought to be a maddening Gideon and a confusing Ethan. "Yea?" he replied with uncertainty.

"You just saved her life, you beautiful son of a bitch." He declared as he bent down to inspect Jen's wound. She relented and assisted in pulling her pant leg up slightly to reveal a blood-soaked cloth wrapped around the wound she suffered back at the auto shop. Ethan delicately unwrapped it and walked it almost ceremoniously over to Gideon. All with a smile of amazement plastered on his face.

"Feel free to explain at any moment." Jen said, grimacing in pain.

Gideon took the cloth from Ethan and in turn showed it to his overseer, who smiled curtly but was genuinely relieved that he would not have to kill any of them.

"I am Silas," the grandmaster stated. "And that little fabric is actually a sliver from the shroud of Turin. The cloth that Jesus of Nazareth was buried in."

Luke's eyebrows shot up in surprise and he was eager to ask questions. When he looked around at his friends who seemed to care less at the moment, he refrained.

"And what does that mean for us exactly?" Matt spoke up.

"The shroud acts a shield from the affliction," Ethan explained. "If you're wearing it on your skin, the plaguers' bites will have no effect." He gave Logan a nervous smile. "You just so happen to wrap her wound in a piece of the cloth I had in my bag... that I was supposed to give to you... like hours ago."

"Well, I guess it's a good thing I didn't get bit." Logan barked.

"That's why you had me wrap a piece of that shit around my arm earlier." Luke suddenly realized.

Logan shot his brother a look of resentment, then extended it back to Ethan. "Playing favorites?" he asked him. Ethan shrugged.

"Come," Silas said, diverting the tension. "We can mend those wounds in the infirmary and get you all some rest." The tone of the interaction immediately lightened as the men behind him lowered their guns and turned to enter the church. "I can answer your questions in the hall over dinner."

Ethan went to step forward when Luke grabbed his arm, holding him back. "Dude, can we trust these guys?" he asked plainly as Logan and Jen leaned in to join.

"We can," he replied with a heavy sigh. "They're just…careful."

"At the expense of others?" Luke asked, indignantly.

"No offense Ethan, but we trusted you for the past, how many years? Not knowing you were some occultist secret agent." Logan said.

"Although that's not entirely accurate, your point is fair." Ethan agreed with no hard feelings.

Logan swallowed hard and his expression turned grim. "Is she really gonna be ok?" he asked Ethan, holding back more tears and refusing to look at his wife who was now staring intensely at the side of his face.

Ethan put a hand on Logan's shoulders, and his other on Jen's. "Yea. For real. And they'll fix her ankle too. You'll see." He smiled as he gently squeezed their shoulders, then turned away.

Logan finally met his wife's eyes and forced an unconvincing smile. She gave him a gentle kiss before he adjusted his arm around her and continued.

The man named Silas ushered his men inside and led the group of survivors into the grand nave of the historic church. Sunlight shone brightly through the stained-glass windows and highlighted a statue of Jesus Christ on display of the building transept. The design was no coincidence and was clearly meant to invoke strong feelings of guilt and thanks for all the Lord and savior sacrificed in our name.

Good marketing, Logan thought to himself when he laid eyes upon the display.

"Good marketing." Jen verbalized to her husband, who was still helping her along. He smirked but said nothing.

Once Shane and Matt were the last two inside, the entry doors closed inward slowly. The loud and irritating squeaking of the ancient hinges were ceased by the thundering boom of the wood colliding with the frame. Matt turned to verify that no one had been behind them to force the doors shut and decided to study them from top to bottom.

"Ok," he said to Shane. "That's not freaky."

"Not in the least," Matt replied, giving the doors his own once over.

Silas stood between the front two aisles as one of his men moved the religiously ordained pulpit from a rather Victorian style rug and placed it on the side. Another man then moved the carpet and a large square outline could be seen carved into the wood flooring. A few choice foreign words spoken by Silas and the section of floor began to slide over, revealing a hidden entryway where the square had been. It was pitch black and ominous looking to say the least. No one moved.

"Not it." Luke said, putting his finger to the tip of his nose. Without even so much as a word of clarification, Izzy followed suit. Then, Betty, Mary, Logan, Jen, Nelly, Ethan, Carrie, Shane, and even Chad. They looked at Matt, the only one too slow to realize that he was clearly going down first.

"Aw, come on," he protested. "It's dark as shit down there."

Silas rolled his eyes and stepped forward. "You are a bunch of children. It's just our bunker below us." He stepped down into the darkness and onto an unseen stairwell that carried him further in until he was no longer in sight.

Everyone slowly pulled their fingers away from their noses and awaited Matt's entry. "You're still going first." Logan said.

Matt relented and after the last of Silas' men was through, he cautiously followed. He was halfway down when he realized Ethan was first behind him. "Why were you afraid to go down? Haven't you been here before?"

"Yea of course," he responded certainly, "but I like to see you squirm." He smiled in jest.

"Fuck you, too." Matt said continuing forward.

The stairs widened as they ascended and led into a ten-foot wide stone tunnel. The darkness that greeted them was short lived as about twenty-five feet from the landing were two medieval era sconces facing each other on opposite walls. Intrigued, Logan stopped for a moment to inspect the ancient looking light sources.

"Purely aesthetic." Chad said, speaking over his shoulder.

"Come again?" Logan asked him, slightly perplexed.

"They're meant to look like old torches, but it's really modern electricity." Chad elaborated.

"Oh." He examined the "dancing flame" closer on what he could now tell was a plastic candle. "Neat." He said plainly before moving onward.

"Yea." Chad agreed walking in-step with him. "Purely aesthetic." He repeated.

Logan eyed Chad for a moment as they continued down the hall. The arrogant and entitled young man was absent and all Logan could see right now was nothing more than a scared child. What he had seen had visibly shaken him, and it was evident that he realized an attitude adjustment was crucial to his survival moving forward.

"That was good, what you did to save Mary." Logan told him softly.

Chad's eyes shot up from the floor to meet his. The previous somber expression melted away and was replaced with pride and gratitude, as if he had been trying tirelessly for his father's approval. He wanted to thank Logan, but no words flowed from his mouth in response. Instead, he caught himself just staring at him.

Logan could see on Chad's face what he wanted to say. The two exchanged firm nods that clearly conveyed the unspoken message. Chad smiled at himself and fell behind Logan slightly, letting the appreciation of his good deed cover him like a warm blanket and finally allowed him to feel a modicum of inner peace.

The hallway ended into a large rectangular room comprised of thick metal walls. Powerful lights lined the tall ceiling and walls and illuminated the room to an almost radioactive effect. Inaudible conversations echoed throughout and bounced off the sound-proof walls back to their sources as a combination of civilians and soldiers hustled and bustled in every direction.

Two men in military gear appeared to discuss the inner workings of their weapons as one removed an attachment from his rifle and presented it to the other. What could be either a lab tech or a doctor in a white coat handed off a small container to a similarly dressed woman and appeared to stress careful instructions with what to do with the item, before turning and hurrying off in another direction. A small gathering of civilians sat Indian style in a far corner, surrounding a woman who rested on a crate and motioned animatedly with her hands as she read to them from a book.

"Arcane studies." Gideon said to Luke as he pointed at the group in the corner. "Around here, the arcane is just as much a necessity to survival as weapons training or hunting."

"Awesome," Luke said in astonishment as he stepped forward with Izzy to take the sights in. His brows furrowed slightly as he tried to focus on a strange symbol he could see carved into a section of the metal. Moving his eyes to the distant wall he could see a slightly different carving. Left and right his head swiveled, spotting several similar yet varying symbols spread throughout the high walls of the compound. "What are those shapes?" he asked Gideon.

"They are Enochian warding," Gideon replied, "Angelic symbols...."

"Given by Enochian Angels to John Dee in the sixteenth century to assist in his studies of divine magic and science." Luke never looked away from the symbols as he finished Gideon's explanation for him.

"Impressive." Gideon replied. "I heard you were a bit of a knowledge-seeker. There is more to it than what's in the history books, which is true about most things you'll learn from us."

"I look forward to it." Luke said, finally breaking his gaze and nodding at Gideon, who smiled at him before shuffling off.

"Your brain is sexy." Izzy said as she got on her tip toes and kissed the side of his head.

"If you think my brains sexy you should see my-"

Izzy punched him in the arm and cut him off. "Shame your mouth always ruins it." She walked away.

Luke rubbed the sore spot on his arm and stuck his tongue out at the back of his fiancé's head before following her.

The man who introduced himself as Silas led the group to a large folding table like you would see in a cafeteria. He waved his arm at the bench to usher them all into a seat. When a female nurse attempted to speed passed him, he gently stopped her by extending his hand out to her.

"Can you have Natasha make sure the rooms are prepped for our new guests?" He spoke as if he was asking a favor, but it was clear that it was more of a politely given order. She nodded curtly and turned off in the opposite direction she had originally been heading.

A wheelchair had been brought over by a large man in blue scrubs who assisted in helping Jen into it. "Anyone else need medical attention?" He asked in a booming but sensitive tone.

Chad raised his hand and winced as he rubbed his lower back and was reminded of his almost fatal incident with the statuesque plaguer outside. He shook his head when another tech offered him his own wheelchair. When no one else volunteered service, the man turned the wheelchair and walked off, Chad and Logan on each side.

"Ethan," Silas said, placing his hands together, "Could you show everyone to their bunks where they can clean and rest before dinner?"

"Of course, Grandmaster." Ethan replied.

"Everyone meet back here at eighteen hundred hours, and I'll show you to the private dining quarters where we may discuss the events that are currently unfolding." He tilted his head to the side and motioned it, "Ethan, a word please?"

Ethan stood and approached Silas as he stepped away from the table. "Where are Logan's Sentinels?" he asked.

"According to Logan, they're dead. They never received the warning." Ethan told him straightly.

"Damn. We'll have to assign somebody else." Silas said, with slight concern. "There aren't many left."

"Which brings me to another point, sir. I saw Matthias at Luke's residence. He tried to kill him." The lack of surprise on his superior's face was troubling. "You knew?"

"We did." he replied, with a hint of shame. "We couldn't risk telling any of the other Sentinels. We knew someone was stealing information and he took off before we could confront him. We could only hope one of you got to him first, which we're extremely glad was the case."

"A heads-up would've helped." Ethan said, frankly. "Why steal information?"

"He was sending it to someone. I assume the person responsible for breaking the first seal."

"What about security measures?" Ethan asked. "Matthias had high level clearance."

Silas was shaking his head. "We updated security codes and even placed fake information in the updated reports, like empty bases, fake names, the works. The real reports are encrypted, so no one should know about this base."

"Matthias said something that didn't make sense to me before I killed him." Ethan said with uncertainty. "He told me 'Mr. Stone is not able.'"

"Mr. Stone? Not able to do what?" Silas asked in confusion.

Ethan shrugged. "No fucking clue...um, sir. Do you know who Mr. Stone is?"

"No, I don't." he said plainly. "But I know who might. I have work to do. See to your friends and don't be late, eighteen hundred."

"Yes sir." Ethan said heading back to the table.

"And Ethan," Silas said, turning Ethan around with his words.

"Yes, Grandmaster?"

"Excellent work, my son. Your father would be proud." Silas said with the utmost sincerity and conviction.

"Thank you, Silas." Ethan said with pride welling in him as Silas walked off. "I'll show you guys to your bunks." The group gave a collective exhausted grumble as they slowly stood from their seats.

The sleeping quarters were small square rooms no bigger than twelve-by-twelve feet. Two thin dressers, four drawers high sat next to each other against the wall with the door. Opposite them were two sets of bunk beds tucked in the corners along the adjacent wall. One would immediately think the rooms to be reminiscent of boarding schools or psychiatric hospitals. Not particularly homey or welcoming, but just enough to keep someone from sleeping on the floor.

Most of the rooms were completely identical and not a one had any trace of originality to it. The only exception was the five or so rooms that had two twin beds opposed to the double bunks. These rooms were given to Logan and Jen, and Luke and Izzy first on the account of them being Legacies. They were also assigned a guard outside their room who was never to leave his post.

Betty, Mary, and Nelly bunked together in one room while Shane, Matt, and Chad bunked in another. Carrie, who had become more attached to Matt, insisted she stay with him and even asked that they share one of the small beds. Of course, Matt was thrilled by the notion.

"Just for sleeping." she had told him when she saw the excitement on his face. He deflated slightly but agreed without hesitation. She smiled at him and took a towel and robe from the dresser. "Well, maybe other stuff." She said coyly, walking past him and out the door, where another woman escorted her to the showers.

Matt turned his now shit-eating grin to Shane who was prepping his bunk and getting comfortable.

"Smile like that too long," Shane said, kicking off a shoe, "and your face will get stuck." All three of them laughed as Matt fell face-first into his pillow and went out like a light.

Chapter 14

"What did he say it was?" Logan asked Jen as he slowly pulled his sweat covered t-shirt over his head. "Because it looked like unicorn shit."

Jen was sitting on her new cot and let out an exhausted chuckle as she examined the new scar on her leg where her deep gash had been only twenty minutes prior. "Grounded amethyst."

The tall man who had escorted them to the infirmary introduced himself as Kareem, the resident shaman. A large, wooden bucket with iridescent purple-hued sand rested on a wheeled cart next to an uncomfortable looking gurney. Foreign tools that more closely resembled arts and crafts than medical instruments lay spread out across a tray for easy access.

Within minutes, Kareem had Jen face down on the gurney and Chad sitting shirtless with his chest against the back of a chair. Kareem began rubbing the crushed crystal on their respective wounds while chanting, in a foreign language, what they could only believe to be an incantation of some sort. Within seconds, Logan could see the flesh on his wife's back being sown back together by an unseen force. Chad tensed as the tear in his lower back did the same.

The whole process had only taken about five minutes. Kareem took a wet towel and wiped the sand and dry, crusted blood from Jen's shoulder and ankle wound to reveal nothing more than a slightly discolored spot of skin. He then did the same for Chad's back.

Logan shook the recent memory and stepped over to the cot where Jen sat. He brushed her tank top to the side and ran his thumb over the scar in the shape of a plaguer bite mark on her shoulder. "You get any more battle scars we're gonna have to get you a red bandana and call you Rambo."

"Now I almost have as many scars as I do tattoos." She stuck her chest out as if she was gloating.

"Let's just stick to tattoos." Logan replied. "I was scared for a while there." He gently kissed the pinkish flesh mark.

"Yea, me too." she said, staring at the floor. One quiet second too many went by and Logan was about to speak again when Jen stood up suddenly, slightly startling him. "I need a shower… like bad."

"Of course." Logan grabbed a robe and a towel from the dresser and handed it to her.

"Aren't you gonna need one?" She asked raising an eyebrow.

Logan almost pulled the drawers of the dresser out by yanking them so hard in his search for more bath wear. The drawers were all empty. He slammed the last one shut and shook his head in disbelief.

Jen sighed and turned out the door. "Oh well. Guess I'll go at it alone." She was halfway down the hall when she heard Logan.

"The hell you are," she heard him yell from behind, "I'll go commando."

Jen turned and saw Logan marching after her, completely naked. His hands were cupped over his delicate area as he strode right passed her on a mission towards the shower. Jen chuckled as she watched his pale ass shake by.

He opened the first facility door on his right and entered. As Jen approached, she could hear Logan let out a slight utterance of surprise.

"Logan, Goddamn it!" an unknown female voice exclaimed. "Get out!"

The door swung open and a red-faced Logan came out, hastily pulling it shut behind him. Jen was bent over laughing.

"Shut up." he said, embarrassed as he knocked on the second door across the hall.

"No, no, please. Just go in." Jen mocked.

With no answer Logan turned the knob and entered. Jen followed, still laughing hysterically.

"So, what happens now?" Izzy asked her fiancé as she dug the side of her head into her favorite spot on Luke's chest. She mindlessly caressed his ribcage with her index finger. This was his favorite thing that she did. That slight touch from her was enough to both invigorate him, as well as bring him to his knees.

"Well, I thought it was pretty obvious." Luke said plainly. She looked at him, slightly confused by his quick response. "I become a full-time bible wizard and you stay at home with our literal miracle babies."

She slapped his chest lightly. "I'm serious, Luke."

"Oh," he replied with a smile when he saw that she wasn't amused. "I don't know. I mean, they seem to think it's a big deal that Logan and I are here. And I don't know what that means for any of us."

"So, we just…live here?" She asked with disappointment.

Luke shrugged and kissed her head. "I literally have just as much information as you do." he whispered to her. She laughed. "We'll just see what that Silas guy has to say and play it by ear."

"Ok." she relented, knowing he had no real answers for her. "Hey Luke? Tell me a useless fact." Whenever there would be silence between them or conversation would just about run out, Izzy would prompt his encyclopedia brain to spew out some piece of nonsensical knowledge. It would usually consist of something so trivial that it could be seen in a VH1 pop-up video bubble. Sometimes, it would be an entertaining historical truth, or the origin of an international myth. No matter what subject matter would come out of his mouth, it would be conversational gold and keep them talking well throughout the night.

"Oh, most golf balls have anywhere between three-hundred and five-hundred dimples on it." He said excitedly. "Though the average number is three-hundred and thirty-six."

Izzy snickered. "Where do you get this shit? Do you have photographic memory?"

"No," he said in defense. "I just don't forget things I see or hear."

Izzy laughed even harder. "That's photographic memory, dork."

"Oh," he said in pseudo surprise. "Then yes. Yes, I do have... what were we talking about?"

She wrapped her arm around him. "I hate you." She said jokingly.

"I know." He kissed her head again. "And no, I don't have photographic memory. I learned about the golf balls from playing Tiger Woods Golf on Xbox."

"Of course, you did." A few minutes went by and the comfortable silence surrounded them like a warm blanket. They were both nodding off and about to enjoy the descent into REM sleep when a knock came at the door.

Without waiting for a response, the door cracked open slightly. "Hey guys, it's time." Ethan announced into the room without showing his face, then shut the door again.

"Sweet." Luke said, almost completely pushing Izzy off the bed in his haste to get up. "Food, food, food." He shouted lyrically, dancing as he got dressed.

"I'm engaged to a giant child," Izzy said rubbing her eyes and stretching.

"Then that makes you a pedophile." Luke retorted. "Let's go, perv." He was already out the door as a groggy Izzy shuffled behind.

Ethan led the group down a series of hallways that twisted and bent like a maze. There were no signs to direct anyone who may have made a wrong turn, and it seemed very easy to get lost in this cavern-like "bunker."

He pushed open an ancient looking wooden and iron door that led into a grandiose dining hall. In the center was a thirty-foot table with benches on each side, and chairs more closely resembling thrones at each end. There were twelve rather large platters of food setup, six on each side, and one at the one head of the table.

Conversation flowed freely as everyone gorged on fresh beef stew and Italian bread. There were highpoints of laughter and levity, and low points of sorrow and heartache. They talked about where they had been in life, and the unknown to come. Friends they couldn't reach and family they would have to search for soon.

Matt spoke about how he hasn't been to the gym in three days. Carrie talked about freedom from Rick's abuse. Nelly reminisced of better times with Tom. Mary stressed about her daughter down in Florida. Betty reenacted a free-spirited cross-country ride on her Harley before almost throwing her back out. Chad relayed a night of copious alcohol consumption and how he was humbled by the barbaric behavior of his frat brothers. Luke and Logan shared drunken bar fights and raucous misadventures they had together. Jen reveled in the idea of not having to payback her medical school loans. Izzy brought up her favorite bands and how much she would miss music. Shane was noticeably quiet during the exchanges.

"Strong, silent type?" Nelly asked Shane as they all settled down from a good laugh.

"Nothing to really say." He smiled nervously.

"Do you have family to go look for?" Mary asked him.

Shane grimaced and gave Mary a saddened look. "I lost them before all this madness." He said with glum.

An awkward silence filled the air for a moment. Logan took a drink of water and wet his lips before speaking again. "Do you have military experience? The way you fight and jumped into battle with those things was impressive."

"I was." he said plainly. "Did two tours in Iraq. I was fighting foreign terrorism while you were fighting domestically."

Logan furrowed a brow in confusion and darted at Jen who was equally confused by his statement. "How do you mean?"

Now it was Shane's turn to look confused. "You were a cop, right?"

"…I was. But how did you know that?" Logan's confusion was quickly turning into wariness.

"I'm pretty sure you mentioned it." Shane said nonchalantly. "And you can tell. The way you handle a fire arm and your training is obvious."

"I didn't know you're a cop." Nelly said in surprise.

"So, I didn't mention it?" Logan asked to form a census among the party. He received several heads shaking in the negative. "I mean, everyone here who knows me knows I was, but I don't walk around advertising it."

"Well why not?" Shane asked with a hint of hostility. "Shouldn't you be proud of your service to your city?"

"I am," Logan said, matching his sharp tone, "but it also makes me a target if I walk around gloating."

"Why would it make you a target?" Shane retorted in an accusatory tone.

"Because I've made mistakes. Which is why I walked away a couple years ago." He stood and leaned over the table. "You ever make any mistakes before?"

"Yea." he said never looking away, "once." The tension mounted to an unprecedented thickness as they stared each other down. No one at the table knew what to do. Even Ethan found himself dumbfounded by the interaction unfolding before him.

The wheels in Logan's head slowly began to turn. He began to recognize the man who attempted to bore a hole in his head with his laser like gaze. From where? From when? The face. Shane's face was familiar, but he just couldn't place how. An eternity seemed to pass as the two men embodied statues with stone cold gazes that refused to falter.

Logan slowly sat down in his chair as the door at the far end of the room opened and Silas casually strode in, Gideon close behind.

"Ladies and Gentlemen," the grandmaster said in a boardroom meeting tone, "I trust the stew was more than satisfying? We have to use as many of the perishables as we can first." He paused just long enough to sense the unease in the room. "Everything... ok here?"

"Peachy." Logan said with an unconvincing smile as he finally broke eye contact with Shane. "So, why were we all brought here?"

"Right to the point." Silas said, taking his seat at the head of the table next to Ethan, "Let's get to it then. You were informed that you and your brother are Legacies, yes?"

"So we hear," Luke said dismissively, "but what does that mean you want from us?"

"What we here at the Order as well as all of mankind *need*, not want, from you is for you to survive." He replied cryptically. He took a long drink from his mug before continuing, "When we learned of Legacies and what they meant to the survival of mankind, we made it one of our top priorities to protect any one we come across. To train them to become soldiers. Hunt the many things that go bump in the night."

Jen gave their host a sideways glance. "These two aren't monster hunting, killing machines."

"No," Silas agreed, "they certainly are not. Years after we started using Legacies as hunters, our many enemies began searching them out and eliminating them. The hunters became the hunted. When descendants of prophets entered dangerously low numbers, we tried a new tactic. We would simply monitor them from a distance and forbid any direct interference unless there was a clear and present danger to them."

"I'm guessing this whole zombie thing falls under that category." Chad chided in.

"Absolutely." Gideon added with a chuckle.

"So, what does that mean for us?" Luke asked.

"You'll all be given food and shelter and we will be more than willing to give combat and other training to anyone who would like to stay." Silas was tapping the tips of his fingers together as he addressed the room. "Anyone who wants to leave once they are rested may do so. We can provide some provisions, a weapon, and relatively safer travel routes."

The room fell silent as some of them began weighing their options. "That's great," Luke said, "but I meant what does that mean for my brother and me?"

"Oh," Silas said glancing down at the table and nervously adjusting his plate, "As I said, you two are important. As of right now, we only have a lock on thirty-two Legacies worldwide. And the fact that the person who wants you the most happens to be in this town, means that I cannot allow you to leave."

"We're prisoners?" Logan challenged.

"Not in the least." Silas answered indignantly. "You are VIPs with an entire military base at your disposal."

Luke and Logan were becoming agitated. Jen and Izzy looked relieved at the information. "Who wants them?" Shane asked, once again staring intensely at Logan. "And why?"

"A man who calls himself Mr. Stone. We believe he is responsible for the plague." Silas informed them. "He wants you two," he said pointing a finger at each of the brothers, "because you can stop him."

Luke rolled his eyes. "This is stupid," he shouted as he stood from the table. "This sounds like a bad plot to a movie. We're not some zombie killing ex-marines or half vampire badasses in some sci-fi novel for God's sake." He was heading towards the exit.

"Luke," Logan shouted at him, "get back here."

"No, fuck him." He responded.

"LUKE." Logan boomed in an authoritative tone. His brother stopped and breathed heavily. "We need to hear this."

"Come on, babe." Izzy said softly as she extended her hand out to him. He relented and made his way back to the table, sitting with his bride to be.

"So, this Mr. Stone wants to spread zombies, why? What's his endgame?" Jen asked, entering the conversation.

"Well, they're plaguers technically." Silas corrected her.

She rolled her eyes. "Whatever."

"He doesn't simply want to spread plaguers." Silas continued. "This is only stage one of the apocalypse. There are pockets left almost seemingly unaffected. Of course, they have no contact with the outside world though."

Mary beamed at the prospect of her daughter being safe. Others had mild looks of relief until Jen once again asked the obvious question that was overlooked.

"What do you mean stage *one* of the apocalypse?" she asked with dread.

Silas sighed. Being so forth coming with information was exhausting him. "As of right now, there is only about thirty percent of the global population affected by this plague. As it spreads, towns and safehouses will build fortified communities. These communities will require resources. Resources other communities have. This will give way to phase two of the apocalypse. War. After which there will be two more phases before we humans are officially eradicated from the planet."

"You make it sound like the Book of Revelations." Luke said mockingly.

More silence as Silas only glared at the many eyes watching him, waiting for a response. Any moment now, the harsh realization would set in.

"Mr. Stone… is trying to unleash… the four…" Logan started to say unsurely but couldn't even believe his own sentence.

"Horsemen of the Apocalypse, yes." Silas was nodding slowly. "Which means that rather attractive fellow that attacked you, is Pestilence. And he is only here to ensure that his siblings are freed."

"No fucking way." Luke said surreally. No one else could say a word. The implications that a literal horseman of the apocalypse was wandering the boroughs of Philadelphia in search of two brothers were absolutely mind-blowing.

"Back in the fourteenth century, I was with a small band of …" Silas started.

Disbelieved headshakes and looks of confusion ran rampant across the dining table. "Wait, wait, wait," Matt said almost comically. "I think we all just heard you wrong. You said back in…?"

"The fourteenth century." Silas repeated.

"Of course, you did." Logan said, to no one in particular.

"Is he fucking serious?" Matt asked Logan.

"Dude," he replied passively, "at this point, I don't doubt it."

Silas was tapping an impatient finger on the table. "I know this is a lot, so I'll give you all a moment to pick your jaws from the floor. Then I would like to continue, so we don't waste any more time."

Gideon chuckled as the rest of the room fell silent so his superior could continue. "In the fourteenth century, I was with a small band of mercenaries in Constantinople when a strange epidemic struck Europe. We came across a man who had some knowledge of what was happening and knew that it was by the hands of a man that this now called Bubonic Plague was being spread. After a few years of following our new captain, we found the one known as the First Plague, Pestilence, who carried with him every disease and affliction known and unknown to man."

"You fought a Horseman of the apocalypse and lived." Luke whispered to his brother, whose eyes widened almost to the point of jumping from the sockets.

"Dude…" Logan said not wanting to think about it, "shut up."

"We managed to seal him away," Silas was going on, "but never found the person responsible for releasing him in the first place."

"Do you know of any way to kill him?" Izzy asked.

Silas again nodded but this time he was grinning almost maniacally. "Only a Legacy can kill a Horseman."

"Oh, who the hell comes up with these rules?" Luke asked slamming a hand on the table.

"There are rules that govern all of creation, both natural and supernatural." Silas snapped. "The horsemen are not creatures directly from the bible, though they are most notably cited in it. Much like all the workings of the great book."

"It's more like vaguely written instructions?" Nelly inquired.

"Exactly." Silas said, putting his finger to his nose. "The bible speaks of seven seals of the apocalypse. There is, in fact, only four. One for each of the horsemen. The other three were simply written as a way for mankind to relish in divine intervention and a fruitful afterlife."

"Good marketing." Logan said, smirking at Jen and recalling her earlier statement as they entered the church. "How does a Legacy kill a Horseman?"

"There are certain relics housed in the Order compounds. There is one in this very bunker kept under lock and key. This is why the Order of Four was founded by my brothers and me, and this is where *you* come in." He paused for dramatic affect as he glanced slowly around the table. "We were caught off guard and now we fight against the clock before this Mr. Stone can break the second seal and we have two horsemen to worry about." Silas stood.

"Everyone get some rest tonight," Gideon addressed them from behind the grandmaster, "and after breakfast, we will see where everyone stands and begin."

With that, the two casually walked out the same rear door they had entered, leaving a speechless room behind them.

"I can't go back out there." Carrie said, breaking the quiet tension.

"Yea, me neither." Betty agreed.

Chad shook his head. "I don't think any of us want to."

"Well I need to find my daughter." Mary said, tearfully. "Will anyone help me find her?" She darted around the room hoping to find a pair of sympathetic eyes staring her back. No one would make eye contact. "Please?" She sounded desperate.

"Let us figure this out first." Logan finally answered her. "Then we can go see about your daughter, ok?"

Mary nodded shakily and calmed for the moment, lost in her own thoughts.

"Nelly?" Izzy asked her friend. "Are you staying?"

"I don't know," she replied. "Without Tom…I don't know."

"We all have a lot to think about," Ethan interjected, "Like Silas said, everyone get some rest. We can figure it out in the morning."

"There's still so many questions, Ethan." Luke said with a look of concern.

"I know, man," he replied putting a hand on his shoulder as he walked by. "We'll get there." He exited the room, prompting everyone to slowly stand and make their way to their beds.

"Hey," Shane said, grabbing Logan's attention. "We cool? I didn't mean to set you off. We're on the same side here." His words sounded sincere and he reached a hand out for Logan to shake.

"Yea we're good." Logan said, reaching out to reciprocate the gesture. He watched Shane's back for a second as he walked away from him. "Something is off about him." He whispered to Jen.

"Maybe he's just hot tempered, like you." She said dismissively.

"Yea, maybe." They headed back to their room in silence.

The mental and emotional fallout of the monster truth bombs that were just dropped on them all would make it extremely difficult for any of them to get a good night's rest. Sounds of power tools and metal clanging seeped through the concrete and steel walls in the early morning as staff and military personnel were already hard at work, making attempts at sleeping in for anybody in the group futile.

"Morning sunshine." Luke said to Logan who was coming out of his room as he took a mouthful of steaming coffee from a mug. "They'll bring you coffee if you want one." He pointed the mug towards the guard who was posted at Logan's door.

"Yea I could use some." Logan said. When he noticed the guard about to speed off, he stopped him. "No, I can get it. Thank you." The man loosened the grip on his rifle and let it hang back in front of him. Logan thought that his guard looked like a kid. No more than twenty-four years old and he was told to lay down his life for his. The soldier began following Logan as he walked with his brother, which caused him to stop in his tracks. This made him extremely uncomfortable being assigned his own personal security detail.

"Do me a favor…" Logan paused to get the young soldier's name.

"Murdocksir." He replied.

"It's Logan, you don't have to call me sir."

"No, that's my name. Murdocksir." He replied, all too seriously.

"Oh." He looked over at Luke who was chuckling. "Sorry, right. Can you just stay here and keep an eye on Jen? I'll be back before you know it."

"Yes sir." Murdocksir replied with military discipline.

"It's… never mind. Thank you." He joined Luke who was already halfway down the hall, still laughing.

"Now you just look like an ass." He said when Logan approached.

"Story of my life." He said taking Luke's coffee and chugging the rest of the contents before handing the mug back.

"What are you thinking?" Luke asked him, looking in the now empty cup but letting it slide.

"I don't know." Logan replied. "But I do know that there is no chance in Hell that you and I are meant to join some rag-tag group of Prophet descendants and take down a goddamn horseman of the apocalypse."

"I agree with you there," Luke said holding up his index finger, "but these guys study and use actual magic. So, in the very least, I am intrigued."

"Now you wanna stay?" He asked raising an eyebrow.

"I thought about it a lot last night," Luke said excitedly. "If, IF, it is the end times being triggered out there and we have a chance to stop it, why wouldn't we? Dude, we would be saving the world. Our names put in history books when humanity resets." He was clearly way more excited about their current situation than he was the previous night.

"Wait, you want to save the world so you can be famous?" Logan asked him, incredulously.

"Well, no, but it wouldn't hurt," he replied, almost hurtfully.

Logan sighed as they finally found a small kitchen room that looked to be staff lounge. He took Luke's mug and refilled it with fresh coffee from the pot.

"You're the bookworm. Any of these stories ringing true? In the bible or other?" Logan asked.

"There's bits and pieces of truth hidden in everything we've seen. And these guys have a lot to teach us." Luke put the mug on the counter. "Dude, there's angelic warding on this bunker for Christ's sake." He thought about that last sentence for a second, "No pun intended. But just think of those implications."

"That means our world just got a whole lot bigger." Logan told him as he picked up the mug and repeated chugging its contents. "Ok, let's tell Silas we're in."

"Fuck yea dude." Luke said as he gave his brother a celebratory slap on the arm. Logan walked off as Luke went for the mug and realized it was once again void of coffee. He grabbed the pot only to find that too, was empty. "Prick." He yelled out the door to his brother's back.

Chapter 15

The decision to stay was unanimous. Mary was the only one with any real apprehension, as she was holding on to the thought of heading south to Florida and reuniting with her daughter. The rest of the group assured her that they would help, but they first needed to be better prepared for such a trek. She relented and agreed to stay with them.

The three days that followed were primarily comprised of training. As the base's Master of Arms, that task lied with Gideon, who divided the group into three smaller ones and gave an extensive tour of the base's armory and its contents. This included handling many aspects of the weapons inside, stoppage drills such as double feeds or stove pipes with the semi-automatic armaments, and close quarter combat techniques with small edged weapons. Gideon would give these lessons once a day until Silas deemed them all fit for combat.

Luke, Logan, and Jen needed little to no instruction while Shane simply recalled his military training and would complete the drills before Gideon was even done speaking.

Matt and Chad took the firearms training the most seriously. They treated the guns and ammo as if they were fragile children, careful not to accidentally shake it for fear of breaking it, while Carrie seemed to excel at the firing range. The raw power of the gun in her hands was as thrilling to her as it was liberating. As each round punched into the paper target, she began to feel reborn. Her soul stitched back together, piece by piece, round by round. In the course of one afternoon, her accuracy and proficiency increased tenfold and it was obvious that she had found her niche.

Betty had somehow located a Smith & Wesson forty-four magnum and proceeded to blow the head of her target off. When she saw that an astonished Silas had wandered over to check-in, she winked and blew him a kiss. He blushed for a moment before leaning over to her while she continued to aim down range.

"Go ahead," he said in his best Dirty Harry voice, "make my day." He smiled coyly before continuing off down the line.

Betty bit her lip as she watched him walk away.

As their introductory to firearms training came to an end, Gideon and a fellow veteran of the Order named Paxton introduced them to close quarters combat and defensive tactics. This included some basics of Krav Maga and knife fighting techniques.

Again, Shane excelled in these categories and was given a carbon steel Kbar upon his request. Both Logan and Luke were also more proficient with bladed weapons and bare-knuckle brawling than the rest of the group that accompanied them.

At the end of the second days' drills, Gideon called the brothers aside. In his hands, he held a rather rustic looking knife with a worn and chipped wooden handle. Pulling the blade from its leather sheathe revealed a dull and blackened edge. The knife was clearly not of the combat variety but rather resembled more of a family heirloom.

"This," Gideon said, turning it over in his palms and allowing its face to catch the light, "is a Moirai Blade."

"Moirai?" Luke asked with interest as he wiped sweat from his brow. "Like the three fates?"

Gideon smiled. "Impressive. Yes, the three Goddesses of fate whose name also means 'parts.' Now, there are only five of these daggers in existence. One was sent to each of the Orders four main bases in different parts of the world. The fifth is held by the Grandmaster, Eli." He sheathed the weapon and handed it to Logan.

"Why is it so dingy?" He asked as he gently accepted it.

"Well there's only five of them because the tips were melted down from the Lance of Longinus." Gideon explained, rather simply.

"I'm sorry," Luke said, with minor disbelief. "The spear that stabbed Jesus?"

"Yea, I was just gonna say that." Logan said, trying join the conversation.

"Why?" Luke asked with heightened interest.

"Religious items have a direct effect on other-worldly beings. Specifically, ancient ones that predate the formal establishment of Christianity."

"So, the knife is part of the spear that pierced His body, and the cloth is *His* shroud?" Luke was understanding now.

Gideon nodded, affirmingly. "That knife won't kill him, but it sure as Hell will hurt him enough to slow him down."

"You only have the one?" Logan doublechecked with Gideon as he extended it to his brother.

Luke shook his head. "Nope, you're better with them. Keep it."

Logan shrugged and put the new weapon on his belt. Gideon placed a hand on each of their shoulders and sighed heavily before walking out.

The Legacy brothers' guards, Murdocksir for Logan and a particularly cartoonish looking young man nicknamed "Duck" assigned to Luke, were always at their sides. They ate every meal with them and their significant other, took the same bathroom breaks, and attended all training exercises with them. They began to wonder if the two guards ever slept or if they were even human at all. It creeped them out at first, especially when Jen could hear Murdocksir outside their door while trying to get intimate with her husband.

"Just pretend it's your parents and we're being sneaky." Logan had told her. Yea that went over about as well as trying to baptize a cat. He had to open the door and spend fifteen minutes ordering the guard away since he had no understanding of privacy, only duty. The mood had passed, and Jen was already falling asleep when Logan jumped back into the bunk.

Back in the armory against the far wall were large metal drawers attached to shelves that stacked to the ceiling. Each one had a different label reflecting its contents. Some were simple, albeit seemingly out-of-place, ingredients such as sage, or pheasant feathers, while others were downright confusing. "Plaguer Bile" with a biohazard simple next to it caught Logan's attention, while Matt stared dumbfounded at a label with "Lamian Blood." He pointed at the drawer with his mouth agape and looked at Ethan as if requesting elaboration.

"Yea," he chuckled in response. "I didn't know snails had teeth either." He picked up a crate and walked off, leaving Matt with no more answers than new questions.

Matt turned back to look at the drawer Ethan mistakenly thought he had been pointing at. The label read "Snail Teeth." Matt shook his head and without ever saying a word about it, and never looked at that wall again.

For all intents and purposes, things were going well. Luke spent every free minute reading any of the thousands of books centered on the arcane with Izzy. Gideon had agreed to show him just how to focus and use some of that knowledge once he read through a particularly thick set of encyclopedias focused on the history of The Order and the magic they use.

Luke was almost a man possessed. He was so enthralled by the readings that by the time Izzy was starting a page, he was already finishing it. He was slightly confused when he came across a specific word that was mentioned several times in many passages but never in detail.

"What's an Agur?" He had asked Gideon in passing.

"An Agur," he said stroking his gray mustache, "is an arcane Legacy, named after the first arcane prophet who gathered much of the magic The Order uses. They can use and adapt spells in ways specifically meant for their bloodlines. Most casters and users aren't descendants of prophets, so its magic they simply can't use. You are a far, far ways off from such teachings. But perhaps, in time."

Nelly causally strode past a doorway and stopped when she heard someone getting thrown to the floor and crying out in pain. She stuck her head in and saw Chad sprawled out on the gym mat, breathing heavily and covered in sweat. An instructor stood over him, no more casual then he had just pushed an elevator button and was awaiting its arrival to his floor.

"You know, you can take a break." She said to the now slumped over Chad who was trying desperately to stand up.

"I keep telling him that," the instructor Paxton said, since Chad clearly couldn't. "But he wants to keep going. Said he owes it to you guys."

Nelly bent beside him as his breathing finally began to slow. "You don't owe us anything, Chad."

He shook his head, moving the wet hair from his eyes and sending beads of sweat to the mat. "I should've… gone in the basement… not Tom." He refused to look up at her.

Nelly was taken aback by the comment. She's known Chad just as long as she knew her love Tom, and there was never really any depth to the former. He was always a selfish, entitled mamma's boy who never seemed to understand how the real world worked. But the pain and regret she saw in Chad's eyes were real. She was surprised when he reached out and saved Mary earlier, and believed it to be nothing more than a fluke. Now, she wasn't so sure. She leaned in and kissed the top of his sweaty head as she began to cry slightly.

"That was Tom's choice." she said with certainty as a single tear ran down her face. He finally turned to face her, his eyes also giving way to the waterworks.

"And this is mine." he said, brokenly.

She smiled grimly and wiped tears from her cheeks as she backed out the door.

"Again." Chad said as he stood, shaking the sweat from his hair.

It was early afternoon on the fourth day when everything went to Hell…

Chapter 16
Mr. Stone

"Matthias' information was incorrect." Mr. Stone said as he primed the tip of a Cohiba Behike cigar and puffed a few times, allowing the tip to burn slowly. "He was compromised."

"Then, where are we going?" the large man sitting across from him asked. His neck was craned to the side as he was simply too tall for the stretch limousine in which they sat.

"St. Andrews Church." his employer informed him. "My other source was very forthcoming with good information. There's even a surprise in it for you."

"I don't like surprises." The bald man said simply in a deep voice that shook the vehicle as it drove.

"Relax." he told Gol as he held up two fingers. "There's not just a Legacy in it for you. There's two."

Gol grinned a comic book villain grin that ran from ear to ear. His deep seeded hate for Legacies transcended generations, ever since he was bested by a prophet thousands of years ago. Their lineage was an insult to his being and any opportunity he would get to eliminate one, he would gladly accept.

The plaguers that lined the streets around the church ignored the convoy of vehicles that approached, and even cleared a path for the limo that was at the tail end. The Humvees pulled around to all sides of the building, surrounding it in a clear show of hostility and dominance. Doors flung open and countless mercenaries poured out into the streets and through the large gates of the church.

A trigger-happy twenty-something year old, who was high on testosterone and caffeine, couldn't wait for the excitement to start. He stared at a plaguer who had the nerve to be within striking distance of him and decided to lash out. He marched right up to the undead man who was paying him no mind and struck it in the side of its head with the butt of his rifle. He let out a celebratory exclamation as it fell and put a three-round burst of lead into it, killing it immediately.

"Hell yea." he yelled to a fellow brother in arms. The like-minded drone validated his behavior by giving an equally "brotastic" appraisal.

"Neanderthals." Mr. Stone said to himself as he exited his vehicle.

"Movement." the squad leader Suthers shouted as he spotted a shadow blur past an open window on the second floor. Like disciplined and battle-hardened military soldiers, the platoon split into three smaller groups, each forming a tactical column and falling behind nearby trees for cover. Once in formation, they awaited further instruction.

"Three up top" one of them shouted as rifle fire sprayed out from each of the three openings above. Two men positioned at a rear column fell as rounds peppered their legs and chest.

"Return fire goddamn it!" Suthers screamed to his squad. The three men who spearheaded the columns poked out and sent controlled machine gun fire upwards. When all three had spent an entire thirty round magazine blindly firing into the dark apertures, they shifted back behind the tree to reload, while the second member of the column then leaned out, ready to continue shooting down target if ordered to.

Dust began to settle as the echo of gunshots faded into the distance. All eyes were locked on the windows, checking for signs of enemy movement, but hoping that the blind fire had taken them all out.

"Charlie," Suthers shouted with authority, "Cover Alpha's advance." Immediately as the lead soldier of the Alpha column stepped out from the tree the gunshots erupted again, striking him four times throughout his body and dropping him dead. The teams fell back and tightened up behind their cover.

Suthers knew that as long as the opposition had the high ground and without an exact count of how many shooters were up there, that he was outgunned and pinned down. He needed a team to flank around back and find a way in. He was weighing his options when he caught a glance at his employer Mr. Stone, who was standing there with his arms crossed and tapping his foot as if he was impatiently waiting for a table at a restaurant.

"Is he fucking serious?" Suthers said to himself as he began to make several hand gestures to his teams. Before he could finish signaling, he watched as the mountain of a man called Gol stepped out of the vehicle and made his way to him.

The mere sight of Gol was as impressive as it was downright intimidating. At six feet seven inches and two hundred-eighty pounds of solid muscle, his appearance could make Olympic bodybuilders weep with shame. He strode forward in his black BDUs and tactical vest, combing his long black beard with one hand and balling a particularly heavy looking fist with the other.

"This is taking too long." Gol said in a gravelly voice as he moved passed Suthers, shrugging him to the side. He stood at the base of the wall and stared up at the center window as lead kicked dirt and cement up around him. Crouching down and pushing off his legs, he leapt thirty feet in the air and grabbed the bottom of the window base. He pulled himself up effortlessly and was face-to-face with the three men who were firing down at them. Before they could even comprehend his presence, he grabbed the first man's rifle and struck him in the side of his head with it, instantly snapping his neck.

The second Order soldier fired wide as he attempted to fall back down the hall and gain space. Gol closed the gap and reached out, taking his rifle from him and placing his large hands on the man's head. He squeezed as if trying to get juice from an orange. And much like the orange, the man's head was crushed. The loud crunching of skull mixed with the wet squishing sound of bloody flesh and brain. The body was still twitching when Gol threw it to the ground and ran for the third soldier.

Three rounds caught purchase into Gol's midsection but did nothing to slow his advance. When the soldier's weapon clicked empty, he thought it the best time to try a new tactic: run. He tossed the gun to the side and took off down the hall. The corridor snaked out onto a small bridge over the nave that opened into the choir area and connected the two sides of the church. He spotted a confessional, and with no time to make it down to the safety of the bunker, he went inside and closed the door. He expelled the fearful air from his lungs and attempted to gain control of his breathing, as to not give away his position.

For long moments he heard nothing and began to believe that the brute had either retreated back to his group outside or fallen over dead from his wounds while in pursuit. The creaking of the confessional door ripped through the uncomfortable silence like a thunder storm when he decided to slowly push the door open and sneak a look. Peaking left and right revealed no immediate danger and he allowed his tense body a moment to relax ever so slightly as he cautiously began to plan his escape towards the trap door.

His right foot came down ever so softly on the carpeted marble, which confused him as to why it sounded like such a monstrous thump. Realizing it was the footstep of another, he turned with panic only to see his pursuer within arm's reach.

"That hurt." Gol said furiously through gritted teeth as he reached a giant hand out and wrapped it around the man's neck, lifting him off the ground with relative ease.

"Please." the soldier pleaded, eyes wide with fear as his feet dangled uselessly.

Gol smiled sadistically.

Suthers was peeved to say the least. He had waited years for his training and skills to be utilized. He had always known that the U.S. military was wrong for dishonorably discharging him. Although he was grateful for the position he was awarded with Stone's special ops unit, the S.O.C., he couldn't help but feel frustrated when he was constantly benched by his commander's lackeys.

He checked his watch impatiently and looked over at a group of his subordinates who were standing by. They all shrugged. "Sir?" he asked Mr. Stone.

Without a word, Mr. Stone held up his index finger at him, telling him to wait. A few seconds later there was a blood curdling scream from the second floor of the church. The soldiers aimed their rifles up, unsure what to expect.

A large unidentifiable object flew out from the window and rained down towards the rear team of soldiers. They scattered as the object smashed into the ground with a wet thud, squirting blood in every direction.

"What the fuck?" a soldier named Curtis exclaimed, as they realized it was a person. Well, a half of person. The upper torso to be exact.

"Where's the rest of him?" another soldier asked, just as a pair of severed legs launched forward from the same window, striking the soldier in the back and sending him sprawling close to fifteen feet.

"What the fuck?" Curtis yelled again, as Mr. Stone began a slow methodical clap, clearly pleased by the barbaric display.

With a deafening boom the front doors of the church exploded outward, revealing a blood-soaked Gol. "The door is open now." He bellowed plainly.

With utter disbelief, Suthers looked from Gol, to the torso at his feet, then finally to his employer. Then again, Gol, torso, employer.

"Today, Suthers." Mr. Stone ordered.

"Yes, sir." he replied as he moved his teams into position and entered the holy building.

Mr. Stone stepped into the center of the large nave and drew a deep breath in, closing his eyes. He raised both hands and spoke words that none of the soldiers could understand, save for Gol. If they had to guess, it sounded Latin. His hands formed a triangle as he spoke and, with the last phrase said out loud, he opened his eyes, which now had a blue filmy look to them.

"Silas," he said in a voice that boomed in the emptiness of the church. "Silas, I know you're here. And we're coming in."

Chapter 17

"What do you mean aggressive?" Silas asked Taylor, who had just rushed down with a message of an approaching convoy.

"They look organized," Taylor spit out with labored breaths, "Private military group, maybe?"

"Our infamous Mr. Stone," Silas concluded. "How many?"

"Five Humvees and a stretch limo. Ivan, Birch and Mac are still up there. They closed the door after me."

"How did he find us?" Silas asked himself. "Get all available soldiers here now. We have to prep for evacuation."

"Yes, sir." Taylor said, before running off.

If Silas had any reservations as to the intentions of the visitors, the muffled sounds of gunfire above was more than enough for him to form a conclusion.

"What's going on?" Ethan asked as he spotted Taylor rushing by.

"We might have unwanted guests." He told him with what sounded like minor frustration in his voice.

"Silas," he heard a detached voice say as it filled the room. "Silas, I know you're here. And we're coming in."

"Mr. Stone, I presume?" Silas asked with a sneer.

"Pleasure." the voice responded. "I believe you have something down there that belongs to me."

"There is nothing of importance down here." Silas replied, doing his best to sound as if he had no idea what his new adversary was talking about.

"Come now. If there was nothing important here, there wouldn't be a large bunker hiding under this church, would there?"

Ethan shrugged. "He's got a point."

"I'll tell you what," Mr. Stone continued, "Give me the relic, and you can keep the Legacies. They're of no consequence to me really. A dime a dozen."

"You and I both know that is a lie, sir." Silas said with a smirk. "I think I may have an idea why these two are of particular interest to you. You will have neither them, nor the relic."

There was a brief pause as Silas' defiant tone almost provoked Mr. Stone to an ungentlemanly shout. He swallowed hard and recollected himself. "Fine. Have it your way. You all die. And thank you for confirming that you have my relic."

The haze that filled the room with the conversation dissipated as an uncomfortable silence took over.

"He sounds awfully sure of himself." Ethan said with concern.

"His men shouldn't be able to get through here as long…"

The grandmaster's words were cut short as the base shook violently with what easily could have been mistaken as an earthquake. The two men were rocked and almost fell over as there was a second colossal tremor. Then another, and another. The symbols that were etched into the walls of the bunker began to luminate. A dull yellow light gave way to a pink hue. The markings darkened again until they shone a crimson red.

"What is that?" Ethan said with concern.

"No!" Silas' irritation was now replaced with fear. "They're removing the warding."

"Isn't there still six inches of reinforced steel stopping them from getting in here?"

Silas scoffed as he went to a console where several technicians sat, confused by what was transpiring. "If they have the arcane knowledge to get passed this warding, the steel walls might as well be tinfoil." He pressed a sequence of switches and sounded an alarm before going over the loudspeaker. "If you can hear this, all non-combative personnel are to evacuate immediately," he said sternly into the comms. "Soldiers to the main entrance, security details with Legacies, other personnel to evacuation point."

In typical sci-fi fashion, red lights that lined the compound began flashing in the universal sign for "danger," accompanied by an audible cringe-inducing, repetitive beep. The blood-red warding blackened as the scratches it was comprised of began to splinter outward. The once unyielding metal screamed as an unseen force twisted and bent the now malleable substance.

Gideon ran into the large room with several armed guards and instructed them to be at the ready. "Grandmaster, where are the Legacies?"

"I'll send Ethan to find them," Silas replied hastily. "Do not go with the others," He said before leaning in and whispering into Ethan's ear. As he did so, he slipped a small item into Ethan's inside jacket pocket. The sleight of hand was so minimal, Ethan didn't notice, but Gideon's eyes followed the transaction.

"No, Silas, you need to come with us," Ethan begged, as he pulled away and digested the information that was just passed onto him. "We need you to…"

"Ethan," Silas interrupted shortly. "You've always been a leader. I'm trusting the Legacies to you." Gideon furrowed his brow, lost in the half conversation he was hearing.

"I…I can't." Ethan stammered.

"You must," Silas demanded. "If this order survives or things have gone differently, I would have loved to have made you a Grandmaster, Ethan."

Ethan swallowed hard. The Order was his family just as much as Luke and Logan had proved to be. "What do I do when I get there?"

A deafening explosion erupted overhead, shaking the foundation they stood on and sending Gideon to the floor. He clambered to his feet quickly as to not miss the next piece of instruction Silas was giving to Ethan. All he could hear over the detonations was his final sentence.

"...that's where you'll find Eli." Silas shouted aloud as he pushed Ethan along. "Now go, my son."

Ethan staggered away as another explosion rocked the base. He gained footing and maneuvered around several soldiers who were pouring into the main room of the compound, ready for action. Gideon began following when Silas called out to him.

"Gideon, my old friend, where are you going?"

"To help with the Legacies." He said, almost defensively.

"Ethan will take care of it," he shouted as a large chunk of metal exploded inward and crashed to the floor, only feet from a gathering of soldiers who all trained their weapons upward at the newly made entrance. "I need you to make sure the staff gets evacuated and taken to the safehouse."

Gideon nodded apprehensively and turned down the hall. Three more large detonations sent giant bricks of steel down to the compound floor. One soldier was crushed under the weight of the debris. When two others attempted to lift the rubble and free their comrade, they were admonished by another who reminded them that there was still an unknown, imminent threat. They acquiesced once they noticed their friend had been dead upon the impact.

Rays of sun shone brightly through the large holes of the ceiling, advertising what could be easily misconstrued as a beautiful spring day outside the church's ground level. The uneasy silence that accompanied the sunshine seemed to last an eternity. The armed men stood like statues with their weapons trained at what loomed overhead. Beads of sweat poured from their brows as their clammy palms tightened their grips on the rifles.

A distant and deep, throaty gurgle broke through the quiet from the ground level of the church. As it faded away, a second similar yet more aggressive sound could be heard. This one was more of a low growl, which was then accompanied by guttural retching of another. A high pitch keening and an unnatural feminine scream of horror joined the frenzied symphony and informed the soldiers of just what was coming through those holes.

Someone was handing Silas an automatic rifle, which he took all too willingly without ever removing his eyes from the ceiling. He did a magazine check by bringing it to eye level and reinserted it, racking one into the chamber.

The first plaguer dropped down with the grace of an elephant. He landed on his coccyx and hit his head on the debris next to him, snapping his neck and killing him instantly. A woman plaguer entered next and landed on her dead cohort. She rolled off and was on her feet in the blink of an eye. Her advance was cut short, as she was riddled with an undeterminable amount of brass from the soldiers' weapons.

Another plaguer landed through the second hole with the unmistakable *pop* of bone and tendon as her right femur and knee splintered out in two very different directions. Not to slow her down, she crawled forward with her hungry eyes locked on her food. When two soldiers both put controlled bursts into her cranium, the one man instructed the team to stagger their shots. This would not only help them conserve ammo but allow some to reload their empty weapons while others could continue firing.

More of the undead poured through the jagged openings. The bodies of the fresh kills acted as cushions for the plaguers raining down inside the bunker. Though most were being disposed of quickly, the bodies were amassing and beginning to enclose the soldiers. They were being slowly pushed outward towards the wall as the hordes of undead filled the large room.

A slightly overweight combatant was reloading his rifle and tactically falling back when he rolled his ankle and collapsed on his side. He hit the ground with a heavy thump and his fresh magazine bounced away uselessly. Before he could get to his feet, two plaguers had already closed the gap on him. The man managed to unsheathe his knife but only sliced at air, as one plaguer bit down into his neck while the other held his outstretched arm and dug into his bicep. The knife clattered to the floor and he let out a blood curdling scream as fat and muscle were torn away from his body by ravenous, flesh-starved mouths. He collapsed again, this time with his attackers on top.

Blood pooled the soldier's now dead body and, once the plaguers sensed that his heart was no longer beating, they stood and moved on to continue their assault elsewhere.

"Graham," Silas shouted to a nearby soldier as he fired indiscriminately into the waterfall of undead that poured through the ceiling. "Get a grenade up there."

The man who was Graham threw his rifle over his back and pulled a grenade from his vest. He ran up and pulled the pin as the Grandmaster covered him to ensure he wouldn't get within biting distance. With a vaulted dive, he pivoted mid-air and threw the grenade, which arced up and through the opening. Graham landed into a roll and sprung to his feet in one quick motion, redrawing his rifle and continuing to fire.

The explosion from the grenade shook the roof of the bunker and sent severed limbs and red mist flying overhead and down onto the combatants. This slowed the plaguers' advance, if only slightly.

Silas and Graham repeated the action for the second hole with the same results. Graham was painted red from head to toe with the blood of the undead from the counter assault.

At the far end of the room, another soldier who was still wet behind the ears observed the amazing feat by his comrades and decided he would do the same. He pulled the pin from a grenade on his vest and smiled up at the hole as he brought his arm back.

The young fighter failed to notice that the one plaguer he had shot was not dead. It crawled silently forward, behind his prey, careful not to make a noise and scare him away. His Burger Hut nametag read Chester. And Chester had not yet eaten since becoming a plaguer. His jaws clamped down into the soldier's calf, ripping through his clothes with ease as his teeth pushed all the way into bone.

The young soldier cried in pain and fell forward. He kicked at Chester's face, breaking his nose and orbital socket, but doing nothing to loosen his bear trap-like grip.

The chaos seemed to freeze temporarily as everyone became hypervigilant to an unmistakable clanking noise that echoed throughout the room. All eyes, alive and undead, fixated on the small green object that now spun on the floor as it came to its final resting place.

BOOM! Human and plaguer body parts danced in the air as everyone within range was reduced to unrecognizable chunks of bloodied meat. Sinew and muscle fibers dangled from unknown unmentionables. Teeth and bone fragments littered the floor with concrete and metal debris.

Some soldiers continued firing as they retreated and split down the large winding halls of the compound. They were being completely overrun.

"That can't be good." Jen said as she removed her earplugs. The obnoxious whining of the siren could barely be heard with the ear protection in place, but the seizure-inducing, flashing lights that accompanied it clearly spelled danger.

"No, it can't be." Logan agreed in a quieter tone as he took the goggles from his face and placed them on the range booth in front of him. "Guys, on me for a sec." He shouted over the alarm as his voice echoed throughout the range all the way down to the paper targets strung up at the twenty-yard line.

Jen, Matt, Carrie, and Betty all approached, eyes and ear protection still on, save for Jen. Carrie was nonchalantly reloading an empty forty caliber magazine. Betty had a lit cigarette dangling from the corner of her mouth with an ash comparable in length to the barrel of the forty-four magnum she wielded.

Logan's private security detail was checking his comms. When he received no response, he spoke. "That alarm means we're under attack, and I can't get through to anyone. I need to take you to the evacuation elevator at the south end. Where is everyone else in your group?"

"I know Luke and Izzy are in the library, where's everyone else?" Logan asked as he himself inspected his firearm in the event that he had to use it.

"Chad's been spending…" the alarm sounded off and Carrie realized she had begun shouting in their faces. "Um," she started over, "Chad's been spending all of his time doing combat training and defensive tactics, according to Nelly." She slammed the now fully loaded magazine she had been loading into the well.

"Shane was in the rec room about an hour ago." Betty said as she took a long drag of her cigarette, mindlessly sending the unnaturally long ash to the floor.

"And Mary?" Jen asked anyone who could answer. Nothing.

"Ok, we need to find Ethan first." Logan said as the door to the range burst open and Ethan ran in with Murdocksir at his side.

"Found him." Matt said.

"You all have to come with me." Ethan said, catching his breath.

"What's going on?" Jen asked as she grabbed an extra fully-loaded magazine from the table and stuffed it in her pocket.

"The man responsible for Pestilence is sieging the bunker. We have to leave."

"And go where exactly?" Logan asked with a hint of desperation.

"There's an exit in Silas' chambers," Ethan explained. "There's a train that will take us north."

Murdocksir was surprised. "What about the elevator, sir?"

"No, Silas said to take them through his chambers. He has his reasons."

"Ok, let's go get the rest." Logan said.

"Silas and a strike team have most of them confined to the main entrance and surrounding corridors," Ethan said as he opened the door to lead them out. "So, these halls should all be …"

A particularly nasty looking plaguer crashed into the half open door, striking Ethan and sending him to the floor as it shrieked with rage. With only one boot on, the undead man stood at an impressive six feet that slouched down to five feet-ten on his left side. He was an older man with flaps of discolored and wrinkly skin that hung over sections of his missing and torn away torso, revealing punctured innards, which dangled freely as he stood. His visible ribcage heaved in and out, but not from deep breaths. The plaguer was bopping back and forth, rallying his hunger and getting ready to pounce on his meal. Blood from his tongue smeared his gray handlebar mustache as he wet his lips with anticipation.

It leapt forward as a loud bang echoed through the hall and was accompanied by a single muzzle flash. The plaguer fell at Ethan's feet, now lifeless. Fresh blood poured from a single gunshot wound from the side of his head. Logan peeked his head out and down at Ethan, who was still on his ass.

"The halls should be what now?" Logan asked him.

Ethan sighed in relief. "Shut up," he said as he got to his feet. "I don't know how they're down in this corridor."

"Isn't there more than one entrance they can come through?" Matt inquired.

Ethan shook his head. "No. Well I mean there's the tunnel I just found out about but that's at the other end of the compound. There's an evacuation elevator for all the employees and…." His words trailed off as a look of pure terror spread across his face.

"Shit," Jen said, reading his expression. "What?"

"Everyone's dead…." Was all Ethan muttered.

The large elevator platform measured eight hundred square feet and rested roughly three-quarters the length of a football field underneath a bifold steel door. On the outside, the door was covered by a patch of green grass and opened into the lower level of a three-story parking garage also owned by the Order. Several locked vehicles ranging in various shapes and sizes waited for escaping members of said Order to enter and drive off to the next safe house.

A mixture of a few dozen doctors, scientists, historians, mages, and VIPs stood on the elevator, anxiously awaiting news of just what was unfolding at the other end of the compound. Three armed soldiers with Gideon at their helm prepared for the evacuation.

"They're not all here, sir." One man said to Gideon as he tried not to focus on the screams that could be heard reverberating through the compound.

"Then, we'll send it back down." he responded as he switched a few switches and dialed a few dials. The orange caution lights lit up the dim elevator as the machine roared to life. Everyone aboard stumbled as the track shifted and realigned, then slowly began its ascension.

The three soldiers hopped on as Gideon stood back.

"You not coming, sir?" The same soldier asked.

"No, I have more work to do. Get them out of here." He turned back and leaned one arm against the wall, taking a moment to rest and ponder. As the elevator rose out of view, he couldn't help but smile.

As the large trap doors parted and allowed the sun to shine down on them, the people on the elevator already started to feel better. There was carnage unfolding underneath, but they would be given another chance. A chance to continue working. A chance to continue living. A chance to help make this mess right. Or so they thought.

Ground level came into view as the elevator approached its stop, but instead of seeing the cars that would take them away, they were greeted with the visage of several hundred hungry, undead faces surrounding them.

The people cried out in surprise at first, then in terror. Some openly wept while others silently and involuntarily soiled themselves. The soldiers spun with their weapons up, unsure where to aim, but didn't fire.

The plaguers did not attack either. They stood there and simply watched with lifeless eyes as the huddled mass of people spread their own hysteria amongst themselves.

"Nonononononononononono," one soldier said as he regained awareness and began to squeeze his trigger down. He kept the rifle at head level as he fired, never allowing the trigger to reset. Some shots struck shoulders and necks, sending the plaguers they struck backwards into the ranks behind them. Several were kill-shots and resulted in almost a half of dozen plaguers falling forward, face down onto the cement.

The soldier's weapon clicked empty as he continued to aim and flail with the muzzle aimed at the crowds' heads. When he realized no magic bullets would materialize for him and the plaguers had already filled their missing ranks, he dropped his gun and let it swing uselessly to his side.

"Where are the Legacies?" a gravelly voice bellowed over the masses and bounced off the concrete pillars.

Heavy wailing and soft whimpers were the only responses that came forward.

"I said…" the voice belted in rage as plaguers stepped aside, creating a path. "Where are the Legacies?!" The bald man named Gol repeated as he stepped through and in front of the gathering on the elevator.

Again, there was no answer. Only sniveling and silent praying.

"Fine," he said as he calmly approached the soldier who emptied his weapon. "We do this the fun way."

The soldier looked defeated and utterly hopeless. He stood in absolute shock with his eyes fixated on the ground at Gol's feet. Even as Gol placed both hands on the man's head, he did not look away from that spot. As if he was having a staring contest with the concrete and the fate of the world was at stake.

Gol placed a large finger under the man's chin and lifted delicately, forcing the man to finally see him. The man let out a low sob as tears began to run down his face. He knew he was about to die.

Gol smirked ominously and, with the speed of ripping off a band-aid, twisted the man's head left then right, violently snapping his neck. It was clear that the man was dead, but Gol did not relinquish his grip. Instead he twisted again. And again. The continuous cracking of vertebrae waned as his neckbones were almost reduced to powder. Then with one final twist, he pivoted his body and pulled upwards, severing the man's head from his body.

Men and women alike screamed from fear at the savagery Gol displayed. A second soldier with the nametag "Tins" aimed a shaky rifle at him.

Gol turned with the head still held in his hand as it dripped thick rivulets of blood and viscous fluids to the floor. "Heads up," he jested, as he hurled the severed head at Tins, striking him straight in his face and breaking both noses. The impact knocked Tins unconscious and sent him flying backwards.

The third and final soldier shook uncontrollably from his legs to his outstretched firearm. He glanced down at Tins and then over to the headless torso before deciding to place his gun on the ground and raise his hands in surrender.

"The Legacies?" Gol reiterated impatiently.

"I… I don't know," the soldier stammered out. "This is our only evacuation point."

"Then I have no reason to let you live." He responded putting a heavy step forward.

"Enough," a deep, disjointed voice said, stopping Gol midstride. "If you keep killing them, I cannot use them."

"Sorry, my liege," Gol said, bowing his head and retreating a step.

The ground shook as the ashen monstrosity called Pestilence came into view and another path was cleared by the plaguers. The people on the platform cowered in such fear at the sight of him that they pressed backwards against the undead blocking their escape with almost no concern.

The First Plague extended his right palm up. As a red sore exploded and purulent discharge ran down his fingers, the sinister white mist from within him flowed outward, surrounding the crowd on the platform. It weaved and wove through and around the legs of each person present, before wrapping itself around limbs like a renegade weed. It held feet firmly in place and cuffed arms down to their sides, minimizing resistance as it then snaked upwards and into their mouths, nose, and ears.

Some vomited into the air as they were turned, others defecated as their internal organs were ravaged with disease. They pulsed and jerked quietly as the process ran its course and filled these new carriers of affliction with crippling pain and suffering. In less than sixty seconds, it was all over.

They all stood in unison. Their white eyes and foul, septic odors matched those of their already undead brethren. The circle of plaguers stepped closer to the newly turned, closing in and completely filling the space on the elevator platform. As if it was being called, it began to descend back to the lower level of the compound.

Like eager children, the plaguers did not wait for the elevator to stop moving. They plummeted into the bunker, breaking arms, legs, heads, and everything else as they hit the floor. Most shook off their injuries and raced down whatever corridor they laid eyes on, broken arms flapping behind like tarps in the wind.

Gideon calmly put his cigarette out on the metal wall, which lit red with the heat. He dropped the butt to the ground and racked a fresh round into the chamber of his AR-15 as the plaguers continued to throw themselves from the elevator.

One sprinted at him, chomping at the air like a rabid dog. Gideon lifted his rifle and the plaguer stopped in his tracks, inches from the barrel. It sniffed the air around the gun, grunted, and ran off down the hall with several other plaguers.

"Why are they not here?" Gol said angrily as he stepped off the now stopped elevator.

"I don't know." Gideon said, lowering his rifle. "The old man was whispering something to his understudy. I couldn't hear."

"That's convenient." Gol said with skepticism.

"Shut up, brute." He retorted, smugly. "I have an idea where they are going."

"Then, perhaps you should tell me." Pestilence bellowed, moving forward.

"My lord." Gideon said as his smug smirk faded and he bowed to one knee. "Silas instructed them to find Eli up north."

"Eli?" The Horseman said with genuine surprise. "The swine yet lives? We have unfinished business, he and I. And what of the relic?"

"It's… not here." Gideon said, timorously.

Pestilence lunged forward and gripped his neck, lifting him up to eye level with ease. "Tell me then, Gideon, where did it go?"

"My lord," Gideon begged with choked breaths, his accent thicker with the lack of oxygen. "I saw him slip it into Ethan's pocket before instructing him where to go."

"Gol," Pestilence shrieked, without looking away from Gideon. "I want that relic before our duplicitous ally finds it. Kill one legacy, allow the other to escape. He will lead me to Eli."

"Yes, my lord." Gol said as he started off towards his new objective.

"Any other information you wish to share?" The horseman asked in a pseudo friendly tone.

"Yes, my lord," Gideon replied, as he finally calmed down. "I gave them a Moirai Blade but ... "

"You what?!" the pale rider barked as he tightened the grip around his subordinate's neck.

"It's...it's..." Gideon choked on the last few words he was trying so desperately to get out. When his face began to turn violet, his master again loosened his grip. "My lord... it's a fake."

"I have to get you to the evacuation point." Duck said, deepening his voice in his best attempt to sound authoritative.

"Uh, yea." Luke said, almost dismissively. "After we find Logan."

"You are my primary mission, sir. I can't risk you to find your brother." Duck said, his voice waning as he finished his statement, losing all authority.

"Tough shit about your mission, then." Luke replied, cramming three books into Izzy's backpack. "Because I get Logan first."

"I..." Duck stammered. "I guess we go get Logan first."

Luke did a once over of a nine-millimeter he had in his waistband then handed it to Izzy, who cautiously placed it in her own holster.

"Good," Luke said, racking the chamber. "Let's go."

They crept out the library and down the spacious hall with no resistance. The sound of battle flooded the empty air of the corridors. Automatic fire and shotgun bursts rang out from all directions and bounced so clearly off the metal walls, it sounded as if they were only feet from the carnage.

"Have you ever even seen a plaguer?" Luke asked Duck, who took lead position and walked in a military crouch.

"Of course." he replied curtly, as he continued scanning ahead. "They create over a dozen different creatures for us to face against in varying battle scenarios."

"Create?" Izzy asked, with an arched eyebrow.

"Well yea. They use cadavers and donated bodies to make them. Other creatures, they have to capture and bring in."

"When we get out of here," Luke whispered, "I want details about that shit."

Duck nodded. "Yes, sir."

"That door on the right." Izzy pointed out as they approached a set of double doors.

Luke pressed his back against the wall and reached his right arm across the slab, then pushed, swinging the door completely open.

Duck stepped inside with caution, his rifle at eye level and ready to fire. One full step in and a pair of hands gripped the barrel from the side and pulled the gun forward. A figure ducked under Duck with an extended waist and transitioned one hand from the rifle to his collar and twisted. In the blink of an eye Duck was thrown over and slammed to the floor with the muzzle of his own rifle now aimed at his head.

"Drop the… Chad?" Luke said in confusion as he was staring at Chad, who had Duck's weapon trained on him.

"Oh, thank God." Chad said, immediately lowering the gun and relaxing. "You scared the shit out of me."

"We scared you? Nice kung-fu, Wang Chun." Izzy said with a smile.

"Yea, I've been practicing a little." He said, bashfully. "We didn't know what was going on, so we were just waiting for someone to come tell us it was a false alarm or something."

"Doesn't sound like one." Izzy said. "Who's we?"

"Hey." Nelly's voice came from behind a wall made of mats. Her face became visible as she finally stood and waved awkwardly.

"Well, come on." Luke said. "We need to get Logan and get out of here."

"I'm good by the way." Duck said, still lying on the floor. "For the record, I knew you were there."

"Oh, that's why you advanced into an open room at a turtle's pace instead of clearing the corners first?" Chad instigated.

Duck brushed himself off and snatched his rifle back. "What, did you read one of our handbooks and now you think you're a badass?"

"Says the guy I just got the drop on." Chad said, stepping forward.

"Ok, you two." Nelly intervened. "Put your junk away and let's get the hell out of here."

"Where is Logan, anyway?" Chad asked as he took a black machete from his otherwise empty gym bag.

"I'm not sure," Luke replied. "But if we make our way to the armory first, then to the escape elevator, we should run into him."

"The armory is this way." Duck said, taking lead again and turning them down another winding corridor. They walked as erupting explosions and varying caliber firearms became more sporadic in the distance behind them.

A low rumble along the walls and floor that intensified slightly with each step gave the notion that something very large ahead of them was moving. In what direction, no one could say.

When Duck noticed that the others were frozen in place temporarily at the low whirring of some unknown machine being brought to life, he glanced back.

"It's the rear elevator. They must have started evacuating." He explained. "We have to skip the armory. Your brother might be waiting at the platform."

"How much further?" Luke asked.

"End of this hall and to the left."

"You two ok?" Luke turned to Nelly and Chad.

"Yea I'm fine, if we keep moving." Nelly told him.

"Yea, let's just go already." Chad said impatiently as he clutched his machete nervously at his side.

As they turned the corner to head towards the large elevator room doors, a deep repetitive belching spewed forth from the other side, stopping them in their tracks.

"Was that from in there?" Izzy said, with a hint of panic. "The room we're supposed to be going into?"

"Um… maybe we should…" Duck took two steps back as the door flew open and the undead poured through like a tidal wave.

"FUCK!" Luke yelled as he opened fire without recourse into the mob of plaguers, killing one and dropping at least two more. It made no difference as the sheer volume of bodies that flooded in were being carried forward by the weight of those behind. Several were pulled under and trampled by their brethren, being practically liquefied by the "dead" weight.

"Go, NOW!" Duck hollered as he ran backwards and held his trigger down as hard as he possibly could.

"Where?" He heard Luke yell back to him.

"The armory has a deadbolt." He shouted as his rifle clicked empty and he turned completely around, kicking into an all-out sprint.

Luke collided with the door, which refused to budge, as he attempted to push the handle down. "It's locked… it's fucking locked."

"Put in the code, damn it." Duck shouted as he gained ground with a female plaguer hot on his heels.

"Code, what code?" Luke shouted at the door in frustration.

"Oh, my God," Nelly said hysterically. "They're coming from the other hall too." Three plaguers were running full tilt right at them from the opposite hall.

"Shit." Luke said backing away from the door and firing at the approaching plaguers. Two of the three fell to the floor with fresh head wounds.

"You had your face in a book when Silas was telling us this shit." Chad snapped as he pressed the seven-digit code; eight, six, seven, five, three, zero, nine. The key panel beeped in approval and he put his body into the door, forcing it open.

"Fucking Tommy Tutone, seriously?" Luke said incredulously as he ushered Izzy in and held the door.

Duck could hear the woman barking in his ear as she closed in, chomping her dry rotted teeth at the back of his head. She was so close he could even smell the halitosis on her breath. He debated on turning around so he could hip throw her and create space, but that two second delay would be all it took for the ones behind her to catch him. He began to panic internally. It seemed that no matter which choice he made, he was going to die.

That's when he swore he could feel the bullet kiss his ear as it whistled by. The bang of Luke's nine-millimeter made him wince as he approached him at the door and, he could tell by the smile he was wearing, that it was a kill shot.

Duck slammed into the open door and rolled along it, pulling Luke in and shutting it simultaneously. As the latch inserted into the strike plate, Izzy slammed the behemoth deadbolt into place.

The heavy door may not have budged, but they could hear plaguers bouncing off it as they attempted to run through it.

"Nice shot, sir." Duck said, trying to catch his breath.

"Please…stop… calling me… sir." Luke replied with the same lack of oxygen.

"Sorry, sir." Duck said reflexively. That's when he threw up.

Izzy and Nelly jumped back with disgust. Luke and Chad just stared in gross disbelief. Duck finished expulsing his lunch and wiped his mouth with his sleeve.

"That ever happen when you were training to kill these things?" Chad asked him with slight.

"Every time," Duck said, dismissing his tone and stepping away from the mess he made. "That should hold a while." He said nodding over to the door.

"Yea, but now we're trapped." Nelly said, leaning on a bench filled with explosives.

"We have a shit ton of weapons in here." Chad said. "Can't we fight our way out?"

"No." Duck said with certainty. "We'll be overrun."

"How good are you with the arcane?" Luke asked him.

"Not at all," he replied simply. "That's why I volunteer for sentry duty."

"Ok." he replied as he turned Izzy around and rummaged through her bag. He pulled out one of the books from earlier and fingered through a section of spells. "While I try to figure something out, you guys should load up."

The mammoth hand cannon rocketed up and back in Betty's hands as she squeezed the trigger. A volcano of blood erupted at the neck of her target as the head exploded from the forty-four caliber round that punched through. Like an elegant dancer, Betty's arms swung as she rode the recoil down into an arc and rested her aim directly on another target. With a second squeeze of her fingertip, the magnum roared as it sent another heavy round into a rotted flesh-encased cranium. The shot ripped through a film encrusted eye and took the right half of the thing's brain and skull with it. It fell, like many others, dead to the floor.

"I'm out!" Betty screamed over the gunfire as she holstered her weapon and pulled a bowie knife from her boot.

The young yet seemingly battle hardened Murdocksir took point and proved his worth in a gunfight with the undead. Like a master of gun-fu, he squeezed the trigger of his automatic rifle with the utmost discipline and allowed every shot to drop a respective target. When the reactionary gap was compromised, he would shift to an improvised Kobudo style, turning his weapon into a club or staff for close quarter combat.

He thrust the receiver of his AR into the throat of an incoming plaguer as he barreled forward to clear the path. With a twist of his wrist and pivot of his forward momentum, he turned his aggressor on his feet and wrapped his weapon around its neck. He forced his hips back and pulled with all the strength his shoulders would allow. As the zombie flipped harmlessly overhead, he freed his rifle and swiveled his arm, again pressing down on the trigger twice and dropping two more enclosing threats. The plaguer he had manhandled lay on the floor, dead from a snapped neck.

It was evident that Murdocksir was a badass. Even Ethan acquiesced and fell back to allow the spry soldier to continue clearing their way forward.

"Matt, take Betty and get that door open for us." Murdocksir shouted as they fired into a large group of plaguers that closed in on them in the open corridor. Their path ahead was now clear, and they were venturing further into the compound, but the horde of plaguers that made it through were hot on their heels. Very soon, the undead masses would be winding their way through every hall.

Matt sprinted past Betty, who was obviously slightly slower given her age. He couldn't see it, but she decided to flip him off when he went around her, reminding her just how much her body had betrayed itself to age.

The door was open, and the path was clear. "Get in, get in, get in." Matt screamed, as they crossed through the doorway, one by one.

Murdocksir entered last and as he turned, saw Matt and Jen already turning the world's smallest deadbolt into the locked position. "That's not gonna hold." He said as he grabbed Matt's empty shotgun and slid it through the U-shaped handles. The door buckled outward from the weight being applied to the other side, but the Mossberg would hold it in place.

"What the Hell?" Matt protested. "Now what am I going to use?"

"Oh, shut up." Murdocksir replied. "The damn thing's been empty."

It wasn't lost on Logan that Matt hasn't used the shotgun or any weapon for that matter since they were hold up at the garage. Matt gave Logan a sheepish expression having been outed. He had hoped no one would notice that he couldn't even bring himself to reload the damn thing, let alone fire it.

"Here." Logan said as he pulled the spare nine-millimeter from his waist and handed it over. "You ok with this? Really?"

Matt nodded with a slight embarrassment that he would have to leave unaddressed for now. He took the gun and checked the magazine like he had been taught. It was loaded to full capacity. "Thanks." he said, softly.

The thumping on the door lessened and shortly tapered off as the frustrated squelches from the other side began to fade down the halls. Somehow, they knew they were not going to get in that way and ventured off in search of an alternate entrance.

The room they entered was one of the entertainment areas. A small oak bar adorned the far corner with stools just in front. A leather reclining couch ran along the distant wall and cut through the center of the open room in the shape of a L, facing a large flat screen HDTV. A pool table off to the side sat with numbered balls scattered atop it from a game of eight ball that would never be finished. Speakers hung in all four corners with unseen wires that ran to a radio/cd combo on a small table next to a vending machine.

"Is it me, or do they seem really pissed off?" Carrie asked with concern as they stepped into the openness of the rec room.

"It's the Horseman." Ethan said, rubbing the back of his head with an open palm. "He changes the way they behave. They can become more aggressive in large numbers. Or, like we saw back at the repair shop, he can make some of them slightly more intelligent." He was pacing now and placed both hands on the side his head as he stared at the floor with eyes so wide, they could see nothing. "They somehow got in on the escape elevator. That means everyone who was being evacuated is dead."

"We don't know that." Murdocksir tried reassuring him. "They could …"

"No." Ethan cut him off. "That's why Silas told me about his quarters. He must have known someone else other than Matthias was feeding Mr. Stone information."

"Well, who knows about the exit?" Jen chimed in.

"Everyone." Ethan answered with a shrug. "They're supposed to know. But these guys up there had such strong arcane knowledge. They just erased our warding like it was…" He closed his eyes as a harsh realization set in.

Logan connected the dots for everyone else who didn't understand. "And I'm guessing there's only a few of you in here who would know how to do that."

Ethan nodded grimly. "Only one person other than Silas. Gideon."

"That sucks." Matt said. "I kind of liked the guy."

"Why would master Gideon do that?" Murdocksir said, with a hint of betrayal.

"I don't know." Ethan told him, putting a hand on his shoulder. "I hope I'm wrong."

Gideon was the Master of Arms at this Order base and personally oversaw all combat training that the potential soldiers received during recruitment. Murdocksir had been like many of the orphans turned-recruits that looked at Gideon as a father figure. The implication that he turned traitorous to the Order and his family was heart breaking.

I hope Luke didn't follow that asshole, Logan said to himself, allowing the thought to exit his head as quickly as it entered.

"Shane's not here." Carrie said, after doing a once over of the place.

"We'll find him." Matt told her.

"Or who cares if we don't," Logan said, with spite as Jen gave an admonishing stare. He shrugged.

"Hey, you guys do know there's another door over there, right?" Betty asked as she pointed a cigarette that nobody saw her light to the opposite side of the room.

"The west corridor and the green mile," Ethan informed them. When they were given the tour of the facility, Silas had mentioned how the "Green Mile," as it came to be known, was one single hallway that ran directly from the main North entrance to the South elevator platform. In the event of some emergency, two large blast doors would close on each end to prevent being flanked. This, in turn, would trap anyone or anything in the corridor with no way out.

"So, which way do we go?" Betty asked as she approached the door. She was about to push slightly and peer out of the crack to ensure their path was clear when a strange sound caught her attention. "Do you…hear that?"

Someone was humming. A quiet, carefree hum of a song she couldn't quite place. Betty opened the door enough to slink out. Bodies of dead civilians and soldiers alike littered the floor. Some bled out from having severed arms or legs. Others had entire chunks of flesh and bone torn from their bodies, while some seemed to succumb to unseen injuries. One sat upright, a deep red and black bloodstain on the wall where its head should be leaning.

A small, frail-looking woman with a long, brown cardigan on, was stepping over a bloodied corpse as she hummed blithefully. Although her back was facing Betty, she knew who the woman was.

"Mary?" she asked, with genuine concern.

Mary spun as if she were dancing on sunshine. "Oh, hello Betty."

Betty was as confused as she was off-put by Mary's carefree demeanor. When Logan and Jen attempted to step out into the hall, Betty politely shied them back inside. "Mary, are you ok?"

Mary tilted her head in confusion. "Of course, I am. Why wouldn't I be?"

"This place is being attacked," she informed her, as she moved closer, her foot coming down softly on bloodied unknowns. "We need to leave."

"Leave?" Mary yelled, uncharacteristically. When she saw Betty recoil at her tone, she adjusted herself and smiled anew. "I can't leave. Becca will be here soon. She's bringing some friends over." With that, she began humming again.

Betty stopped moving forward. *Oh shit*, she said to herself when she realized that her friend was losing her mind. "Listen, girlfriend. Let's all get out of here and we can meet Becca and her friends later."

"No." Mary said with impudence. "You were all supposed to help me find her."

"And we will." Betty reassured her. "But we need to leave here."

Mary shook her head adamantly at her. Betty had been so focused on her friend and the several bodies lining the hall that she failed to notice the door Mary stood next to. The metal slabs did not push inward and there were no thumps or thuds like someone was trying to get through. But the faint moaning and shrills that bled through made it perfectly clear just what was on the other side of that door.

"Logan." Betty yelled in a whisper as the rec room door pushed open and Logan stepped behind her.

"Mary? Hey it's …" Logan started.

"You liar!" Mary screamed at him.

"What?" Logan asked, noticing Betty backing up closer to him and pointing over at something for him to take notice of.

"You said we would find Becca. But you didn't help me." She began crying hysterically. "I needed your help and you lied to me."

"Mary, I…" Logan said softly, unsure where to let his words land next. "We will find Becca." He took two large steps forward.

"Don't do that." Betty warned him.

Logan met Betty's eyes and saw the concern they held. She jerked her head a few times, again pointing at something for him to see. When he looked back, Mary was smiling again. Tears streamed down her face and she began humming blissfully once again.

The rest of the group had now entered the hall and Betty ushered them along in a quiet rush. "Go. Now." She said to them.

When Mary reached out to a door that Logan failed to notice she was standing next to and undid a large latch, he finally realized what Betty was trying to tell him. He turned to warn the others, only to realize his "bodyguard" was the only one still standing there.

"Sir…" Murdocksir said to him with heightened alarm as he too began to backup.

Mary pulled the door open with a sobbing grin as plaguers poured through the door. "Becca, my little angel." She said as a young, blonde woman grabbed her by the shoulders and bit into her face. The plaguer pulled away with Mary's nose and cheek muscles, titillating her undead taste buds.

Mary's screams echoed down the hall as Logan kicked into high gear to catch up with his group.

"The library's up ahead." Ethan shouted, as they turned a corner that was the same drab gray as every other corner.

"Feels like we're going in circles." Matt said as he huffed in thin air.

The doors burst inward as they ran inside. Ethan, Logan, and Murdocksir pressed their backs against the single metal slab as they felt the weight of at least a dozen bodies slam into the other side. They fell forward slightly and regained footing, then pushed back with all their combined bodyweight. It was only a matter of time now before the monsters would be inside.

"We need something for this door." Logan shouted as he fought to keep his body plush against the metal.

They spread out in a panicked search for any kind of blockade. "The bookshelf!" Matt yelled as he tried to slide a bookcase that was too heavy for his beach muscles.

"The tables?" Carrie screamed, as they effortlessly moved the wood tables only to realize it would be too light and insufficient.

"Come on, damn it." Ethan said pressing with all his strength. Matt squeezed between them and did what he could to help them keep the door close. The hinges screamed in protest as the door threatened to give way. Jen curled into a ball at the base of the door and pushed as Carrie ducked under Matt and leaned in as hard as possible. Even Betty pushed her fragile frame against a small unoccupied piece of the steel.

"We're losing it." Murdocksir screamed, as he locked his knees, beads of sweat falling from his forehead with the substantial amount of energy he was exerting.

All it took was for Ethan's extended foot to slip out from under him. The corner of the door was forced in and down, sending Ethan, Logan, and Murdocksir tumbling outward. Jen was thrown off balance and knocked into Carrie, who sprawled across the floor. Betty dove to the side and collided with a book cart, which lifted with the impact and buried her in countless works of returned literature. The door crashed down on Matt as several dozen plaguers found their way in.

A middle-aged man landed on Ethan and attempted to bite down as he drew his knife and drove it into the side of the man's temple. He pulled the crimson covered blade out and tried to get his footing, only to be toppled by two more plaguers.

Unsteady footsteps of the dead marched mercilessly inward, stomping down on the mangled and broken metal that was the door. Matt's cries of pain could be heard over the sound of unknown bones in his body being crushed under the weight.

Murdocksir pulled his sidearm and managed to get a single shot off before being bum rushed and taken savagely to the ground by several of the horrid creatures.

Jen and Carrie huddled under the wooden table, unloading their final handgun rounds into the mass of hungry undead that quickly overrun the room. Festered and boil-covered hands, oozing puss, and bodily fluids extended outwards, grabbing at them from under the confines of their maple cover.

Logan's eyes locked onto Jen's struggle for survival. "NO, Jen!" He screamed as a tall plaguer he failed to see slammed into his side and took him down. He turned as they tumbled to the ground and pushed his forearm under its chin. It gnashed and bit at him, flinging blackened droplets of saliva as it did so.

"Fuck…" Logan screamed into the plaguer's face with pure, unfiltered rage and hatred. He felt his arm fatiguing as he tried desperately to hold on for dear life. Until finally, he couldn't. His arm gave out and the plaguer's mouth leaned in for the kill.

Suddenly, the plaguer was gone. Logan's body trembled as his eyes locked onto the peaceful mural on the ceiling of a sunny afternoon at a local outdoor market. He found himself focusing on the most minute details of the beautiful artwork as he laid there with his arms on his chest, grasping at air. It took him a second to realize that he was not bitten, rather he was completely covered in blood. His entire body from head to toe was red with the crimson life fluid.

"It's not my blood," he said as he sat up, wanting to check on his wife. He looked over and saw the same looks of terror on Jen and Carrie. Although they were clearly in shock, they seemed to be physically fine, but also covered in blood.

Ethan was on all fours and the first to stand. He stretched, wiping some of the blood from his arms to reveal his brown skin. He let out a light chuckle.

"Did they just…explode?" Betty asked, as she shook uncontrollably.

Ethan nodded. "Someone… made it to the armory…"

Chapter 18

"Son of a bitch." Mr. Stone exclaimed as he looked over the walls of the church that were now covered in countless gallons of plaguer blood. There had been a momentary high-pitched frequency that spewed forth, giving him the slightest warning that his undead army was about to explode. It had given him just enough time to shield his Kiton suit from the bloody projectiles. "That was close."

The caravan of mercenaries that he brought with him stood in total disbelief. They were all painted red while their commander sat there unscathed, wiping a single droplet of blood from his Venezia leather Berluti shoes.

"What are you waiting for, Suthers?" Stone asked as he tucked his handkerchief back into his pocket. "Get in there."

"You want me to take my men," he started with his blood-soaked face as he pointed to the hole with his rifle, "down there?"

"No," Stone replied with a hint of aggravation. "I want you to take *my* men down there and finish *your* goddamn job."

"Yes, sir." Suthers said apprehensively. "Alpha and Bravo, on me." With that, Suthers jumped down into the bunker, as his fireteams followed closely behind.

Sporadic machine gun fire could be heard below, followed by inaudible verbal commands. More gunfire would issue forth as a response followed by more indistinct yelling. After a few moments, Suthers could be heard shouting up.

"All clear." He said to Mr. Stone.

Like a sorcerer from medieval stories of knights and wizards, Mr. Stone descended the hole in the bunker ceiling, floating through without ever touching anything until his feet came down on the floor.

"Excellent job, Suthers," he said, patronizingly as he patted him on the back. "Go, find me Silas and the relic. Kill the Legacies."

"Yes, sir." Suthers said as he made an excessive amount of overly dramatic hand gestures to his men. Mr. Stone rolled his eyes. He knew this made his employee feel valuable, but he just couldn't understand the point. He watched with boredom as they split into teams and made their way down the various halls and corridors of the facility.

Mr. Stone walked over to one of the terminals and fidgeted with the keyboard. He couldn't help but feel like he was being watched. Placing one hand casually into his pocket, he spun quickly and drew his Micro SR9 twenty-two caliber pistol.

"I just sent my men looking for you," Mr. Stone said as he smiled ominously at a battle worn Silas.

Silas coughed as a spittle of blood ran down his chin. He was unarmed and had clearly been fighting. He studied Mr. Stone long and hard for a minute before realizing he knew exactly who he was.

"Ha!" Silas said with exaggeration. "I like it. *Mr. Stone*. Matthias said you are not able. I get it now." He was clearly amused.

"All these years and you just discover who I am?" Stone said, with a hint of indignity.

"You were excellent at covering your tracks." Silas responded, resting on a broken office chair for a moment. "But now, I know how to stop you."

"Good luck with that." Mr. Stone said as he threw the gun to the floor and sped toward Silas.

Silas sprang to and pivoted, grabbing the chair and launching it at the approaching Stone, who smacked it away mid-air with ease. Silas then held up his thumbs and forefingers to form a triangle and glided backwards, shouting an incantation as he did so. A large cement slab with a rebar protruding from it lifted from the debris and rocketed at Stone. It was too heavy to push aside and moving too fast for him to evade. The chunk of concrete struck dead center in his chest and stopped his forward progress, knocking him to the floor.

Stone raised one hand and closed his thumb over his two middle fingers, shouting an incantation of his own as he sat upright. The dead bodies surrounding them began to twitch and tremor. The deafening sound of a hundred bones snapping filled the room as jagged ivory spears punched through the corpses' arms, legs, and chest cavities. They rose to the air, spilling all manners of organs and innards to the floor with a wet and bloodied splash. These floating husks of ravaged flesh and sharpened marrow now resembled deep sea mines made of man.

Before Stone could extend his hand outward and hurl his Frankenstein weaponry at his fast-approaching foe, Silas pushed his hands at the ground at Stone's feet. The makeshift human missiles fell to the floor harmlessly with a wet thud as Stone was again sent reeling back.

Stone realized his attacks would take too long to cast and if he was to win this confrontation, he would need to get distance and wait for Silas to go on the offensive. When he saw that Silas was entirely too close for him to create space by arcane means, he took a slightly more archaic approach. The concrete he had been struck with was in reaching distance. He grabbed the rebar and swung the cement end out like a club, hitting Silas in the ribcage and sending him nearly thirty feet back.

Silas screamed in pain as at least two ribs shattered from the blunt-force trauma. He gripped his side and locked eyes on Stone, who dropped his new weapon to the floor. Silas again placed his hands together and uttered another incantation. Long, sharp blades of glass formed in the air around him like icicles. He thrust his hand forward and the spikes shot towards Mr. Stone.

Two of the spikes flew passed him, harmlessly shattering against a wall. One found purchase in his left arm as he continued forward, grimacing in pain with the impact. Stone held his right hand in the air, fingers in summoning position as the remaining four stopped midflight as if hitting an invisible barrier. They turned and hovered for a second before their solidity gave way to elasticity and heavy balls formed on the ends like bolas.

Mr. Stone then heaved his right hand forward, sending the bolas spinning through the air back at Silas. He crouched as he attempted to dodge, making himself a smaller target. Two of the bolas went wide while the other two curved midflight to match Silas' evade. The third wrapped around his left arm with such speed and ferocity that sent him reeling backwards. As he staggered and tried to rebalance himself, the fourth coiled around his right leg like a razor whip. His legs kicked out behind him and he was brought down hard on the sharp rubble laden floor. Blood spewed from his mouth as his face hit rock.

Silas could feel his consciousness beginning to wane from the impact. He attempted to lean on the floor so that he could stand but neither his arm nor leg would move from the weight of the bolas. If he could not get his fingertips together, he would not be able to summon any arcane means of combat or escape.

He craned his neck and got a hazy view of Mr. Stone casually strolling towards him as if he were taking a walk through a park on a beautiful, sunny afternoon. *Arrogant prick,* Silas thought to himself.

"You must think me a fool, old friend." Stone said as he bent down next to him. "I know the relic is here, and before nightfall, I will have both it and the legacies."

Silas wriggled his trapped arm in frustration and reached his free hand over at Stone, who simply stared bemused as it lashed at the air inches from his face. Mr. Stone stood and slapped Silas' hand away like he was disciplining a child who was caught with a hand in the cookie jar.

"You're embarrassing yourself." he mocked.

Then, Silas did the unthinkable. He let his hand fall to the floor and began to laugh. A light chuckle at first, which quickly grew into a maniacal heckling.

"What could you possibly find so amusing?" Stone said with a look of disgust.

"I understand your motives now." Silas said, spitting another mouthful of blood. "You freed the Horseman, thinking he would be in your debt. And now that you two don't particularly see eye-to-eye, you want the relic to hold over him. You're afraid of him."

Stone's face turned stone-faced. "Preposterous. I fear nothing." Stone kicked Silas in his already broken ribs, fracturing a few more for the insult.

"What is it you wanted from him?" Silas goaded, as he absorbed the pain. "Everyone else said no to letting you get a do over for your heinous crime, so you figure you'd try bargaining with some of the Allmother's pets?"

"You have some gall," Stone told him, as he pulled a strange looking knife from his waistband. "Why don't I see what they look like." He lifted Silas' bloodied chin and placed the sharpened edge against his throat. "Any last words?"

"Yes," Silas choked out in defeat. "Limbus infernum." He muttered.

"What?" Stone asked, crinkling his nose.

Silas grinned wide with red stained teeth. "Limbus Infernum!" he shouted into Stone's face as his free hand formed a fist and punched down on a sigil at his side. It was essential that Silas irritate his adversary and keep him talking just long enough that he could scribble a banishing sigil with his bloodied hand.

"No!" Stone said as he shot up and back to avoid the blast range. A whitish-blue light emitted from the symbol and swept through the room like a tidal wave. In the blink of an eye, the light faded back into the marking. Everything that lay strewn across the floor only moments ago was now gone. The twisted metal and rubble along with the mangled corpses were no more visibly present in the large empty room than the air they previously breathed. The walls stood as the only witness that there had ever been a skirmish between the disappeared Mr. Stone and Grandmaster Silas.

"Did it work?" Izzy asked after a long moment of uncomfortable silence.

"I don't know," Luke said plainly. "I'm in here with you, remember?" He wiped the soot from the burnt spell bag on his pant leg.

"Well, someone should check." Nelly said nervously.

"Agreed." Chad said, looking at Duck.

"Why the hell should I check? You want to be Mr. Badass, right?" He shot back at him.

"Well," Luke said, sifting through the ingredients that lay across the table. "You are my security detail. So, you could secure our exit."

Duck looked betrayed. "Yes, sir. You're right." He said with false confidence as he adjusted the grip on his rifle and stepped towards the door. The wince-inducing whine of the large bolt seemed to last for hours as Duck pulled it back from the locked position at a snail's pace. He placed his hand on the lever and paused a moment longer to listen for any signs of danger. Nothing. Not a single sound emanated from the hall on the other side.

Taking several deep breaths, the rookie Duck let out a battle cry as he pushed the door open and stepped out with his rifle pointed forward. He jumped back slightly and squeezed the trigger, letting out a three-round burst of fire and an involuntary gasp. Everyone still inside rushed to the door to aid Duck when they discovered that he had been startled by someone in the hall.

"Fuck, you almost shot me!" Shane yelled at the bent over Duck who was trying to stop his heart from jumping out of his chest. He looked at the wall next to him with the fresh bullet holes and shook his head in disappointment. "Trigger control, soldier."

"Sorry, sir." Duck said, gaining his composure.

"Glad you're ok, Shane," Luke said. "Where the Hell have you been?

"I was with Mary in the rec room, but she started acting funny. I think something's wrong with her, so I left. I went to take a nap in my room and the next thing I know, the base is overrun."

"Um," Izzy said pointing a bashful finger at him, "Why are you covered in blood?"

"I'm sure you guys saw there were plaguers everywhere in here. For some fucking reason, they all just..." He looked up as he tried to think of the correct verbiage to use. "...exploded."

"Exploded?" Izzy repeated. "A lot of them?"

"As far as I can tell," Shane replied, "all of them did."

They all finally took notice of the new, shiny red paint that coated the entirety of the walls and floors.

"You made them explode." Izzy told Luke with a hint of derision.

Luke pursed his lips and nodded with certainty. He scanned his work and gave himself a literal pat on the back, clearly impressed by his efforts.

"I thought you tried to do that fire thing Ethan did." Chad said.

"The important thing is that they are dead now." Luke told him.

"I guess we're lucky you didn't miss and get us with that thing." Nelly said in gest.

"Yea," Duck interjected. "We are lucky. That's why I don't mess with that stuff."

"Holy shit," Nelly exclaimed, "He really could have done that?" Duck nodded in confirmation.

"Can we just go and change the subject?" Luke said, as he stepped back inside the armory for his gear bag. "Shane, you're ex-military. You want to check some guns over and grab essentials?"

"Sure." Shane said, as he picked up a rucksack from a bin and stocked up on everything he could carry. Supplies included fragmentation grenades, magazines for various caliber weapons, attachments, and the like.

"Hey, Shane," Luke whispered to him as approached his side with caution. Shane looked over but remained quiet. "Whatever's up with you and Logan…. However you think you know him… I don't know." Luke was struggling to get his words in the right order. He took a concentrated breath in and continued. "You can trust him. And me."

Shane's face showed no concern one way or another for his comments. "I know." He said simply, and continued filling his bag.

"What about this?" Chad said with excitement as he placed the lid to a crate down. Inside was a Russian made RPG-7 anti-tank rocket-propelled grenade. He hefted it up like it was a piece of treasure and he was Indiana Jones making the claim of ownership.

"It's a beauty, but tough to run with if we have all this stuff." Shane told him. Chad reluctantly put it back.

They each grabbed a prepacked go-back that lined the walls along the many racks and shelves of weapons and accessories. Gunfire erupted in the distance and prompted them to load their respective packs even faster. Two minutes and they all had fully-loaded automatic rifles slung around them and a sidearm at the ready. Luke had a fanny pack strapped to his waist with as many arcane ingredients he could fit inside.

"Cute fanny pack." Izzy mocked, as she gave him a kiss on the cheek.

"Just wait til' later when it's the only thing I have on."

"Let's go." Shane said with urgency as the gunfire drew closer. "We have to go back the other way."

They ran back the way they had come from when they heard a soldier yell out to his unit. "I got runners down here." Machine gunfire cascaded the walls and floor around them as the unidentified man finished his sentence.

They turned the corner just as more guns joined the fray and fired indiscriminately at their backs. Shane pressed against the wall and peered around to see a small band of fully-geared men approaching.

Duck bent down in front of Shane and reached his TEC-9 automatic handgun around the cover and fired blindly at the men. He was laying down cover fire as Shane fetched a grenade from his new bag of toys. He popped the pin out of place and hurled the explosive.

"Come on," he told them as he rushed forward, not waiting for the follow-up explosion. They followed as the men behind shouted commands like "take cover" or "fallback" at each other. Shane and the rest were halfway down the next corridor by the time the grenade went off.

They passed the cafeteria and turned left at another corner, almost running straight into a second outfit of armed men. "Fuck," Shane said as he fell back behind the wall. "There's more."

"How many? Luke asked.

"A lot."

"Order member," a voice shouted out to them. "Do you have the legacies with you?"

"Nope, just me," Shane shouted back. He turned to Luke. "Hear that?"

"Yea," Luke replied. "Means they haven't found Logan either."

"We can't fight them here," Chad told Shane. "The cafeteria is right over there."

"Yea," Shane stated as he pulled another grenade from his bag. The head soldier in the hall was yelling something about Shane coming out with his hands on his head. No one was listening and nobody cared. "Go set up some tables as cover, I'll be in. Duck stay with me."

Duck stayed as the rest cut into the mess hall and immediately began flipping tables over in typical, action movie fashion.

"This is your last warning," The soldier said as he tapped one of his men on the shoulder, prompting him to creep up the hall in a military crouch, weapon ready.

"Fuck off," Shane said to himself as he swung his arm down and back in a reverse underarm throw. The green explosive clanked between the legs of the man who had been ordered forward and rolled to a stop at the feet of the one who believed to be in control.

As the grenade exploded soldiers were sent flying in every direction. The blast killed a few and maimed several more as fingers, hands, feet, and many other appendages were separated from their masters. Those not caught in the blast were scattering for a tactical position. They were told that the only Order soldiers that were still alive were already being made prisoners. This made their approach a little laxed to say the least. Now, they were scrambling.

Without mercy or hesitation, Shane and Duck stepped out, pressing their triggers down as hard as they could, spraying lead into anyone and anything still standing. They both clicked empty and again went behind cover.

"Reload and fall back." Shane told him. "They're gonna have grenades too."

Right on cue a fragmentation grenade ricocheted off the wall in front of them and landed at their feet. Without a second thought Duck swung his foot and kicked it to the side. It slid across the floor into a clear area and detonated as they half jumped, half fell, forward to avoid the explosion.

Their ears were ringing with the sounds of war that drummed through the metal and concrete halls. Duck could see Shane's mouth screaming at him, but he heard no words. Shane grabbed him by the collar as he stood on shaky legs and led him back to the lunchroom with the others.

"Lock it," Luke told them from behind an overturned table. He did so as Duck grabbed the end of a nearby table and slid it against as an added measure. Duck took position next to Luke, while Shane crouched in the right corner, taking full advantage the blind spot allowed him.

They could hear the clanging and movement of what sounded to be at least a dozen men outside. It halted suddenly and fell eerily silent.

Luke felt his pulse quicken to unprecedented heights. Any moment now, that door was about to be forced in by countless armed soldiers who wanted specifically him dead. Long seconds passed and turned into even longer minutes. Nothing happened.

He looked over at Izzy who had her rifle propped on the table for stability but still had no idea just what she was doing. For a moment, he was distracted at just how hot he thought she was sitting there with an actual military grade weapon in her hands. *But dressing up like Lara Croft for me was a 'Hell no,'* he thought to himself.

"What's going on?" Chad whispered, loud enough for everyone to hear.

Shane warily rose to his feet, keeping his weapon trained on the entrance. "Maybe they…"

"Hey dickhead, you in there?" a voice broke through the silence like thunder. Luke's already itchy trigger finger was given all it needed to squeeze down involuntarily. The unexpected *bang* of the firearm jolted everyone present. Even Shane winced in surprise as the bullet punched just shy of dead center.

"I think that was your brother." Izzy said, with concern.

"Dude, it's me!" The voice said with indignation.

"Oh, shit. Logan? Luke asked, as he lowered his handgun with a hint of embarrassment.

Chapter 19

"Is everyone ok?" Logan asked as he made a b-line for Jen and Carrie.

Jen nodded fervently as she helped Carrie from under the large wooden table.

"Where's Matt?" Carrie asked, shakily.

"Get this fucking door off of me!" Matt yelled. The door had fallen on top of him and he was trampled by at least a dozen plaguers before reprieve.

Ethan and Logan pushed it aside to see a bloodied and injured Matt. His arm was cradling what was assumed to be a few broken ribs. They helped him to his feet to assess the damage.

"Ribs?" Logan asked him.

"Yea, and my arm." He said as he pointed to his forearm with his head. It was swollen two sizes too big not to be broken. When he tried wiggling his fingers, he would only wince in pain.

"I'll wrap it." Ethan said, tearing a ribbon of his t-shirt and creating a makeshift sling for him.

Betty was the slowest getting to her feet. Her aging body throbbed and ached from her impact with the cart. It felt as if it had been hit by a truck. She rubbed her neck and stretched her back out, wiping tears of relief from her face that she let no one see.

"Guys…" Jen said grimly, staring down.

It was Murdocksir. He was lying still on the floor, devoid of life. Although chunks of flesh were torn away from his throat and arm, his blood was indistinguishable from that of exploded plaguers' blood. In his hand he still held his forty-caliber handgun.

"Shit," Logan said, as he bent down next to him, a lump forming in his throat and a tear freefalling down his cheek.

Ethan leaned in and placed the blade of his knife against Murdocksir's temple. "He was an exceptional soldier," he said as he clearly fought back his own tears.

"He was just a kid God damnit," Logan said in anger. "Why should he have died for us?"

"He died in the line of duty," Ethan pointed out. "It's an honor in death."

"It's pointless," Logan shot back.

Ethan could tell he was upset. This young man had displayed an intensity in combat while remaining cool under fire. But for the past few days, Logan had known him as just a really nice kid, barely even twenty-one years old. He had so much potential. But here he was, dead on the floor in an underground library protecting a stranger.

"We need to keep moving." Ethan reminded him as he slowly slid the blade into the dead man's head.

Of all the things that recently transpired and the fact that they were all covered in blood, the wet sucking sound of the knife being extracted is what made Logan's stomach churn.

"Let's go then," Logan said with red watery eyes as he stood. Jen embraced him tightly for a moment.

They found a roll of paper towels in the bathroom at the back of the library and wiped off the best they could before they moved out.

The group swept silently throughout the compound. A large majority of the gunfire had died down as the number of survivors dwindled drastically. They could hear groups of armed enemy soldiers scanning the halls and rooms.

Ethan took lead as they slid with their backs pressed firmly against a wall. Logan was close behind as Carrie assisted an injured Matt and Jen kept a close eye on Betty. They were approaching a small team of enemy scouts and stopped to eavesdrop on their transmission.

"…Delta Two was engaged by a small band near the mess hall. One of them recognized a legacy with them. Delta One is closing in on them." The man with the radio told his partner.

Ethan and Logan held a whole conversation with just a stare. "Luke," Logan mouthed to him.

Ethan leaned his head over the edge, just enough to allow his one eye to see the two men. When he saw the transmitter was not wearing a helmet he decided to act. He stepped out and fired a single shot into the radio holder's head. Brain matter spewed out as he fell over. The second soldier, being caught off guard, realized his weapon was leaning against the wall ten feet away.

"Don't," Ethan told him, as the man almost reached for his sidearm, "hands up." The man abided as Logan came out and quickly removed the gun from the man's holster.

"What do you want?" The skinny man asked, nervously. He had to be in his late twenties.

"Information," Ethan said. "How many are there?"

"Uh… uh…" the soldier stammered. He had clearly never had a gun pointed at him before.

"Don't lie to me"

"I'm not, I'm not," the soldier pleaded. "We're just radio guys. Our team was wiped out and we just wanted to leave. This shit's not for us." The man was almost in a full sob.

"If you want to live, tell me how many." Ethan was growing impatient.

"Uh… six. There's six teams that each split into two." The man spit out.

"So, twelve teams then, asshole? How many soldiers?"

"There was twelve to a unit. They split into two teams of six. So…. thirty-six?" the man's math was clearly off.

"Are you fucking with me right now?" Ethan asked, with agitation.

"I think he's just an idiot." Logan said.

"The gun is making me nervous," he blurted out. "Seventy-two. There was seventy-two of us, not counting Suthers, Mr. Stone, and the big guy."

"The Horseman?" Ethan asked.

"No, I think they called him Gol." The soldier told him.

"Gol…is here?" Ethan asked in disbelief. "Jesus, Stone must definitely be someone of influence."

"Who's Gol?" Logan asked.

"Tell you later. But he's a bad one," Ethan said as he wiggled the gun at the soldier's nametag. "Ok, Bronson. Is Suthers your boss down here?"

"Yes," he nodded.

"And do they know your unit's dead?"

He shook his head in the negative, "No, sir."

"You're about to get on the radio and tell him you have a legacy with whatever relic they're looking for trapped in the hall connected to the Western corridor."

"Why?" he asked nervously.

"Because if you don't, I'll shoot you in the head." Ethan told him as a matter of fact.

"That's a good reason." Bronson replied. He went over his own headset with the message first. "Unit Charlie Two, Unit Charlie Two, we currently have a small group trapped in the hallway connected to the west corridor."

A rugged voice crackled over the comms in response. "Suthers to Unit Charlie Two, so fucking what."

Ethan rolled his eyes and waved his gun at Bronson, prompting him to really sell it. Bronson clicked his headset again.

"The other legacy is with them and we verify the relic in their possession," he said, "Requesting the closest unit available for backup." This time he sounded extremely convincing.

The voice who identified himself as Suthers crackled over a little bit more excited this time. "Verify on second comms!"

Bronson bent down with his hands still raised to show Ethan that he was going for the large radio attached to his comrades back. "I need to verify with that one." Ethan waved him on to continue. "Charlie Two, verifying previous comms. Need another Unit here. We have a legacy with the relic in the hallway connected to the western corridor."

There was a moment of silence on the other end of the radio. "You were really good," Logan told Bronson to create some levity. He could see the man wasn't cut out for combat and even pitied him slightly.

"Thank you," Bronson said. Ethan gave Logan a sideways glance, to which he shrugged off.

"Delta One," Suthers shouted through. "You're closest, disengage that legacy and get to Charlie Two's location. Gol will handle the mess hall."

"Oh shit." Ethan said with the name drop. "Ok, we gotta go now." He stepped closer and put the gun to Bronson's temple.

"Whoa, whoa, whoa, man!" he pleaded as he shrunk into himself.

"Wait." Logan said in his defense, putting his hand up to Ethan's gun.

"We don't have time," Ethan growled, "and we can't take him with us."

Logan thought for a second. "Take his radios," Logan said as he leaned down to the fallen soldier and snapped the transmitter antenna clean off. Bronson was already removing his headset and handing it over. He waved it in front of Ethan, who was weighing his options.

"Fine," Ethan said as he clocked Bronson on the side of the head with the pistol, knocking him unconscious before he hit the floor. "Should have just killed him," Ethan said, with brood.

"Man, you're grumpy." Logan told him, waving the others over.

"We need to get to them before Gol does," Ethan told him as he transitioned his brisk walk into a cautious jog.

"Yea you said that. Who is he?" Logan asked, trying to keep pace.

"Well," Ethan said with a chuckle, "you might know him as a Philistine giant from a certain piece of literature."

"What like Twilight?" Jen asked. Both Ethan and Logan had to stop and furrow a brow at her. "Or not, jeez."

"I mean from the Bible," Ethan said, picking up speed.

"Never mind," Logan replied. "I never really had an interest in reading that."

They turned left at the intersection of hallways and came to a halt. Another squad of heavily armed soldiers was up ahead. Ethan placed his finger over his mouth to ensure silence among the group. He peeked around cover to see them moving away from them. When he believed the coast be clear enough, he signaled them to cross the opening. When Betty was last to go, he moved.

Within a few minutes they could see the entrance to the cafeteria. Soot plastered sections of broken walls and floors. About a half dozen soldiers lay in the hall, dead from dismemberment or gunshot wounds.

"Yea, Luke was here," Logan said, as they approached the door. He tugged on the handle only to find that it was locked. "Hey dickhead, you in there?"

There was a long second, with no response. He was about to pull again when a small section of door exploded outward simultaneously as he heard the unmistakable sound of small arm fire.

Ethan and Logan both jumped aside. Matt almost fell out of Carrie's grip.

"Dude," Logan shouted through the splintered door. "It's me!"

"Oh shit. Logan?" he heard Luke say.

"Yea, can you open up before they come back?"

"We could just leave him out there." Shane said loud enough for Logan to hear.

"Oh, awesome, Shane made it." He replied, in the same tone.

Luke slid the table away as Duck unlocked the door. "Man, it's good to see you guys," Logan said as they were all ushered inside.

"What happened to you?" Nelly asked a cradled Matt.

"A door fell on me," he said vaguely.

"Listen up," Ethan said, taking control of any further conversation. "Silas told me there's a secret exit in his chambers, which is right down the hall. The main escape elevator's compromised and we have a particularly nasty asshole on his way here right now, so we have to move."

"Don't have to tell me twice," Luke said as he went to exit. His hand touched the crossbar just as the door was forced inward. It struck Luke, sending him airborne. He hit the ground and slid backwards, out cold.

"What the fuck?" Logan said in disbelief as the door was ripped from its hinges. In the opening stood a behemoth of a man. He was solid muscle from head to toe, and wore a sinister grin on a battle-hardened face. A single scar ran from dead center between his eyes and over his bald head, stopping at the base of his neck. Dried blood coated his naked torso and further added to his both awe and fear-inducing physique.

"Gol…" Ethan said, with despair.

Shane didn't hesitate as he was the first to unload several rounds into the clear and present threat. Bullets riddled his midsection as well as the wall behind him. His face grimaced with displeasure more so than pain as he advanced on Shane's position.

"Which one of you is the legacy?" Gol bellowed as Shane's magazine drew empty. At least half the rounds fired met their mark with almost no effect. At best, they may have slowed Gol's already monstrous stride. He reached a hand out towards Shane, who was fumbling to put a fresh magazine in the well of his rifle.

"I am," Logan said as he pulled his nine-millimeter and squeezed relentlessly, sending thirteen of his seventeen rounds directly into his target in a matter of seconds. One round punched through Gol's cheek, sending a flab of flesh careening through the air. "Come get me, big guy."

Gol gritted his teeth and growled in response, letting blood cascade through the newly made hole in the side of his face. He reached down and hefted a bi-fold table over at Shane like it weighed no more than a feather. The table spun through the air and crashed against the two joining walls, not striking Shane but throwing him off kilter. He ran headlong at his new target, Logan.

Logan was amazed by the speed and agility the colossus possessed and misjudged his reaction time by a hair. He dodged left just as Gol reached and swung right. Although he managed to evade the brunt of his boulder-like fist, his leg was caught by the sweeping motion he made as he sped past. Logan was sent tumbling head over feet and came down hard on the solid floor.

Gol stopped his forward momentum, landing him face-to-face with a fear-stricken Betty. Her arms shook like wet spaghetti as she tried to raise her magnum to face her foe. Gol flicked the gun from her weak grasp mockingly and placed his large palm over her face. He lifted her slightly off the ground and pivoted as she grabbed at his tree trunk of a wrist.

She was thrown sideways at an approaching Jen and Carrie, who's weapons flew from their hands as they were forced to catch Betty and were all toppled to the ground.

Ethan was moving his hands spastically and speaking quickly in unknown tongues. Once Gol noticed that he was attempting an incantation, he picked up a bench and tossed it at Ethan with great force. Ethan put his hands up and braced, which did little to lessen the impact. He hit the ground hard, and a small object was sent flying from his jacket pocket.

Gol focused on the white shine of the object as it slid across the floor. "The relic," he said to himself as he began to ignore all others in his presence and head toward his new goal.

Gol was sent off balance as the buckshot of a Mossberg shotgun was sent into his abdomen. He roared a-la the Incredible Hulk and turned to see Duck with the smoking barrel of said shotgun in his hands. The ground shook with every enraged footstep Gol took. Duck swallowed hard and fired a second time. Bits of midsection and bone flew outward as Gol was again sent reeling back.

Duck racked the forearm and attempted to chamber a third round. "Shit," he exclaimed, realizing he had a stove pipe. Gol darted in before he could clear the malfunction and extended his massive boot forward, front-kicking Duck square in his chest. Duck soared through the air as if he was yanked backwards on pulleys. He crashed into and over a dining table, sending abandoned lunch trays in every direction.

Gol grunted as he stuck two fingers into his new wound. He pulled his digit away and grunted at the sight of his blood. He was starting to feel pain. And the more pain he would feel, the angrier he would become.

A sudden stinging in his right shoulder caught his attention. He turned to see Nelly holding a twenty-two-caliber handgun and firing in his direction. He scoffed as he leapt at her, closing the gap and making her last two shots go wide. He smacked her hand aside, snapping three of her fingers as the gun came loose and fell away.

Nelly screamed in pain as Gol wrapped his hand around her throat and drove her back into the wall. Her head bounced off the metal, instantly sending her into a semi-conscious state. Her ears were ringing, and her vision became hazy. She felt his palm close like a vice around her throat as air became increasingly elusive and her windpipe threatened to cave in. She waited to blackout and never wake again.

Then, she suddenly felt the grip loosen as Chad's face appeared behind Gol's giant frame. Chad had drawn two large knives and vaulted up at Gol's backside. He lashed out and dug the sharpened steel into his shoulder blades, dragging them down and cutting through his enormous muscles and back.

Gol dropped Nelly to the floor and spun, backhanding the air as Chad slipped just out of reach of his wrecking ball of a fist. He dragged one blade across a bulky thigh, severing more flesh and muscle, and bringing Gol down on wounded knee. Chad pivoted again and brought his second knife overhead, then swung downward with all his might, aiming for the man's scarred cranium.

It was stopped several inches away when Gol reached an open hand up and intercepted the edged metal with his palm. Blood cascaded from the protruding blade and dripped to the floor in thick rivulets. Chad pushed with all his strength, but it just wasn't enough.

Gol wrapped his free hand around Chad's face and in one seamless action, lifted him effortlessly from the ground as he stood. "Cockroach!" he roared, before smashing him to the ground. Gol took a moment to remove the knife from his hand and stretch his fingers, assessing the damage, if any, that had been done.

Chad lay there, paralyzed from the manhandling and gasping for air. Both lungs were collapsed and several of his vertebrae now crushed. He locked eyes with Nelly who was just beginning to come to. When she saw the panic in his eyes, she reached out to him, unable to do anything more.

Chad's lips quivered and he gave her a small, heart-felt smile. Nelly could feel her heart breaking for him.

"I...love...you." Chad mouthed to her as he closed his eyes.

"CHAD!" Nelly screamed as Gol again grabbed him by his face and rammed the back of his head straight down on the cement flooring. His occipital lobe shattered like a head of lettuce as Gol's palm pressed down on his face, crushing every bone within. He admired his work as he removed a few of Chad's stray teeth that had been embedded in his fist. Nelly buried her face in her hands as she laid there sobbing.

Izzy fixated on the savagery with frozen fear. She hugged the wall with her back and silently prayed that Gol would pay her no mind. He strode past casually and headed for a wobbly Logan. He drew the new knife he had been given when he spotted the weapons bag in the corner with a trapped Shane.

"Shane," Logan shouted to him, pointing at the bag. Shane wriggled his upper torso and reached down, trying to reach the sack. The table that had him pinned was lodged into the wall next to him and would not budge.

Logan ducked under Gol's bloodied fist as it punched out at where his head had just been. Logan could hear the brute cut through air as he threw several more missed haymakers and wide hooks. He didn't know just how much longer he would be able to keep this up. He glanced at Shane, who had made only inches in progress. Before he could turn back and check on his foe, it was too late.

"Hold still, worm," Gol growled as he clamped down on Logan's arm and pulled him closer, grabbing him by one of his legs and lifting him over his head like a ragdoll. The knife he hadn't even had the chance to use on his foe clanked down uselessly to the floor. He felt every joint and fiber in him threaten to snap as they were being stretched to capacity. Gol was literally pulling him apart.

Carrie was helping a limping Betty away from the carnage as Jen was up and firing a fallen rifle she had picked up. She aimed low as to not hit Logan as the five-five-six rounds tore through Gol's stomach and already filleted thigh. He stumbled back and, with an irritated grunt, he hurled Logan at her.

"Not again," Jen squeezed out as her husband homed in on her like a cruise missile. His elbow caught her in the eye as his head bounced off the floor and he rolled into a seated position against a bench. The rifle slid away, too far for anyone to reach it.

"You're both coming with me," Gol grumbled as he bent down and grabbed Logan's ankle, dragging him away from Jen and over to the relic. "Now I'm going to take my time with you, legacy," he bellowed as he picked up the small white gem.

Its sparkle was reminiscent of a brilliant diamond, but with almost no clarity. It was a thick white, like a chunk of arctic ice, but was warm to the touch. There was a small engraving on the front of a bow and arrow.

The shine began to intensify in Gol's hand. A small hum emanated from the white rock and he could feel his body start to tingle. He could not peel his eyes away from the beauty of the relic and found himself transfixed. His eyes moved from side to side, but his legs and arms would not follow instruction to do so. He was frozen in place.

"Logan, here!" Shane shouted as he had finally made it to the rucksack in front of him. He threw his arm out and rolled a small green object along the floor. As if Logan were holding a large magnet, the object rolled directly into his waiting hand.

It was Shane's last grenade. Logan popped the pin and scrambled to his feet, ripping the piece of cloth he had been wearing from his arm as he did so. He reached it out and yanked the relic from Gol's hand, wrapping it safely in the cut shroud as he jammed the live grenade into Gol's mutilated midsection.

"Everyone down!" Logan screamed as he turned and vaulted over the nearest table he could find.

Gol's eyes widened with terror as he was given back command of his body. He plunged his hand into his own intestines in a frantic struggle against time. He grinned as his hand found the foreign object, but it was too late.

The grenade detonated, splitting his lower extremities in two and his upper half into several hundred bits. Blocks of muscle flew through the air like fish, as if there had been an explosion at Sea World. Jagged bone fragments and teeth rained down like hale as ribbons of intestines and blackened organs snaked across the floor in a sea of red. His one leg stood in place for an extra second, completely detached from the rest of his frame at the hip. It fell over with a wet thud as more flesh bits and unmentionables flopped around them.

Ethan grunted as he sat up and rubbed his arm. Izzy ran over and shook a slow-waking Luke. Carrie went to an inconsolable Nelly, who was crawling across the floor to get to what was left of Chad. Logan helped Jen to her feet, then made their way to Shane, who was struggling to get free. Matt appeared at the far wall, using his good arm to assist an unbalanced Duck.

They huddled over Chad's mangled remains, each clutching fresh injuries from the titan they had just faced. It was silent, save Nelly's unrestrained sobbing. None of them ever took the time to actually reflect on what was truly happening. They still have not been given the chance to properly mourn the people they lost. Izzy might be the only one who knows Nelly best out of anyone in the group, but it's understood universally that they witnessed her lose two people that were close to her. She lost her long-time love Tom not four days ago. Now her douchebag, best friend who revealed he may have only been a douchebag because he was in love her, died saving her life. They gave her a minute, as they each began to weep a little themselves.

"What happened?" Luke said, softly.

"He saved her," Logan responded, wiping a stray tear from his cheek. "He did good."

"Nelly…" Izzy whispered as she crouched next to her grieving friend. "We have to go sweetie."

She rocked back and forth as she shook her head vehemently. "No."

"We have to," Izzy repeated, cradling her face softly and turning her watery eyes to face her. "We have to."

"Leave me here," she cried with spittle escaping her lips. "Just go. I can't do this anymore."

"Listen," Izzy said firmly. "You have to sweetie. You have to do this just a little longer and then we'll be ok."

"I can't. He died to save me. Why would he do that? Jerk!" she said angrily.

"He died for you so you could live," Izzy said plainly. "Honor that." Her words seemed to hit their mark.

Nelly gained a slight measure of control and wiped her eyes. She took a deep breath and expelled the air. "Ok," she said softly.

Izzy helped her to her feet and held her tight. Shane grabbed the rucksack as the rest gathered their own bags and weapons.

Duck turned away and cascaded a large section of the already messy floor with vomit.

"Jesus," Matt exclaimed, as he jumped away from the chunky discharge.

"I'm good," Duck said, wiping his mouth.

A glint in the corner of the room caught Luke's attention. He went over to investigate what looked like Gol's tactical rig, or what was left of it. Protruding from a damaged sheath was a familiar-looking, rustic knife. The dull and blackened edge was unmistakable: it was a Moirai Blade.

"I thought he said they were rare." Logan said, walking over.

"Yea me too. At least I have one now." Luke said removing his carbon tac knife in favor of the antique looking upgrade.

"You can't do any worse with it than I did." Logan said in gest. "I didn't even get to swing it at him. I kind of just dropped it."

"You dropped it?" Luke said, with a chuckle. "Thanks for setting the bar pretty low. Only way I could top that is if I stab myself."

"Har har. Did you not see that I crammed a grenade into him like I was stuffing a turkey?" Logan said in self-defense.

"Yea, that was pretty cool." Luke relented. "I'll give ya that."

"We have to go," Ethan told them as he peered outside and down the hall. They were back on the move.

Chapter 20

"Silas' quarters are right up here," Ethan said.

"So, how did you get past the soldiers back there, anyway?" Shane inquired.

"We tricked them into going to look in the green mile. By the time they get past those blast doors, we should be out of here."

"There's a ton of them down here." Logan said. "We just have to make sure we're not followed." He was implying Gideon.

"Gideon doesn't even know about this way out," Ethan explained. "At least Silas told me as much."

They pushed the wooden door of Silas' chamber open and stepped inside. Memorabilia and collectibles from ages of pop culture adorned the entirety of the room. Movie posters spanning from the silent nineteen-twenties to the B-horror genre of the eighties checkered the wall on the right with replica props safely encased in glass booths in front. Vintage records with photos of classic music bands that spawned them sat atop a large baroque bookshelf standing as tall as the ceiling. At the far end of the room, six portraits in six very different, yet equally impressive and refined frames hung. Each person in the portraits looked to bear an uncanny family resemblance.

Luke strolled across the room, bypassing anything considered of value and stood at the base of the portraits. Each one reflected a man from a different time period, each in his late thirties or early forties. One sported a clean-cut look and pasted brown hair with a silver badge on a black and white suit, like a midwestern lawman of the nineteenth century. The caption under it read "Sheriff S. Corbin."

Next to it was one that resembled a stock photo of a United States soldier from World War II. The caption under it said, "Staff Sergeant S. Creedwater."

"Holy shit," Luke exclaimed. "It's Silas."

"Well, this is his room," Logan said. "What's weird about having family pictures?"

"No," Luke said, correcting him. "They're all Silas. Each portrait, from different times." His voice fell away with astonishment.

"I'll be damned." Logan said, walking over. "He really is like eight-hundred years old."

"And he's always loved pop-culture," Ethan interjected. "Music, movies, fashion fads, you name it. The eighties were his baby." He spoke with a fondness for the man who raised him.

"That explains the code to the armory," Logan recalled.

"He said Bowie would show me the way." Ethan recalled stepping over to an autographed photo of Silas with the superstar from his Ziggy Stardust days. He removed it from the wall to reveal two switches, labeled "one" and "two" respectfully. He flicked the first as the wall of portraits began to vibrate. A small crack they previously ignored widened and formed the outline of a door. When it stopped, Ethan hit the second switch. The section of an outlined wall slid upwards, the loud grinding rock doing its best to draw attention.

The passageway widened inside, but they required flashlights to navigate. It was eerily quiet, but the coast seemed clear. They moved in a single file line with Ethan at the head. The terrain was not particularly difficult to navigate, but it wasn't the flattest of surfaces.

A large explosion somewhere overhead and behind them rocked the walls of the passage. "I think they just got through the blast door," Ethan told them. "Let's pick up our pace."

They traversed a total of just over a mile and a half with no resistance. Just ahead was a literal light at the end of the tunnel. A doorway arched as artificial light shone behind it. Ethan figured lamps and lighting meant electricity, which meant that there had to be a backup generator running nearby. They filed out and into a long subway tunnel lined with tracks.

"That's us," Ethan said, shining his light on a "Keystone North" sign.

"Are trains running?" Izzy asked.

"He said this one would be," Ethan shrugged. "If not, we find a different way. But we can't be on the streets right now."

"Hey Ethan, not for nothing but...do you know how to drive a train?" Luke asked.

Ethan stopped mid-step. He was completely floored by the simple overthought. He was so focused on getting them to the escape route that the very thought of who would drive the train eluded him.

"Relax," Shane said, slapping him on the shoulder. "I can."

"Buses and trains?" Ethan asked. "What else can you drive?"

"I drove military vehicles. I can drive anything with wheels and three things without them," Shane said proudly.

"What doesn't have wheels?" Matt asked.

"Helicopters, boats..." Shane raised an eyebrow at Matt, "...women."

They all laughed for a second. Carrie looked a little disgusted by the humor but let it go. It was good to hear a little laughter.

They climbed onto the platform and opened the operator's car. Shane looked everything over while everyone stood outside, taking a long-deserved break.

"So, what happened back there?" Logan asked Matt as he ushered him away for a little privacy.

"Back where?" Matt was confused.

"With Gol. You just…hid." He didn't bother to hide his disappointment this time.

Matt looked away. Although he appreciated his friend pulling him aside for this chat, he did not like being put on the spot for a second time in the same day. He was afraid whatever words he said next would result in him crying uncontrollably. Instead, he pointed at his slung arm and shrugged.

"Look, Matt. We've all been through a lot these last few days. And God knows you saved my ass when it all started, but we need you here." He hated preaching to his friend, but he had to hope it wasn't too late. He had to believe that his friend wouldn't just roll over and let everyone around him die, and then join them without a fight.

"I'm…" Matt started as a tear threatened to escape. "I'm good."

"You better be," Logan scolded him. "Carrie needs you. So, get your shit together."

Matt only nodded with affirmation before letting Logan walk off. He took a deep breath before following after.

"Train's good," Shane said, wiping his hand. "It's like Silas had it sitting here this entire time, ready to go."

"Alright," Ethan said. "Let's fire it up."

"Legaaaaaaaaaaaacy." A shrill voice belched out from the tunnel ahead.

"No way." Luke said.

"Was that…?" Logan asked Ethan, whose distant stare provided an answer with no words.

"Legacy!" It said again, as the grotesque First Plague stomped into view.

"Holy shit. How did he find us?" Logan asked with dread.

"Didn't you say he could smell our blood?" Luke asked Ethan.

"Well yea. That's how he found you at the garage, but the Shroud of Turin blocks him from tracking you," he explained in a hurry.

"…oh, shit," Logan dipped his head. He pulled the strip of the shroud he was given from his pocket. He took it off to swipe the relic for fear of it doing to him what it did to Gol. He had completely forgotten to tie it back on afterwards.

"Smooth move," Luke said with a sting.

"Not now," He shot back, pulling his Moirai Blade. Luke reached back and grabbed at the handle of his own to ensure it was at the ready.

"Didn't happen to find a third one that I could use, did you?" Ethan asked.

"No, but can you use this?" Logan said as he peeled back the cloth and revealed the glint of the gem.

"Wait, I've seen that before," Luke said with interest. "I've seen that before," he repeated with more excitement. "Izzy, go inside and grab the red book from the bag. Look for this symbol." She did as he asked.

"Stand before me, legacies," The Horseman ordered, approaching the platform.

"Everyone get inside! Shane, get this thing moving." Logan said with authority.

"I'm staying right the Hell here." Jen said, defiantly.

"Jen, get inside." Logan told her with no hint of gest. "I'll be in shortly, I promise," he said, as he kissed her head and gently turned her around.

She pushed back slightly at first but acquiesced with his sense of urgency. "You better be. I love you," she replied as she apprehensively entered the car.

Logan stepped forward, adjusting the grip of his knife in his sweaty palms. Luke stood next to his slightly younger brother and took deep controlled breaths while Ethan and Duck were positioned at respective ends. Their hearts threatened to punch through their respective chests.

"You do know I'm supposed to keep you two alive, right?" Ethan asked, as if they are doing this all wrong.

Duck checked his shotgun and racked a shell into the chamber. "*We* are supposed to keep them alive, sir," he corrected Ethan.

"Four of us versus one of the four Horsemen," Luke chuckled, terrified.

"I do not wish you dead, legacies," The Horsemen grumbled as he stopped moving forward. "It has come to my attention that I may have use for you."

"No," Ethan told him, in no uncertain terms.

Pestilence emitted his signature white mist from his open palm and, in a millisecond, it completely enveloped Ethan. "You may be wearing the shroud, servant. But that does not mean that I cannot remove your head from your body." The mist acted as a rope for the Horseman and pulled an immobilized Ethan closer to him.

Duck sidestepped and unloaded five slugs into the ashen monstrosity. Chunks of pale shriveled flesh burst away from his stomach and shoulder. Before the tarry thick globules of green and black blood hit the iron tracks, his body was whole again. He regenerated everything down to his puss-filled boils that were blasted off of him.

The horseman fixed his gaze on the assaulting Duck. "Ah, I can smell your blood mortal," he said, with merriment. "You do *not* wear the shroud." As he held Ethan in place the beast unhinged his massive jaws and opened wide. A gaseous belching spewed forth and was accompanied by a low hum that quickly turned into a loud buzzing. More mist poured from the gape, but this time, it was laced with small, black dots that were intertwined with one another.

Flies. Millions of flies were soaring through the sky in the mist and were heading right for Duck. The tentacle of insects slammed into Duck, sending him backwards with the impact. As they collided, they wrapped around his body and yanked him forward, stopping his kinetic movement and almost snapping his neck. At the very least, he would have whiplash.

Duck dropped his shotgun and flailed wildly at the flies that crept into every crevice of his clothing and began to bite at him. His skin began to burn with each nibble as thousands of the tiny white-eyed flies each took a nibble. He screamed in torment as enflamed sores popped up along his skin from the bites.

This gave Logan the chance to go on the offensive. He ran at the mythical creature headlong, who cut off the flow of mist and insect hybrid vomit to focus on his new threat. The flies continued their assault on Duck for a moment longer however, covering him in a thick swarm from head to toe before flying off down the tunnel. Duck fell to the floor in anguish, feeling as if he was being burned alive, but thankful for the reprieve from the assault.

Pestilence swiped his free arm at the approaching Logan, but he was too fast. He crouched under the boney appendage and came up with the Moirai Blade straight into the horseman's neck. Emerald tar pushed out the exit wound with the tip of the knife and ran down the creature's neck like tree sap. Logan's grip on the knife slipped and he came down empty handed as the monster reeled.

Ethan fell to the ground, the mist that held him dissipating instantly. The horseman's outstretched hand now clutched at the wound on his neck as he choked for air and fell to his knees. His head dipped down as his breathing slowly stopped. Logan couldn't help but let a smile spread across his face with satisfaction.

"That was easy," he said turning to Ethan and Luke.

Ethan sat up. "No. He's not dead."

"What?" Logan turned back as Pestilence was already standing to his feet. He could feel his heart pound with primal fear as the horseman towered over him. "Oh, shit," he whispered as a massive hand enveloped his throat and lifted him from the ground with ease.

The horseman pulled Logan close and turned him to face his friends. He applied just enough pressure to his windpipe to ensure compliance. Logan wriggled in his grasp with futility as his feet dangled in the air.

"Ha," Pestilence mused with the most sinister of smiles. "This is not a Moirai Blade, legacy. My pet made sure of that."

"Gideon?" Ethan barked at the pale man who nodded with confirmation.

"Now that I have your attention," the horseman said casually, "about my offer."

Luke and Ethan exchanged desperate glances. They had to at least hear him out.

"I will let you live, for now. In exchange for the relic." His retched voice oozed with deceit and his Cheshire grin did little to convince them that this was out of the goodness of his heart.

"Why?" Luke asked, not arguing with the idea of being allowed to live, but needing to hear a valid reason.

"I have no reason to lie to you," Pestilence replied, "I will have use for you later when your ancestor tries to kill you."

"What ancestor?" Luke asked, in confusion.

Pestilence chuckled. "The Order has not been very forthcoming with you have they? Your beloved "Mr. Stone" is of the same bloodline."

It was Luke's turn to reel back. "The guy who's doing all of this? No, that's not right. There is no prophet named Stone."

The horseman turned to meet Ethan. "No, there is not. But I believe your Sentinel may know more than he claims to."

Luke glanced at Ethan, who shrugged unknowingly. "Doesn't matter," Luke said. 'You're not getting this relic."

The horseman's faceless expression changed from bemused to irritated. His hairless brows furrowed, stretching the wrinkled skin down and tearing a small laceration across his forehead. He said nothing but squeezed his grip on Logan's neck, making him gasp violently for air and illustrate his intentions for any further disobedience.

"Ok, ok," Luke said throwing his hands up in a placating manner. He put the sleeve of his hoodie over his hand and bent down, picking up the relic. He approached Pestilence with extreme caution.

"Don't give him that," Ethan said, finally getting to his feet.

"Shut up, Ethan," Luke told him, never looking away from the growling monstrosity that was dangling his brother like a plaything.

Luke stopped a few feet away and bent to one knee. He slowly lowered the relic and ensured Pestilence's attention was fixed on it.

"You said that Moirai Blade is a fake?" Luke asked him. The horseman again said nothing. He placed the gem on the floor and stood. "Because I'm pretty sure…"

The horseman reached his free hand down for the relic as Luke pulled his knife from behind and darted over, slicing his outreached arm. It cut across, separating his pale flesh and leaving a bright trail of white light where the metal met skin. He pulled back and shrieked in genuine pain this time, dropping Logan to the floor.

"…this one's real." Luke quipped, as he stayed on his target and drove the blade into his bleached abdomen, dragging it across in a fashion that would disembowel any human. The knife sliced through him like a lightsaber would through butter. No bodily fluids nor discolored discharge spew forth from the large wound, however. Only white light lined the sight of incision. Pestilence fell to his side on one knee, clasping his good hand over his fileted midsection.

"Let's go," Shane shouted from the conductor car as the train's ending chugged to life. It crept forward along the tracks at a turtle's pace at first, and gradually began picking up speed. Ethan was lifting a taught and aching Duck to his feet, ushering him along at a quickened pace as he did so.

Luke pulled his brother up, who in turn snatched the relic with his bare hand. They raced to the train as it picked up steam. The relic shone brightly in Logan's hands, but he did not feel any discomfort or tingling.

"Luke," he called out to his brother as they ran. He lifted the relic slightly to show his brother it was not the gem luminating like before, but now an engraved bow and arrow. They huffed and puffed as their legs pushed and closed in on the train.

An incessant buzzing sound made him glance back as he saw the swarm of flesh-starved insects closing in behind him. Logan grabbed the rear guardrail of the car in motion and pulled himself up. He turned to see his brother only two steps behind with the swarm hot on his heels. He reached his hand out to him to close the gap.

Luke's hand was only inches away when the swarm of mist and flies encased his legs and lifted him upward. The fear and shock on his brother's face as he was lifted away would haunt his dreams.

"No...NO!" Logan shouted as the relic rumbled in his hand. Like a grenade comprised of light, the gem detonated in his grip. The blast sent him flying backwards into the door of the cart, the gem falling from his hands and down onto the tracks. A single, long projectile with the visage of an arrow soared from the explosion and struck the "neck" of the swarm. The mist and any insect intertwined with it was instantly disintegrated. The horseman could be heard roaring in what could have been frustration, pain, or any combination of the two.

Luke was tossed aside like an unwanted toy. He hit the ground hard but was of sound enough mind to ignore the pain and keep moving. He tumbled and moved into the impact, rolling forward and up to his feet into a full stride.

"Gotcha," Logan said, as he successfully grabbed his brother's arm and yanked him up. The two fell backwards, hitting their rear sides against the car and collapsing into a seated position against the car door. Their lungs fought for air as their chests heaved in and out. They watched for a second as Pestilence, the first of four horsemen, sat hunched over on the tracks. In what seemed like a lifetime of seconds, he faded from their view.

"Did you...just shoot... a fireball?" Luke asked between struggled breaths, his arms resting on his knees.

Logan chuckled. "It was the relic. It didn't have the same affect that it did on Gol. I had it in my bare hand."

The door slid open and the two tumbled backwards to the floor. They were looking up at Jen and Izzy, as well as Ethan, who was still trying to catch his own breath.

"As long as I'm supposed to protect you two," Ethan said, with humored resentment, "don't ever, *ever*, do some dumb shit like that again. You weren't supposed to just run at him."

"Yes, father," Logan chided as Jen helped him up. "You good?" he asked his wife.

She wiped a stray tear from her face and kissed him gingerly on his lips. "Like Ethan said," she told him softly. "Don't ever do some dumb shit like that again!"

"Ok," was all he replied with a kiss to her forehead.

Izzy slapped Luke across the back of the head. "You don't get off that easy," she admonished him, before wrapping her arms around him.

"Hey," Luke protested. "I might have a concussion. How's Duck?"

"I'm fine," they heard him grumble as they maneuvered the length of the car to find their friend lying across a row of seats, stripped down to his underwear. "A little chilly without pants," he said, his voice strained as if he was fighting a throat infection.

"Will he turn?" Logan asked Ethan with concern.

He shrugged in response. "I don't know. I've never seen that before."

"We'll look after you." Jen said, running a hand through his drenched, dark hair. He had no visible signs of being afflicted with any plague aside from the red sores which more closely resembled bug bites.

"Thanks." He said as he shivered with hot sweats. He leaned over the side and threw up. "Not from the bites," he choked out, waving a hand up at them. "That's just my nerves again."

"We can't stay on this train, you know?" Shane yelled back to them. "They know where it goes. We have to find another way."

Ethan ran a finger over the map posted on the car wall. He followed the Keystone tracks and tapped at a spot that could be beneficial. "There's a three-point junction a few miles away. We'll get out there and find another route north. First, we need a weapons check and round count. Everyone take five."

"Ethan," Logan said softly. "I lost the relic..." He looked defeated.

"It's ok, man. I'm glad you're both still alive." He squeezed his shoulder.

"What was it... that shot out of it?"

"To be honest, Logan," Ethan said, with a slight shrug, "I have no idea."

Logan didn't know whether to believe his old friend or not at this point. He had lied about being in a secret society the entire time he's known him. Looking back now, it worked out for their benefit, seeing how his brother and their significant others were all safe. Sure, they were being pursued by zombies and mythical monsters, but right now, they were safe. And they were given a fighting chance that so many others would never receive. He decided to let the discussion go.

Ethan turned and went to check with Betty, who was wrapping Nelly's broken hand, compliments of Gol. Shane kept a close eye on the controls. Carrie slept soundly with her head in Matt's lap as the car rocked gently from side-to-side. His broken arm hung to the side in his sling as he stroked her hair. Duck passed out from exhaustion, though the fever was already dying down. They had all taken a beating.

Izzy had been sitting down with the book Luke asked her to look through. It was a red, rusty looking book that had clearly seen better days. The title was "Runes and Relics of the Allmother's Creations." Her eyes locked onto a particular page that she scanned several times over before jumping to her feet with a clear expression of panic.

"Uh, guys." She said, nervously, garnishing all the attention in the car with her tone. "Where's the relic?"

"We dropped it." Logan said, with a particularly bad feeling creeping through him. "Why?"

"I found what it is…" she said with a pause. "You want the bad news or the worse news?"

"Out with it Iz." Jen said impatiently.

Izzy turned the book and pointed to an illustration of the gem. "It's his bow. From when he arrives in the Bible."

"Shit," Luke said. "Now he has a weapon?"

Izzy crinkled her nose. "For us, it's a weapon. A Legacy can wield it and use it to kill him. It's the only thing they know of that can."

"And I gave it right to him." Logan said with disappointment. "Son of a bitch."

"That's just the bad news," Izzy said turning the page over to a similarly illustrated red gem with the image of a sword etched into it. "He needs the bow to open the second seal…" The words hung in the air, heavy as boulders.

"He has the key he needs," Ethan said, with dread, "to release his brother, War."

Epilogue
Pestilence

The pale rider watched as the train retreated from his view. He craned his neck back and let out a harrowing roar of frustration and fury. He had clearly underestimated these humans. He stood slowly and allowed his own mist to snake around his body. It flowed through his open wounds that bled white light and painfully, oh so painfully, stitched his ashen skin back together. He grimaced and snarled with the unfamiliar stinging upon his flesh.

In all but three minutes, the horseman was fully healed. The glint of an object in the distance caught his eye, and he towered over to investigate. He snickered with bewilderment as he bent down and retrieved the fallen relic. It emanated the purest white light in his gargantuan palm. His hand began to tingle, and pain radiated through his arm as white lightening crackled from the gem and along the horseman's body.

He shrieked and dropped the relic. Twice in one day, he had felt physical pain after a millennium of feeling nothing. "Warded," he said plainly to himself. He tore a piece of his own discolored and stained sarong and wrapped the gem. He squeezed it tightly in his hand as the mist once again enveloped him and he was teleported back to the main entrance of the church.

"Where is Stone?" he bellowed to a small group of soldiers who were removing items of their own personal interest from the base.

"We don't know, sir," Suthers told him as he approached with caution. "We swept the entire base. There's no one else inside and no trace of the legacies. The information about the west tunnel was a rouse."

"I see that, human," he said with frustration as he reached over and lifted a random soldier by his midsection. "I know where the legacies are headed. Now, find Stone before I decide to eat everyone still here!" He roared his command as he lifted the man above his head and twisted his legs and upper half in opposite directions. The snapping of every vertebrae in his body was overshadowed by the wet tearing sounds of his flesh and organs as the horseman then ripped him in two. Bloodied innards and ribbons of intestines flowed freely to the ground as Pestilence threw the two halves of the lifeless man aside in differing directions.

Suthers retreated from the savage imagery with the calmness of a true professional. "Yes sir," he said with military discipline before turning to see Gideon fast approaching.

"My liege," he said, taking a knee before the crimson splattered, ashen giant. "There are traces of a banish spell in the main entrance. It's possible Stone and Silas were caught in the blast."

"Can you tell where?"

"Not yet, lord. But I can with time and some materials." He could see something ruminating from his master's waist. "The relic my lord?"

"Yes," he replied, warily. "It is warded against us. It will simply destroy any mortal aligned with us. Find Stone. He will be able to break the warding. Then, we will have no more use for him."

"And what of you my lord?" Gideon asked, standing.

"I will follow them, alone. They will lead me to Eli. And I will strip their bones from their bodies," he grinned as he let loose a demonic chuckle that sent a shiver down the spine of every man within ear shot.